RUSTLING RANCHERS

"Let's talk business, Bramwell," Lee Morgan said. "Over the past two years you've rustled over three thousand head of stock from this ranch, rebranded them and sold them in the Miles City stockyards. We'll expect a thousand head on our border by noon day after tomorrow. If they aren't there, we'll just have to come and get them. Understand?"

"You have a vivid imagination, I certainly won't—"

Another shot slammed into the early morning. The slug tore through the Englishman's pant leg.

"At noon, day after tomorrow!" Morgan roared. "If you think you're lucky you might try making some additional comment that will upset me. When I get angry my six-gun here just seems to go off."

The Englishman glared at Morgan and Willy Joe, stepped into the rig and drove away. He didn't look back.

The Buckskin Series:

RIFLE RIVER
GUNSTOCK
PISTOLTOWN
COLT CREEK
GUNSIGHT GAP
TRIGGER SPRING
CARTRIDGE COAST

DOUBLE EDITION:
  BOLT ACTION/TRIGGER GUARD RECOIL

DOUBLE EDITION:
  GUNPOINT/LEVER ACTION

SCATTERGUN
WINCHESTER VALLEY
GUNSMOKE GORGE
REMINGTON RIDGE
SHOTGUN STATION
PISTOL GRIP

BUCKSKIN SPECIAL EDITION:
  THE BUCKSKIN BREED

PEACEMAKER PASS
SILVER CITY CARBINE
CALIFORNIA CROSSFIRE

DOUBLE EDITION:
  HANGFIRE HILL/CROSSFIRE COUNTRY

COLT CROSSING
POWDER CHARGE
LARAMIE SHOWDOWN

GIANT SPECIAL EDITION:
  BOUNTY HUNTER'S MOON

DOUBLE ACTION
APACHE RIFLES
RETURN FIRE

NIGHT RIDER'S MOON

KIT DALTON

LEISURE BOOKS   NEW YORK CITY

A LEISURE BOOK®

January 1991

Published by

Dorchester Publishing Co., Inc.
276 Fifth Avenue
New York, NY 10001

Printed in the United States of America.

Chapter One

When a rifle round slammed through the brush a foot over his head, Buckskin Lee Morgan dove for the safety of a log near the banks of the Tongue River in eastern Montana. The sturdy cottonwood log had been there for a few years, but it soaked up two more rifle rounds before Morgan could fire back toward the splotch of brush now sporting black powder smoke.

He rolled to the heavier end of the log. Right at that moment he wasn't sure where his horse was. The mare had been grazed in the shoulder when he caught the first bullet through his left forearm.

Both rounds came so close together that he knew there probably had to be two men.

Morgan listened. There had been no movement he could pick up from the brush. If there were two of them, they were both dismounted now. One would circle to the left, since that was the only area with enough brush to cover a man, while the other would keep him pinned down from the first spot.

Buckskin Morgan checked behind him and saw there was enough cover to get away downstream.

Hell, no! He was going upstream toward the Circle-S ranch. Damned if he was gonna let a couple of snot-nosed bushwhackers hold him up for long.

He had come into Miles City only this morning and had not attempted to hide his face. He'd had no idea those old wanted posters would be way up here in Montana. Evidently someone had seen both the poster and his face and made a match.

He'd gone straight to the livery, rented a good horse, a sorrel with a touch of blonde on her mane, and headed upstream across the big sky country of Montana toward his old friend, Milburn Scoggins, who ran the Circle-S ranch.

Another rifle round jolted just over the cottonwood log. He checked the lightly covered area to the left where the circling man would have to pass.

Buckskin Morgan lifted his rifle over the log and aimed at the far right side of the lightly screened section.

Morgan took a deep breath and then another, his eye looking down the barrel at the front sight.

Now!

He tracked a figure and fired. The .44 caliber slug spiraled through the air, missed the light brush and hit the bushwhacker in the side as he ran. The bounty hunter jolted six feet to the left and crumpled dead in the leaves and mulch of the small woodland.

For a moment there was silence along the Tongue

River.

"Bastard!" the remaining hunter bellowed.

"Bastard yourself! You shot first, you yellow-bellied bushwhacker!" Buckskin Morgan roared back at him.

Then the real battle began.

The bounty hunter sent four rounds at the log where Morgan lay.

Morgan crawled out of sight along the log to the bank of the river. It had gouged a channel here during flood stage and now left a dry shelf along the water. Morgan dropped into the dirt and ran upstream to get behind the bushwhacker.

But by the time he had covered 30 yards and looked over the edge of the bank to check where the other man had been, he could see the man running through brush toward his horse.

Buckskin Lee Morgan drew down on the running man. Two rounds slanted off brush and missed. The third caught the man's left leg and toppled him, but he continued to crawl toward the mount.

Morgan sighed, lifted his sights and shot three times quickly. The second shot hit the horse, and it went down screaming.

Now Morgan took his time working toward the wounded man. He came through the brush like an Apache, not making a sound.

The bushwhacker had tied up his left leg and now lay with his rifle ready and a six-gun positioned nearby. The only trouble with the bounty hunter's plan was that he was facing the wrong way, looking in the wrong direction.

Morgan was in an open spot to the left side of the bushwhacker. He took careful aim and slammed a round into the forward stock of the bounty hunter's rifle in front of the breech. The heavy .44 round jolted the rifle out of the man's hands, and the stock spun around and slammed into the gunman's left arm.

"Don't try for the iron," Morgan said sternly. "It would just pleasure me no end to put a slug through your head. You a bounty hunter?"

"You're wanted, Morgan. Saw the poster last week."

"The damn wanted poster was recalled three years ago. There's no paper out on me."

"Says you. Never seen a wanted man yet who would admit it."

"You're never gonna see another one to check your theory. In ten minutes you'll be as dead as your partner over there."

"Bastard!"

"You play with guns, you stand the chance of getting hurt. You try to kill somebody, you stand the chance of getting killed yourself."

"You gonna talk all day or help me get to town so I can get my leg fixed up."

"Start walking."

"Can't walk."

"Too bad. Should'a thought of that before you started shooting."

"You can't just leave me here!"

"Why not? You been a damn big help to me so far today. You shot me through the arm. You shot my horse. You tied me up for an hour, so I'll be late getting where I'm going."

Morgan turned as if to leave.

The bushwhacker grabbed his six-gun and rolled and

fired all in one move.

He was too late. Morgan had turned back around. His rifle barked once, and the round bored through the bounty hunter's neck, spewing bright red blood into the brush and leaves. His dying finger pulled the trigger, but the round bored into the ground ten feet away.

By the time Morgan walked up to the man he was dead.

Morgan stared down at the dead man and kicked him gently in disgust. "What a hell of a waste," he said, then walked back to where he had seen his horse grazing. He got out some white cloth and bandaged his left forearm.

He soothed the mare and rubbed some ointment on the bullet burn across her shoulders, then mounted and headed on upstream toward the Circle-S ranch. If he hurried he might be in time for supper.

As he rode, he wondered if there would be any more trouble with bounty hunters. The poster from Arizona hadn't been withdrawn. There had been no real trouble about the dead man when he was there six years ago. Then the county sheriff got home and decided to prosecute, well after Morgan had ridden on.

It was bad paper, but convincing some trigger happy bounty hunter of that was easier done with lead then talk.

He followed the wagon road along the river. It looked like it had been used lately. There were two ranches in this direction, at least there had been five years ago when he'd been through here.

The Circle-S was owned by Milburn Scoggins, one of the best cattle ranchers that Morgan had ever seen.

Scoggins had built up a herd of scraggly wild cattle into a fine producing ranch of beef cattle. Each year he bred them with better and better range bulls. Soon he was selling brood cows to other herds.

The other big outfit nearby was the Bar-B as he remembered. It was over on the Pumpkin River nearly 20 miles due east. He rode along remembering that last contact with Scoggins. The old man had been nearly 60 then and tough as a range steer beefsteak and about as cantankerous. Oh, Milburn Scoggins was honest and straight with his crew and his neighbors, but he liked to do things his way—or not at all.

He had a daughter and an older son. The son was probably running things now.

If so, why had the daughter written the telegram asking Morgan to come, that her father needed him or he could lose the Circle-S ranch? The wire had caught up with him in Denver, and he had grabbed the first train heading in this direction.

Even so he'd had to go back to Omaha, then up to Minnesota and across on the Northern Pacific to Miles City. But it was a lot easier than making the 400-mile horseback ride—faster, as well.

He looked ahead now and could see the gate.

When he'd been here before, this little valley had been covered with brown-coated steers, and across the way a pasture had been fenced in for the brood cows due to drop calves. Scoggins had had the whole thing down to a science.

Ahead he could see the ranch house. It looked the same, four square and solid, built for a big family that Scoggins never had. After his wife had died giving birth to their second child, he had concentrated on his ranching. The ranch house must have 14, maybe 16 rooms on two floors. It swept to either side from a big covered porch. Inside was one of the biggest fireplaces he had ever seen.

But now, somehow, it was different. Smoke came from the chimney to the left where he knew the kitchen was. The bunkhouse had no smoke. There seemed to be only a few horses in the small corral and none at all in the big corral. At the side were fenced-in pastures for the horses and some of the prize brood stock. But curiously, they didn't seem to have many cattle in them.

He saw no hands working, and no one at the corrals.

Maybe they were out on a roundup.

At once he knew that wasn't possible. It was the wrong time of year for that. He stopped 50 yards from the big ranch house and stared at it. It took him back five years. Where had that much time vanished to?

He moved ahead and was almost to the front of the house when he saw the screen door open and a young woman appear. She shielded her eyes against the setting sun, then gave a little cry and rushed forward, her bright blue print dress dusting the ground as she ran.

She had dark hair and a pretty, pert face, and all of a sudden he realized that this was little Heather, only she wasn't so little now. She'd been only 13 when he had left.

''Heather?''

''Lee Morgan, I'd know you anywhere with that almost-blond hair!''

He dropped down from the mount, and she caught his hand. Her face shone radiantly, her smile so

11

engaging that he had to grin. He kissed her cheek.

"Little Heather, you have grown up into a beauty! It isn't only prize beef cattle your father raises on this ranch."

She blushed but kept holding his hand.

"I'm so excited that you're here that I'm all choked up and can't say what I want to. Oh, first, Daddy is a little worse. Please don't be shocked when you see him. He had a small stroke, and his left side is paralyzed. So he can't ride, and sometimes he doesn't talk plain. He's in a wheelchair we got for him."

Morgan stopped. "Milburn Scoggins is stove up? A stroke?" Morgan shook his head. "Damn—pardon me. I never thought I'd see the day. Then your brother Ken must be running the ranch."

She looked away, blinking back tears. She shook her head and wiped her eyes and looked up at him. "No . . . no Ken is dead. He was killed in some trouble with the Bar-B. A new man has taken it over and bought it, some Englishman who thinks he's the king of Montana."

"I've met one or two of them." He dropped the reins of the horse and held out his arms. "Looks like I got here just about in time."

She leaned into his arms, and he held her tightly for a moment. "Little Heather, you are going to get at least two good tight hugs a day from now on, Dr. Morgan's orders."

He let her go and she looked up. "I'm so glad to see you I'm not sure whether to scream for joy or cry." She reached up and kissed his cheek.

"There, that will be a compromise. Now come on, we'll put your horse away and then take you in to see

12

Daddy.''

He looked around as they walked toward the small corral. "How many hands do you have?"

"Only four."

"Four? You used to have thirty."

"We don't have as much stock now. We couldn't pay the hands one month, and six left and then another five. Our foreman even left and went over to the Bar-B."

Morgan scowled. "We'll see what's going on here. First, take me in to see your father. I owe your dad a lot of favors, and it's about damn time I start paying some of them back."

Chapter
Two

Buckskin Lee Morgan was shocked.

He looked down at the old man sitting in the wheel-chair and wanted to cry. Milburn Scoggins was 64, but he looked more like 94. His once-powerful body at six feet had shrunken and wasted away, so his bones showed through his flesh. His black hair was almost gone, leaving wisps of gray over a blotched bald head. His face had caved in, and one side continually twitched.

One eye stared at him in recognition, while the other wandered to the other side of the room. One hand lifted up a few inches and then fell back in his lap. Only the right side of his body had any life in it at all.

Morgan tried to cover up his surprise and shock but knew he did a terrible job of it.

"Well, Milburn, it's been five years since I've seen

you. Good to be back in Montana. Before I forget, I wanted to say what a great job you've done growing up this young'un. She's just as pretty as a buttercup in spring.''

Milburn Scoggins lifted his right hand and said something, but the words came out so garbled and soft that Morgan had no idea what they meant.

"Yes, I know she was bound to grow up sooner or later, but you have to admit you got the whole process started. I'm sorry to hear about Ken. He was a good man. Now, I'll have to see what I can do about taking care of a few overdue accounts I owe around here. Do you think I should meet this Englishman?''

He paused, and again some garbled words came out of the old man's mouth.

"Good, I'll pay him a social call just as soon as I get my feet on the ground here." Morgan patted Milburn's good shoulder.

"You take it easy now. Don't worry about a thing. This lady you've grown here and I will take care of everything. You just ease back and relax, Milburn, you've earned a rest. All of those years of pounding leather have finally paid off for you. My turn to do some of the work around here.''

He nodded at the distorted face and turned and walked away from the back porch where the old man sat watching the sun go down with his one good eye.

Back in the kitchen, Buckskin Morgan leaned against the doorframe and took a deep breath. "Oh, God!''

Heather looked up from where she stood at the kitchen range.

"I should have told you how bad he is. Seeing him every day, I forget.''

16

"How long has he been this way?"

"It started about a year ago—just a small stroke, the doctor said—and he was out riding again a week later. Then about a month after that this big stroke hit him when he was on the range. Two of our hands brought him back.

"The doctor from Miles City said sometimes the brain can rebuild some of the nerve pathways, but he said after a stroke this bad there was not much hope it can reverse itself. He might never get any better, and at any time there could be another stroke that would end it all." She looked away quickly, trying to blink back tears.

Morgan balled his fist and slammed the side of it against the wall. He hit the wall three times, then stormed out of the kitchen, slammed the door and stalked into the yard. He went past the bunkhouse to the corral and around it and onto the Montana plains.

For a half hour he walked, kicking the ground, screaming at the sky that such a terrible fate could drop on a good man. When he got back to the house an hour later, Heather sat on the back porch waiting for him.

"I'm sorry," she said.

He held out his arms and hugged her, surprised by the strong hug she gave him in return.

"I'm the one who's sorry. I owe that man a lot, more than I can ever pay him back, but I'm going to start paying a little on the account books."

Heather watched him. When he first arrived she had been thrilled to see him. When he had been on the ranch years ago, she had been totally in love with him. Now she knew her feelings hadn't changed, just matured a little. He was the most wonderful man she had ever known. Of course she had known him only as a child. Now she had to find out about the real Lee Morgan.

"First, before anything else, it's time for some supper. I've got a stew I've been working on for a day, but it's all new to you."

Inside the two of them ate at the highly varnished, big-plank kitchen table. The stew was good with lots of big chunks of beef, a thick sauce drowning carrots and parsnips, lots of potatoes and whole baby onions, quartered turnips and a mess of navy beans.

He had three helpings and three thick slabs of home-made bread and freshly salted butter and a quart of coffee.

When he pushed the dishes back he watched her.

"What I need is an honest appraisal of the ranch—how much stock is left, how many horses, the crew, if the Bar-B is on your land and how much hell they've done you."

"Yes, I can show you all of that."

They both looked up when they heard a rider coming into the yard fast. "It's Willy Joe. Usually he doesn't ride like that."

The man jumped off his mount and ran for the back door where they met him. Willy Joe was tall and slender, with a pleasant face, a thick moustache and piercing green eyes. Right now dust and sweat covered his face.

"Miss Heather! Damn Bar-B is making off with about two hundred head over in the Engelmann flats. Must be six men over there taking Circle-S stock."

"Rustling is the word," Morgan said. He held out

his hand. "Name is Lee Morgan. I'm a friend of the family from way back. You get a fresh horse and then we're gonna ride so you can show me where these rustlers are."

"Just the two of you?" Heather asked, brown eyes wide with fear and wonder.

"That's plenty. Oh, Willy Joe, bring a good rifle, a repeater if you've got one. I'll get my horse."

Willy Joe grinned as if he were glad for some action for a change and led his horse back to the corral where he roped a fresh one.

Heather touched Morgan's arm. "You be careful. Some steers we can replace . . ."

"Pretty lady, I got shot once today, and I don't intend to repeat that mistake. We'll be back well after dark, I'd say, so don't worry."

It was fully dark by the time the two men rode down a small draw and saw the herd of 200 head moving slowly to the east.

Morgan stopped and motioned to Willy Joe. "You can cut out now if you want to. Ever killed a man?"

"No, but I'm damn ready. I'm with you."

"Good. We'll ride around and get in front of them. Then we pick off the two point riders before they know what hit them. After that we each pick a flank man down the side of the herd and ride him down, blasting him. Four is the best we can hope for. Then we turn the herd and drive them back where they were or maybe even closer to the ranch. Ready?"

Willy Joe nodded grimly. They circled around the cattle and riders and came in about 100 yards ahead of them.

They parted then. There were two men on each side

of the small herd and two riding drag.

Morgan lifted his rifle out of the boot and made sure there was a round in the chamber. Then he settled on his mount and waited for the cattle to come toward him so he could see the point man clearly.

When he did he aimed and fired. The cowboy slammed backwards off the saddle, while a dozen steers around him bawled.

A moment later, Morgan heard another shot from the other side of the herd. He worked through the cows and rode hard until he saw another rider.

"What the hell was them damn shots?" the other man called, thinking it was his friend coming back.

"Hell is the place," Morgan answered. He was now within 20 yards of the man and had out his Colt .45.

Far too late the man realized a stranger was coming. He whipped his horse to the left to get away, but Morgan's gun barked twice and the rustler spun to the side and fell off his mount.

Three gunshots came from the other side of the herd. Morgan rode back to the head of the pack and began turning them back the way they had come. It took him ten minutes to get the lead cows and a few old steers to move in the right direction.

At last he had the head of the column turned and heading down the draw to the west, back toward the Circle-S ranch. It was another ten minutes before Willy Joe found Morgan.

"I done it. I killed my first man, got him with my rifle, but the second son of a bitch got away. He nicked me with a lucky shot, but I put the fear of God into the bastard!"

"Three out of six ain't bad. How far are we from

the ranch house?''

"Five, maybe six miles."

"Them Bar-B boys are getting mighty brave, but we'll put a stop to that. First we get these critters driven back well into Circle-S lands. Then we go back and strip those three bodies of guns and rifles. Next we pay a little surprise visit to the Bar-B. What is it—another fifteen miles east?''

Willy Joe gulped but nodded. "Yes sir. Hell, this'll give them something to think about. Ain't been a man killed out here since they done in Ken near a year ago.''

"Tell me about that," Morgan said.

"Six of us was on the spring roundup out in the Garland area, upstream. We was shagging strays out of the brush when ten Bar-B riders stormed out of the east, shooting rifles. We hunkered down in the draw and tried to fight back, but all we had was three six-guns between us.

"They rode right over us, shooting and laughing. They stampeded the thirty head we'd gathered, and when they was gone, we found Ken with a round right through his forehead. Nobody saw it happen, but it didn't make no damn bit of difference by then.

"That was about a month after Mr. Milburn had his bad attack. They been walking all over us ever since.''

"All of that shit stops tonight, Willy Joe. After tonight they'll know there's a whole new game that they have dealt into.''

It took them another hour to drive the scattering herd back into the close northern pasture, only four miles from the ranch buildings.

Willy Joe rode up to Morgan in the soft light from a crescent of moon.

"We really going to the Bar-B tonight?"

"Damn right. First we strip those bodies of guns and ammunition. We might need some extra."

They had no trouble finding the bodies and stripping them of weapons.

It then took them three hours to get to the fringes of the Bar-B. There were two windows in the main ranch house that showed lights.

"Good," Morgan said. "One of the cowboys who got back is talking to the boss. The three riderless horses probably got back to the corral as well. Should give them something to think about. Now all we have to do is see if they are smart enough to have any guards out."

The two men left their horses in some brush near the Pumpkin River and slipped through the darkness a quarter of a mile toward the nearest barn. Morgan carried his rifle.

They lay in some grass and weeds 20 yards to the side of the barn and surveyed the whole yard. There were seven buildings—another barn, some kind of an equipment shed, a bunkhouse, a cookshack, a smaller house, probably for the foreman, two corrals and a horse-breaking pen. The whole place was well laid out.

After a while, Morgan decided there were no guards. He had seen no glow of sneaked cigarettes. He told Willy Joe to back him up with the rifle in case there was any shooting.

Then Morgan stood and walked toward the barn as if he belonged there. He slipped in the back door and found what he wanted. In the dim light he could tell the entire barn was one big haystack. He didn't know where they had cut or cured so much grass hay, but it didn't matter.

Morgan took four matches from his pocket, quickly struck them and set the hay burning in four places. When he was sure it was going to catch and burn fast, he slipped out and ran back to where he had left Willy Joe.

Together they lay there, watching the barn. It was ten minutes before smoke came out of the rear door, then a tongue of flame shot out a side window, and soon the fire ate through the roof.

A shout came from the yard, and someone ran toward the fire.

Morgan took his rifle and sighted in on the ranch house. When a light blossomed in an upstairs window, he fired three times through it.

Then Morgan stood and stretched.

"Looks like our work here is done for the night," Morgan said. "Guess it's about time we wander back toward the Circle-S and get some sleep. We've got some figuring to do about what we do next."

"God almighty, I can't believe this has happened," Willy Joe said. "I've dreamed about doing something like this to the Bar-B for months. I didn't think that we could. Won't they send over a bunch of guys tomorrow and burn down our whole ranch?"

"No. First it'll take them a few days to realize the game has changed. Then they'll have to know for sure that the attack came from us. Then the Englishman will try to figure out what to do. By then we should be ready for whatever it is."

"Damn, the fat's in the fire now!"

"It was in the fire the moment they killed Ken. Now for the first time some of that fat is going to splatter back on the Englishman. We'll see how he likes it, but my bet is that he won't like it one little bit!"

Chapter
Three

The riders made it back to the Circle-S just as dawn broke.

"No reason to tell the other hands what we did tonight," Morgan said to Willy Joe. "They'll find out in time. We might need a little space here, understand?"

Willy Joe nodded. He would agree to anything right then for a chance to get to his bed.

When Morgan came to the ranch house, Heather pushed open the screen door, one fist on her hip, a frown on her pretty face.

"Didn't say you'd be gone all night."

"We saved the ranch two hundred head of cattle. I'd say that was worth two men spending all night." He watched her a minute. She was as pretty as a flower, and one he was not going to touch. He owed that much to Milburn.

"You want coffee first or a bed? I've got both—in either order." She held open the door. She wore a robe over something else he didn't want to know about.

"I couldn't sleep, I'll have you know. You and Willy Joe out there getting shot at probably." Her anger was short-lived, and she hurried into the kitchen and poured him coffee from a pot on the stove.

"Anybody get hurt?" she asked, her face softening as her concern came through.

"Not on our side. You got any alcohol to splash on this arm of mine? Picked that up before I came under your employment and control." He rolled up his sleeve and showed her the bloody bandage.

"Yes, we have some things." She brought back a small metal box that held medicines, bandages and some ointments. She picked out some things, then cut the old bandage away and looked at the wound.

"At least there's no infection." She painted the wound with some red fluid. "Kills the bad germs," she said. Then she put on some ointment and bandaged his forearm. She tore the end of the bandage and tied it neatly.

"That should do until you get shot again. Now tell me exactly what happened out there. This is my ranch to make go or to go broke. I need to know."

When he told her, she sat down quickly.

"Bramwell will be over here this morning with fifty men and burn us to the ground."

"No, he won't. First he has to figure out who did it. Then he won't believe it. Then he'll try to figure out what he can do that will be bad for the Circle-S without being something we can prove against him. First he'll be in shock. The anger won't come for a few days. In that time we'll get organized. Who is your best man?''

''Willy Joe.''

''The next best one you can trust?''

''Clint, Clint Dawson. He's been with us the longest.''

''Good. Send him into town and tell him to hire fifteen hands. We want men who can use a six-gun and a rifle.''

She blinked, and he was afraid she was going to cry.

''Lee, I'd love to do that, but I can't. We don't have enough money to pay for the four hands we have now at the end of the month. How can we hire any more?''

He unbuttoned his shirt and fumbled a moment, then pulled out a money belt and dropped it on the table.

''Look inside.''

She opened the flap and saw dozens of hundred dollar bills.

''Where in the world . . . ?''

''Don't worry, it's honest money. I didn't rob a bank or anything like that. Had a lucky streak. Is Clint in the bunkhouse?''

''Yes,'' Heather said, unable to take her eyes off the money.

''I'll go tell him you have something to say to him. That way he can get an early start and be back before dark with the new hands. Oh, you have any extra rifles around here?''

"Two or three."

"Send some money with him and have each man buy a Spencer or a Henry repeater. They should be able to find them for about twenty dollars used."

"Is this something we need to do? It sounds like a war."

"It could be a war. If it is, best we have something to shoot back with. I've found the best way to stay out of trouble with a bully is to show him that your gun is just as big as his is."

She watched him. She was so glad he was here. Now maybe they would get some things done that needed doing.

He finished the coffee, then went to the bunkhouse and brought back Clint.

In the ranch house Clint looked uneasy as he waited to talk to Heather. Morgan stared at the pretty girl. "Now, if you could show me to a stall in the barn or a quiet corner somewhere, I need some sleep."

"I've got a spare room for you with a real bed and clean sheets."

"Sounds good. Wake me up at ten o'clock. I've got a job to do."

"What job?"

"Come and help me if you want to."

He went to sleep four seconds after falling on the bed.

By 10:30 that morning he and Heather were down

at the gate, a half mile from the ranch house. He put up a ladder and repainted the sign that carried the brand and the name of the ranch. He made the brand black, the Circle-S name in bright red and the background white. Those were the only colors of paint they could find on the ranch.

"A place is usually as good as it looks from the road," he said. "Now you have a good impression to start out."

It was noon by the time they got back to the house and had coffee and sandwiches. In the afternoon Heather took him on a ride around the ranch, showing him where most of the cattle were and what they had left.

"Bramwell has been draining off our herd a little at a time for the past six months. He rebrands them and sells them. When Pa got sick we had close to four thousand head. Of that number we had about a thousand head of brood cows. That means we could figure on about nine hundred new calves each year and from those four hundred steers and another five hundred head to add to our brood herd."

"How many animals do you have now on the whole place?"

"We need a roundup to figure it for sure, but Willy Joe and I been talking. He figures at the most we have maybe twelve hundred head. That's brood cows, bulls and steers."

"So Bramwell owes you three thousand head of cattle."

"More or less. If we'd kept the brood cows he stole we'd have more than that by now. Our drop this spring was pitiful.''

They rode back to the big ranch house.

"I hope you don't have a range cook."

"No, he moved on four months ago."

"Good, I told Clint to hire a cook as well and bring back a couple of hundred dollars worth of food and supplies."

"Lee," she said sharply, "you know I can't pay you back, at least not right away."

"Young lady, your father was more than a friend to me when I didn't have anyone who would even admit that they knew my name. I owe him more than I could repay in six lifetimes. There'll be no talk of paying me back or what things cost. What I want you to do is tell me if you don't agree with something I have in mind for Mr. Bramwell. You're the manager as well as the owner of this ranch, so you better manage it."

"Maybe I should hire you to manage the place."

"I'm not for hire."

"Will you do the foreman's job while you're here?"

"No, Willy Joe needs that promotion." He paused. "You know, the man is head-over-appetite in love with you."

She glanced away. "Yes, I suspected. I haven't given him any encouragement, not with things the way they are."

"But you do have some feelings for him?"

"Oh, yes, he's sweet and gentle and a top hand."

"You might give him some small hint, just a little encouragement."

He checked the clock on the mantle and saw it was

3:00. "Too late to ride over and meet Mr. Bramwell. I'll go first thing in the morning. Always like to size up the competition."

"You're just going to ride in and say hello?"

"Of course. I'll be looking for a job. That way I can find out something of what's going on over there."

The rest of the afternoon Buckskin Morgan rode the west range and checked the remuda. The horses were good, fed well and strong. He knew horses, and these were some of the best he had seen. There were about sixty of them all together, enough for a full scale roundup.

It was May, and there had been no roundup in the spring. So they would have one in the fall and sell off all of the marketable steers. By then he hoped to have most of the cattle back from Bramwell, one way or another.

The one thing about range with no wire fences was that rustling worked both ways. Now it was about time to start the flow going from the Bar-B back to the Circle-S, but just how to do it was the question. He sat on his horse watching a March calf nuzzling for his supper. There was plenty of grass in this valley along the Tongue River. Later in the summer they might have to drive the main herd higher into the hills south of Brandenberg.

He rode back to the house and saw the new hands coming in from town. Clint had found 11 cowboys and a cook who drove a light wagon loaded down with supplies. Each of the men rode a horse, although some of the nags looked worse for wear than an old shoe.

Clint took them to the bunkhouse and got them situated. The cook was about 40, bearded and slightly fat. Morgan grinned. He hated to see a thin cook. A beard and the stub of an unlit cigar indicated a stubborn streak, also a vital ingredient for a range cook.

The cook met Heather, who showed him the cookshack and where to stow the goods and how to set up for the hands. He got a fire going at once since he was as hungry as the crew.

In the ranch house, Morgan found Heather in the kitchen, looking at account books.

"I want to talk to the hands," Morgan said, and let them in on the situation. Tell them we may have a small war, but I really don't think so. A good crew will forestall any more rustling."

"We've started it, and now I don't see any other way. Lord knows it wasn't working my way. We were about two months from a sheriff's sale for back taxes."

"You promoted Willy Joe yet to foreman?"

"No, I guess I should do that. I'll go with you and introduce myself to the men."

Morgan went into the bunkhouse first and yelled to get the men's attention.

"You're working for a lady, and I want you men to remember that. Her name is Heather Scoggins. She's boss, and her word is law. She wants to say hello and tell you a few things."

All of the crew was there, new and old. They sat on bunks and watched the door as Heather came in. She was a bit embarrassed at first, but then she relaxed.

"I'm your new employer. We have a big job to do, and I want you men to help me do it. This place is a little run-down, and we have some cattle on another spread. I expect every man to do his best.

"I don't know if you've met your foreman yet. This is a surprise for him as well. You'll be taking your orders from Willy Joe Dawson. Willy Joe, you're the foreman of the Circle-S, so stand up and say howdy."

Willy Joe stood, his face suddenly red. He was flabbergasted. He quickly waved and sat back down.

"I caught him by surprise, but I guarantee that he can talk. Now I want you to listen to a friend of my father's and mine as well, a man who came yesterday and stirred up a hornet's nest, but I'm sure he can take care of the situation."

Briefly Morgan told them that Bramwell had appropriated over three thousand head of Circle-S cattle, and that men from that ranch had killed the owner's only son about a year ago.

"Last night we caught six Bar-B men rustling two hundred head of Circle-S animals. They were within six miles of the ranch house. Willy Joe and I persuaded them to go back home. Six of them came on the raid, and only three got home. That same night a strange thing happened. The big barn filled with winter hay on the Bar-B ranch caught on fire and burned to the ground. It must have been spontaneous combustion from that green hay."

The men laughed.

"So, it looks like we may have some visitors. We'll

be posting guards. There will be three men out in a circle around the ranch buildings. I want you three hundred yards out, on the ground in a blanket with water and a rifle. If you see anything coming our way, you fire two six-gun shots in the air, then empty your weapon at the intruders. No need to warn them, just blast away. They aren't used to resistance. Chances are they'll cut and run so fast you'll have trouble spotting their dust.''

Morgan glanced at each man, trying to look him in the eye.

"Any questions?"

"What if they don't turn back?" one of the new men asked.

"Then you play Indian. Cover up in your blanket, and they'll ride right past you without spotting you. By then the whole ranch will be up, and we'll meet them with twenty guns."

He looked around. "Like Clint told you in town, thirty dollars a month. Any man who can't stand the sight of blood and won't shoot to protect this ranch and his job is excused right now. It's only a four hour ride back to town."

Nobody said a word or left.

"Good. The cook is getting used to his new gear. Soon as supper is ready you'll hear the triangle ring. Thanks, men. We're going to put the Circle-S back in business. Welcome aboard."

He turned and walked out of the bunkhouse with Heather. When she reached for his hand, he looked down.

"I . . . I just hope that we're doing the right thing."

"We are, Heather. Bramwell started it when he killed Kenny. Then he stole your cattle. Now is the day of reckoning, whether he's ready for it or not."

Chapter
Four

Just after ten that night, Morgan took a walk and checked on the three guards. They were alert and ready, each with a repeating rifle.

A little after midnight when shooting awoke Morgan, he got off his bed fully clothed and raced toward the sound. As he ran up to the guard post to the east he heard four rifle shots and some horses pounding away in the darkness.

The guard, one of the new men from town, looked to be about 25. He was reloading his Spencer as Morgan went up to him.

"Yes sir, Mr. Morgan, there was three of them. I yelled but they didn't stop, so I popped my six-gun twice and then fired at them with the Spencer. Don't know if I hit anything. They was maybe fifty yards away but it's damn dark out tonight. Soon as I popped my Colt they swung around. I'd say they was just checking up on us."

Morgan nodded. "I'd say about the same thing. We'll be having guard duty every night now for a while."

The men were set up on four hour shifts, which might mean some of them would be a little groggy in the daytime, but there wasn't a lot of ranching to do now anyway. Willy Joe promised to lay out a work schedule. He was going to be a good foreman.

Morgan met Heather coming out from the ranch house.

"Everything is fine. One of the hands chased off three riders. Bramwell was just checking up on your place, I'd say."

She put her arm through his and walked back to the house.

"Lee Morgan, what's going to happen next?"

"Not sure. Part of it will depend on how Bramwell reacts and if he listens to whoever is advising him. I should be able to tell a little better after I ride in there today. I'll want to borrow one of your dad's old shirts and an old hat so I don't look like I'm eating too well."

After a quick breakfast and a change of shirt to a ragged blue one a size too small for him and a battered black hat, he set out for the ride to the Bar-B.

He knew it was on the Pumpkin River. He'd ride due west, hit the water and work downstream. He hoped they didn't have any trigger-happy guards out.

By the time he found the river, it was nearly noon. He couldn't be too early and work his grub stake line.

He would pretend to be one of those down-and-out cowboys who rode from ranch to ranch asking for work but not really wanting any. The scam was to ask for a job, plead sickness or some problem that he couldn't do that specific job, have a good meal and maybe sleep in the barn, then ride out in the morning looking for the next ranch.

Shiftless cowboys had been working the dodge for years, and everyone knew the score, but the ranchers played the game, hoping they were never in the same fix.

He could see the ranch downstream when he came on the first Bar-B rider. The man had a rifle over his arm and rode out of some brush near the river.

"Where you bound for, stranger?" the cowhand asked pleasantly enough.

"Next ranch. Looks like that's it yonder. You know if the ramrod is hiring?"

"You really want a job or just riding the line?"

"The line? Hell, no. I had a job, couple of months ago, then we had a difference of opinion."

"So you rode out. Yeah, you're riding the grub line. Seen fifty just like you. Boss probably give you some grub if you ride on down to the cookshack. Foreman is Jed. Tell him Al sent you along. What place you come from?"

Morgan scratched his head a minute. "Didn't make much impression . . . Circle something . . . back over there west a ways."

"That's the Circle-S, our closest neighbor. You go see Jed."

He rode on, grinning at his play acting. Hell, he

could join one of them variety troops of actors who come through now and again.

Morgan saw a few other hands. Two men worked some cows and calves, moving them higher on the river. Nearer to the buildings he saw another man with a rifle but he only waved Morgan forward. The rider wore a white high-crowned hat called a Montana peak.

"You looking for Jed?"

"Yep."

"On the grub line?"

"Yep."

"Really want a job?"

"Not really, no."

"Thought so. Go on over to the cookshack. Jed is busy with the owner. Have something to eat and light out of here. We got some trouble and no room for strangers or loafers."

"Trouble?"

"Yeah, lost three men the other night and two windows. Now git!"

Morgan rode to the cookshack, tied his horse outside and went in. The cook looked up and grunted.

"Riding the line?"

"Looking for work," Morgan said without meaning a word of it.

"Yeah, I bet. Sit. I'll rustle you up something."

Five minutes later, the cook came out with a tin plate filled with fried eggs, bacon, refried potatoes, two big slabs of bread and a mug of coffee.

"Too early for dinner, so you get breakfast."

Morgan had a light bite back at the Circle-S and was still hungry. He ate it all and emptied the coffee cup.

When the food was gone the sweating cook brought him something wrapped in white paper.

"Push this in your pocket and ride on. Jed just get mad and ornery as hell he find you here. Three men got killed the other night. Boss went out and brought them in. Gonna be hell to pay once they figure out who done it."

"Killed?"

"Dead as door rats." The cook shook his head. "I been here since way before the new boss. Don't like what he's done to the Bar-B. Hell, we don't need to rustle stock. Got a good ranch going here. He's just in too much of a hurry."

"Thanks. I appreciate the breakfast. Where's the next ranch?"

"Not much more out this way. Best to head downstream to Miles City. Several smaller outfits around there."

Morgan shook the cook's hand and went out to his horse. He mounted and could see the two windows on the house that had been covered up with cardboard. At least Bramwell knew he was in a war now. Two men came out of the ranch house and stood on the steps.

One was tall and slender with a moustache and thinning hair. His face was pale. The other man had on range clothes and a white forehead, but from his eyes down his face was tanned. He had to be the foreman or a cowhand.

The tanned man walked out toward Morgan.

"Hey, who the hell are you?"

"Morgan's the name," he said.

The tanned man scowled. "What you doing here?"

41

"Just had some eats at the cookshack. Guard up there told me to come in."

"Riding the line?"

"Looking for work, sort of."

"You shoot a gun?"

"Only at rattlesnakes. Only reason I carry a firearm. Don't believe in shooting my fellow man. Goes back to a passage in the Bible that says . . ."

The foreman held up his hand. "I've heard that passage. If you don't want work, you just hightail it on out of here. I got a bellyful of trouble already."

"Trouble? Maybe I could help. Been known to do some preaching now and then."

"Not that kind of a problem. More like gunfire will settle it, not words. Get on out of here, preacher."

Morgan touched his hat brim and rode north along the Pumpkin River. When he looked back, it seemed like the foreman was getting a group of hands together. It could be range work, or it might be gun work.

He passed the first guard at the edge of the yard, then a second one a half mile out. When Morgan was out of sight of the second guard and behind some trees, he turned and stared at the Bar-B range.

He could see clumps of cattle grazing. They looked like a mixture of steers, range bulls, cows and calves. No roundup yet this spring for the Bar-B either. Morgan wondered why not. The Englishman was new to all this, but that foreman looked like he was a cattle man.

Buckskin Morgan made a sketch of the range, the rivers and where the main buildings were, then he rode north for three miles and sketched in where there were more cattle.

If worse came to worst, he might have to do some reverse rustling here to even up the score. One way or the other he was going to get those 3000 head of beef stock for the Circle-S. Just how he did it depended a lot on how Bramwell reacted.

He scouted north another three miles and saw that Bramwell had a lot of stock close to the ranch. As Morgan turned west and rode for the Circle-S, he came to the shared territory between the two rivers.

Most claims along a river ran outward a day's ride, roughly 20 miles. No other rancher was supposed to run his stock on this land. It wasn't law, but it was the westerner's way of doing things and establishing guidelines.

In this case the two rivers were only 20 miles apart, which meant opposing ranches couldn't reach out for 20 miles. In this situation, they split the land to a center line. The only trouble was that cattle didn't know where that center line was, and a roundup was usually needed to separate one brand from another.

Most of the Circle-S cattle on this side of the Tongue River were closer to the water for better control. Morgan guessed that much of the stock lost to Bramwell had been on this side of the river.

He got back to the Circle-S just after three that afternoon. Morgan put on his own shirt, then found Heather. She was in the office talking with Willy Joe.

"Lee, come in," Heather said. "We've been making plans. First Willy Joe wants to make a ride south to see what we have down that way."

"Sometimes those draws and little creeks can shield a lot of animals," Willy Joe said. "We'll need a roundup in the fall, but now I want to know about how many head we have to work with."

"I want to ride with you," Morgan said.

They left the first thing the next morning. It would be a hard, all day ride. As they rode, Willy Joe made a map and wrote in the number of cattle he estimated in each area.

By midmorning they were far up the Tongue and getting into some small hills. They came to a small valley leading away from the Tongue and saw a half dozen black hawks descending on one spot along the creek. When they investigated they found the remains of two steers that had been butchered. The hide was gone, and a pile of entrails to one side had been nearly eaten up by the birds.

"Who would slaughter two beef way up here? Isn't this the area where Lonesome Wolf retreated with a small band after he fled the reservation?" Morgan asked.

"Lonesome Wolf, that old Indian? Yeah, seems he did come this way. Nobody around here has seen him for years."

"Which means he's found a way to live and not touch the white man, except maybe use a few of the cattle since the buffalo have all been driven away or killed."

Willy Joe stared at the carcass for a minute and then shrugged. "Hell, guess we can't begrudge them red-skins a beef or two now and then. Ain't but about thirty or forty of them left from what I heard before. Just so they don't come down and drive off a whole herd."

They worked on up the main stem of the Tongue, counting and estimating what Circle-S cattle were left.

At noon they stopped under some willows and worked on some sandwiches that the cook had fixed for them. They drank from the clear cool stream and were about to end their short break when an Indian warrior stepped out of some brush. He held a rifle in his hands as if he could use it.

For a moment neither of the white men moved.

"Easy," Morgan said to Willy Joe. "He doesn't want to hurt us or we'd be dead by now."

"That is exactly correct," the Indian said walking forward, the rifle not pointing at them. He stopped six feet in front of them.

"One of you is riding a Circle-S brand. I am here to express my appreciation to you for the kind way you referred to my people when you found the two dead steer below a few miles."

"You were listening?" Willy Joe asked.

"I was. After all, I am an Indian. I have the skills."

"You also speak English very well," Morgan said. "You are with Lonesome Wolf?"

The warrior before them was nearly as tall as Morgan, which was unusual in the Plains Indians. He wore a pair of blue jeans that had been cut off at the knee, moccasins, and a necklace of beads that held a gleaming Phi Beta Kappa key. Morgan noted the key at once.

"No, Lonesome Wolf is now with the great spirit. He took leave of this physical world nearly a year ago and his spirit soared from the highest peak in these mountains to return to the Mother Spirits."

"But you had been with him and his band for some time?" Morgan pressed.

"Yes. I was with him in the reservation. I

45

returned to the tribe after my schooling with the white eye.''

''And after you achieved academic excellence and earned your Phi Beta Kappa key. Is all that learning wasted here in the wilds of Montana?''

''No, learning is never wasted, Mr. Morgan. Lonesome Wolf spoke of you often. I saw you five years ago, but you did not see me. I am called Young Wolf. Lonesome Wolf was my father.''

Morgan began to smile. ''Young Wolf, would you honor us by sitting down in the grass and talking for a few minutes? I have a problem that you might be able to help us with.''

Chapter Five

Morgan and Young Wolf talked, and Willy Joe listened.

"Then you can mount twenty-five warriors and older boys who can make a good show?"

"Yes, but I don't want to take these men into war."

"If a war comes it will be between the Bar-B and the Circle-S, not with you. What I want you to do is to scare the hell out of the Bar-B people who won't know why you're there."

"And for this we will have the friendship of the Circle-S owner and foreman?" Young Wolf asked.

"Not only our friendship," Willy Joe said, "but you will be free to harvest from our supply of beef when you need to. When the deer are scarce or your hunters can find no other game, then come and use our steers. We would prefer the cut steers to the producing cows.''

"I know what a steer is." Young Wolf nodded. "Then that is fair. Quid pro quo, as my Latin speaking friends would tell me. Yes, something for something.''

"Good," Morgan said. "You know where the lightning-scarred tree is at the second rock in the river below here? When we want to talk to you, I'll leave a message in a closed fruit jar there at the base of the tree. We might need you in three or four days.''

They rose then and shook hands, and the Indian slid into the brush and was gone in a flash.

"How does he do that?" Willy Joe asked.

"He's an Indian; he has the skills."

They made the rest of the ride south until they no longer found cattle in the rapidly lifting landscape. They were in the foothills before they turned and rode quickly back toward the ranch.

"Why would an educated man like Young Wolf go back to his tribe?" Willy Joe asked.

"I've seen it happen before. The outside world isn't as kind to a 'white Indian' as the academic world is. There is little chance for them to get ahead in business, to do well in any field. They are always just that 'funny Indian' who worked there. By coming back to his tribe, Young Wolf can bring the best of the white eye's culture and progressive ideas to his people. He can make life easier for them and their children, who eventually will have to try to blend in with the white eye world.''

They got back to the ranch just before supper.

"Willy Joe, let's not say anything to anyone except Heather about our talk with Young Wolf."

"Good idea," the foreman said. "I'll get my figures together and show you what I think we have out there." He waved and walked toward the bunk house.

What was he going to tell Heather about the Indians, Morgan wondered. Nothing right now, he decided. There would be time. He was curious about the Englishman. What was he planning? What might he try? Buckskin Morgan shook his head. They couldn't win if they sat still and reacted to what the other side did. What they needed was another bold strike.

He went over several possibilities, then came on an idea—a midnight roundup. Morgan grinned. He hurried into the house and found that the cook had brought in their dinner.

"What did you find upstream?" Heather asked. He noticed that she had on a different dress, one that clung to her like a wet sheet. Though it covered her from neck to wrist to ankles, it was obvious what was under the cloth.

"Pretty dress," he said. She thanked him automatically.

"What was upstream?"

"Lots of cattle. Willy Joe will have an estimate for you tonight or tomorrow. We also found two slaughtered steers."

"Butchered out?"

"Yes."

"I know, it's the Indians. Dad told me about it before he got bad. He said he had a kind of arrangement with the old chief Lonesome Wolf."

"Glad you knew. Lonesome Wolf is dead. His son Young Wolf is now leading the band. We met the young man, a college graduate and very smart. We're continuing the arrangement about the beef. He also has agreed to help us in our struggle with Bramwell."

"He'll fight on our side?" she asked, eyes wide.

"Not exactly, but Bramwell won't know that. At the right time he can send over twenty-five armed warriors as a threat and scare the hell out of Bramwell."

Heather grinned. "Morgan, I like the way you do things."

"I hope you continue to. What I'm suggesting is that tonight we go on a midnight roundup over into the Bar-B range."

"Steal their cattle?"

"No, just return some of our cattle that strayed over into their territory."

"No matter what the brand?"

"Especially no matter what the brand."

"We're talking about a running iron?"

"Yes, and rebranding and blanking out old marks, whatever it takes. Tit for tat."

Heather broke a biscuit in half and spread it with freshly churned butter and some dark, unstrained honey.

"I'll be there for the branding. There's a hollow

about six miles west of here where we often do branding—a natural pen of sorts and also a little out of the way.''

Morgan laughed softly. ''I thought you had the eyes of a fighter when I first saw you a couple of days ago. We should have some critters over there by daylight. How's your pa?''

''About the same. Doctor says he could go on this way for years. Pa don't want that. One day when he could still make sense, he told me to bring his six-gun. I . . . I told him I couldn't find it.''

''He knows a horse with three legs ain't much use around a cow outfit.''

''He would have shot himself dead that day. I wouldn't let him. Maybe I should have.''

''That's your decision, and I don't envy you having to make it.''

Morgan finished his supper. ''I better go tell the hands they start earning their pay tonight. If anybody is going to town, we could use eight saddle boots for those new rifles.''

''I'm keeping track of the money I owe you, Morgan.''

''I asked you not to.''

''I'm a woman who pays her debts.''

He watched her a minute and then walked out of the kitchen toward the bunkhouse where two games of poker were underway.

''How many of you men been on a roundup?'' Morgan asked. Most of the hands went up. ''How many ever been on a midnight roundup?'' No hands lifted.

One man chuckled. "That what I think it is?"

"Probably about what you're thinking. Tonight we're going to do a roundup over to the east. You see, a batch of our Circle-S critters strayed over that way too far and mixed with some of the Bar-B, and tonight we're bringing them back home."

Two of the men guffawed.

"That's right," Morgan went on. "A newfound friend of mine calls that quid pro quo. That's Latin meaning something in exchange for something. Or to put it another way, since they stole cattle from us, we're going to do them the honor and steal some cattle from them. By count we're about thirty-five hundred or so short. We might find four or five hundred tonight if we're lucky.

"We take anything we find?" a hand asked.

"Right. Outside of range bulls, we drag cow and calf and steer and anything out there."

"Going tonight?"

"Right. It'll be dark in about an hour. We won't be nowhere near into Bar-B land in that time. We'll leave in a half hour so get your gear ready. You with saddle boots, bring your rifles. The rest of you carry your six-guns. I don't expect any trouble. If they have a guard out we'll try to take him out without killing him or getting off any shots. My guess is that this will be a picnic in the park. Now, let's get ready."

In the barn, Morgan found a grass rope about 40 feet long. Somebody had tied a good honda in the business end. He pushed the rope through and formed a loop. It felt good. Yes, he could work with this rope. He coiled it and tied it to his saddle.

For the ride that night he picked out a new horse that hadn't been ridden all day. She was a big buckskin with black points in a line down her spine. He saddled the new mare and gave her a turn or two around the yard.

Morgan got off and waited until the men were ready. Four hands wouldn't be making the ride. They had previously been given guard duty. Three would be in the usual spots 300 yards out from the buildings and the fourth on duty near the well house.

They finally pushed off and rode a mile north, then cut due east. Willy Joe rode the point with Morgan, and the rest of the men strung out behind.

"We gonna have some rebranding to do, Mr. Morgan?" Willy Joe asked.

"I'd guess. Heather said you usually branded in a gully about six miles west of here."

"True. We can send a man down to the shop to get the irons when we come back past the ranch."

An hour later they found the first stock. A quick look in the full moonlight showed the Bar-B brand.

After they rode another half hour, Morgan figured they had passed at least 300 head.

"Let's make a line about here and start pushing everything west," Morgan said. They had seen no riders from the Bar-B. They moved into a line with the men a dozen yards apart and began moving the animals west.

A half hour later they had a good-sized herd, and six men kept them walking the same direction in a solid mass. They weren't happy to be walking at night, but none were wild. The other six men fanned out and drove in six or eight animals at a time from a wider arc. After another half hour they were finding fewer and fewer cattle. The outriders were brought in, enclosing the cattle with two men on the point guiding the lead steers, two swing riders on each side to keep the critters in line, and two more flankers along the second half of the line to maintain the march.

Behind them came three drag riders to sweep up any stragglers or strays.

Not a shot had been fired. As they moved back toward the Circle-S lands, Morgan let out a breath. He had figured that the Englishman would have had some security. Now he knew better what kind of a man he was up against.

The cattle had spread out in a long line, and Willy Joe had just ridden the length of it.

"Figure we have a tad over four hundred out there," Willy Joe said. "Damn near all of them hold the Bar-B brand."

"Any ideas how to change that to a Circle-S," Morgan asked.

"Just burn it out with one iron and put the Circle-S on the other hip."

"About all we can do."

"Gonna look damn strange with two new brands that way if anybody investigates."

"They got to get on our land first, and it's gonna take a court order for that to happen. Circuit court judge been through lately?"

"Danged if I know. I'm trying to figure out what

we can use as a brand blotter. Ain't the usual kind of iron we keep around the place.''

"Got a forge?''

"Used to be an old one in the shop. Ain't been used for a time.''

"Reckon I better use it,'' Morgan said. "Melt some bars together and jam a handle on them. Might just put the bars on over an old Circle-S iron. That would be quicker.''

They kept the critters moving even though they were getting harder to handle. A half hour later they smelled water and walked faster. When they got to the Tongue River they waded in and drank.

Once they were lined up and heading out again, Willy Joe gave the herd to Clint and told him to take them to the branding gully.

"We got to ride back to the ranch and get the irons. I'll meet you there soon as I can.''

Morgan and the foreman rode for the ranch house. It was only a little after midnight when the first guard challenged them. They called out their names and rode on in.

Morgan roused the cook and told him they needed the chuck wagon up and running.

"You couldn't tell me that last night? I need time to get it working.''

"You have from now to daylight. I didn't know for sure we'd need you when we left last night. You drive out to the sink which is about six miles northwest. You'll see our branding smoke. We'll need breakfast and a big noon meal. Miss Heather might want to ride with you.''

In the shop, Willy Joe had lit four lanterns and had pulled some lumber and boxes off the old forge. He found some wood and got the fire going.

"Should have coal, but this might get hot enough," Willy Joe said.

He picked out two of the Circle-S brands that had been damaged. "Might put some iron across these. I better get moving and be sure Clint and them hands find the right spot and keep them critters bedded down."

Morgan found the bellows pump. The bellows had a hole in the stiff leather, but it would work well enough. He blew the wood into the hottest fire he could and pushed in some half-inch, thick iron rods. It took him half a dozen tries to get the rods to melt fast to the face of the Circle-S brand. He worked four more strips on the iron, then looked around for something easier to use on the next one.

Morgan built up the fire and pumped the bellows, then slid a four-inch square of iron that had been sawed off something with a hacksaw. With tongs he held the plate against the second red hot branding iron, and this time it melted enough to weld itself tightly to the brand face.

Now, if the Bar-B brand was no larger than that, they had a chance.

He put a top over the forge, hauled his two blanking irons out to the water trough and cooled them down. Then he looked at the house and the bedroom but shook his head and mounted up.

Morgan turned and rode northwest, hoping he could judge six miles in the dark and hoping he didn't miss the gully all together.

He grinned. He had no idea that rustling cattle could be so much work.

Chapter
Six

Parrish Bramwell stared at his foreman, his eyes cold with fury. He sat behind his big mahogany desk he had brought from Chicago and tapped the ash off a long brown cigar.

"How in hell could you let something like this happen, Hackett? I pay you well to keep everything running smoothly around here."

Hackett, 28, held his hat in his hands, turning it slowly.

"Just no way I can explain, Mr. Bramwell. Don't know what got into old Scoggins all of a sudden. Thought the old man was still bad off."

"He is, and that leaves the daughter, who is about eighteen. You think she's been doing this?" He scowled in disgust at the shorter man. "Hell no, she isn't the one. Someone new has come to the ranch.

In town they told us one of the hands hired a dozen new men and a cook and a wagonload of supplies and food. Doesn't that tell you something, idiot?''

Jed Hackett backed away a step. ''Don't like to be called names, Mr. Bramwell. I put up with a lot from you, but not that. You want me to collect my wages and move on, you just nod once and I'm riding away.''

Bramwell turned. ''No, Jed, I don't want you to leave. But we should have known this was coming after we lost those three men. Then the gunshots into the house and the barn burning down. We should have been ready.''

''We sent our three men over there,'' Hackett said in his own defense. ''They damn near got their asses shot off. Two of the horses got bullet wounds.''

''That should have told us something else. The Circle-S is now guarded. We won't be able to borrow any more of their cattle. And to make matters worse, they rustled some of ours off the west pasture. How many head you think we lost last night?''

Jed pushed his hat into the other hand and crinkled his forehead. He wasn't too good at numbers. ''I'd guess maybe three hundred head or a few more. We didn't have a whole lot of our herd over there. Mix of steers and cows and calves.''

The Englishman sat behind his desk and tapped ash off his cigar again. It gave him pleasure just holding it and watching the smoke curl. He looked back at Hackett.

''So, the Circle-S is not there for the taking anymore. They are fighting back, killing our men, burning our barn, stealing our stock. What we have to do is figure out what to do next.''

"I could take all twenty-five of our hands over there with rifles and chase them right out into the prairie and then burn down all the buildings," Hackett said with a spark in his eyes.

"You could, and the sheriff would have both of us in jail in two days. Smart, Hackett. We've got to think smart here. That certainly is an option but one we won't exercise.

"Now what's left? I could buy her out. Yes, that might be a possibility. Offer to buy what she has left, her water rights and land and get her out of the country."

Bramwell stood and walked around his desk, then looked out the window. "I could sell out myself and move back to Chicago where they have some of the civilized necessities to which I am accustomed." He watched Hackett. The man was good with his guns, knew cattle and how to get them to the rail yards. Bramwell knew he needed this man and shouldn't make him angry.

Bramwell went back to his desk and tossed a cigar to Hackett, then held up a pair of matches and helped him light it.

"What else can we do? We can put up a fight. We can make small raids on the cattle. We can send snipers out to cause hell around the place during the daylight and send a few rounds into their windows at night. Yes, I like that idea. We also keep a guard force out ourselves. I want half our men reassigned as full-time guards. Three around the buildings here, the others guarding the cattle at night out on the range." He smoked the cigar and thought a moment.

"Might put them on a picket line along our western

border. If anyone hears a bunch of riders coming into our territory, all they have to do is fire three warning shots and we all charge out and meet whoever is invading us.''

"What comes first, Mr. Bramwell?''

"The guards. Be sure that they go out tonight. Cut down on the range work that we need to do. Get half the men on guard. You pick the men and who goes where. Each guard will have his revolver and a rifle.

"Today I'll work up an offer for the Circle-S and head over there tomorrow. Some cash money right now for that spread and the cattle she has left might be a good bit of news to that struggling young woman.''

"Might be at that, Mr. Bramwell. What I'm wondering, sir, is where the Circle-S got all the cash all of a sudden. She doesn't have any money in the bank, and the man in town said that the new cook paid more than two hundred dollars in cash for that load of food.''

"Cash? Now that is interesting. You go get your guard roster worked out and let me think on that.''

"Yes sir, Mr. Bramwell, I'll get right on it.'' He lifted the stogie. "And thanks for the smoke. Ain't had one this good in four or five years.''

When Hackett was outside, Bramwell left the office and went to the second floor of the big ranch house. Though the window there still had a blanket and a piece of cardboard covering it, the glass had long been swept up.

He didn't bother to knock as he went in. The girl on the bed sat up suddenly, pulling a sheet over her chest. She was blond with long hair swirling around her shoulders. Bright blue eyes looked at him. When she saw who it was she grinned, then laughed. Slowly she let the sheet slip down revealing her chest a half inch at a time.

"Hi there, cutie pie," the girl said. "I've got a little surprise for you. I figured out a brand new way to make love. Want to try it?"

"Elly, luv, there isn't any new way. I've tried them all and tried to devise some new ones, but the human body is so constructed that the convolutions are only possible in certain configurations."

Elly giggled. She let the sheet drop all the way down, revealing her pink-tipped breasts with bright red nipples. She had rubbed cherry juice on them to make them redder since he liked them that way.

Slowly she pushed up on her knees so he could see that she was naked. Her blush of blonde hair at her crotch showed streaks of wetness.

"Little darlin', you promised me you'd bring in that big long stick of yours and poke me this morning. I been waiting and getting all excited."

Bramwell grinned as he watched her. He had found her in a saloon in St. Louis. She swore it had been her very first day spreading her knees for pay. He bought her anyway and brought her with him. She'd more than served him in the past year and a half. She was one woman who seemed like she could never get enough of a man's prick.

Bramwell pushed the door shut with his foot and walked over to the bed. She grabbed his waist and kissed the fly to his pants.

"Oh, glory, he's rising already. Just like the sun, he rises every morning, and then at night he plays like he's the moon and he rises again. Glory, glory, glory!"

Bramwell laughed as she tore at the buttons on his pants. He let her pull them open and unfasten his belt, then push and tug and pull his pants and underwear down until his now-erect penis popped out.

"Oh, glory, I done died and gone to heaven. Look how big that telegraph pole is! I swear I never seen one as huge before. I just got to kiss him!"

She bent to kiss the head of his purple and red shaft. As she did, he nudged forward and the purple head slipped between her lips.

Elly gurgled a response and pulled him down on the bed. She took him in her eager mouth for a moment, then pulled away and pushed him down on his back. She sat on his thighs, facing him.

"I want to do it this way, my feet up beside your arms. Can you get in me that way?"

They turned and tried and twisted and at last made the connection, but she was kneeling by that time. She fell forward and kissed his cheek, then began to ride him like a young bull on an old, experienced cow.

Elly began to sing then grinned down at him. "I'm gonna cut them off at the pass, podner. I'm gonna cut out that little white blazed doggie. You get the strays, I'll ride drag. Hey, I'm talking cowboy here. Can you hear and get fucked at the same time?"

They both laughed—and then he could hold back no longer. He pounded up a dozen times with his hips, lifting her sleek little ass high off the bed each time until he shot deep inside her, then he dropped back spent and panting like a steam engine.

He couldn't even open his eyes for five minutes, but then he came alive and pushed her off him. She hadn't even ruffled a hair on her pretty little head.

"Don't you ever get excited, ever climax?"

"Did once in St. Louis, but mostly I just get worked up a little and then it fades away." She shrugged. "Hey, some girls do and some girls don't. No earth-shaking problem. Hey, I'm happy. I'm taking good care of you, ain't I?"

"Yes, of course, and that's the important thing." He rolled off the bed and pulled up his clothes. "Well, I say I now have a rather important decision to make. Be a good girl and go make me some tea, could you?"

She jumped off the bed and headed for the door.

"Elly, it might be better if you put on some clothes first. One of the hands or the cook might be in the house."

"Oops! Forgot. Just get used to running around bare assed, I guess." She came back and slipped into a print dress that covered her but didn't hide much. She hadn't buttoned it beyond the middle of her breasts.

"Now I look good enough for church." She hurried out the door, heading for the kitchen.

Bramwell went down the hall to his master bedroom and sat at a small desk. At least the wench could make a good pot of tea. It had taken him two months to train her, but at last she caught on. A woman who could make tea and was as good in bed as Elly didn't need to know how to do anything else.

He settled down in the small hard chair behind his

desk and went over the alternatives in his mind.

First he would make an offer to buy the Circle-S. He'd paid $80,000 two years ago for the Bar-B with about 2000 head of stock. Say the Circle-S had 1000 herd left at $30 a head—that was $30,000. Another ten for the ranch buildings, corrals and the land claims. He'd offer them $45,000 and might have a sale. That would be much easier than fighting to claim the land and the cattle without an outright purchase.

He knew the Circle-S spread was worth a lot more than that, but with the problem of her father and the hands leaving and being short of money, the girl might just decide to sell out—even though she apparently had gained some fresh money and fight from somewhere.

That worried him. He knew the family. With the old man out of action and the son gone, it was only a matter of time until he could take over the whole place. Only he wanted it quicker than that. He had been systematically thinning out their herd, stripping them of the whole damn thing.

It had worked well until two nights ago when he lost his cattle and three hands. The next day two men quit and rode off. He couldn't stand a lot of that. Even gun hands could get cold feet. Better if he just bought them out and had the whole twin valleys to himself. Then he could go after the smaller outfits back toward town.

He swore softly and poured himself a stiff shot from a whiskey bottle. Not even any fine whiskey in this ridiculous country! Now in Chicago he could get good whiskey and women who had a brain or two. Damn, why did it have to be so hard? Now he had even been stripped of some of his own cattle. He always took the stolen Circle-S herds to the far side of his ranch and rebranded them, keeping them there until the hair grew back in.

Who the hell had come to the Circle-S ranch to get them all stirred up that way? It was too late to send a man over to hire on and spy for him. They would not take anyone now without knowing for sure where he worked before. Damn!

So his best first step was still to go calling on them tomorrow morning in a buggy, just a social call and a business proposition. He would take along a thousand dollars in gold coins as an indication of his sincerity. It could be a binding down payment.

If they did take the $45,000 offer, he would have to sell some bonds in Chicago to get that much cash, but that would be no problem. He smiled. For the first time in three days he was feeling better, almost human.

They still had that roundup to do on the steers to sell. He had made a commitment for 500 head by the end of the month. It would be harder weeding them out of the cows and calves without an overall roundup, but Hackett said it could be done.

What he really needed was a new woman. He enjoyed it when the girl got as much pleasure from sex as he did. Elly didn't, but that was the only complaint he had. She never had a headache or put him off, not once that he could remember.

Bramwell walked to the window and looked out across his range. He wanted it all, for as far as he could see, for as far as he could ride in a week!

He saw a rider come around the bend in the lane and head for the ranch house. The way the man sat on his horse was vaguely familiar. Then he saw the sun glint off a badge on the man's chest. It was Sheriff Straud from Miles City. Damn, what had happened now? Bramwell went down the stairs to meet the lawman at the door.

Sheriff Straud left his horse tied outside the fence around the ranch house and walked through the gate. He saw Bramwell on the porch and waved.

"Figured it was about time we had a meet," the sheriff said.

"Might be, Sheriff. Come on in and I'll see if I can find the good sippin' whiskey."

A few minutes later they settled down in the parlor with half-filled glasses of Tennessee whiskey.

Sheriff Straud was medium-sized, but he had long powerful arms that ended in ham-sized hands that could crush any man's grip in the state. He wore a moustache but no beard, and his hat stayed on like the cowboy he used to be. Flint green eyes stared at the rancher.

"Hear you had a man killed out here couple of days ago," he said flatly.

"True. An old range bull got on a tear and caught one of my hands off his horse and not watching what he was doing. Damn horn went in his chest and ripped out damn near his chin and took half of his heart with it. We destroyed the bull. Took the man's personal items and mailed them to his parents back in Kentucky."

"I heard it was three men and all died of lead poisoning," the sheriff said. He lifted his tone slightly but just short of making an accusation.

"Not likely. One bull to get three cowboys means they got to be sleeping. We had a couple of hands get

spooked after that and ride off. You know how unhappy cowhands talk. Tales get told that just grow and
grow.''

Sheriff Straud nodded. ''Know how stories can get
started. Ain't really why I rode down here. We got
ourselves a small problem. Railroad put on a new man
to check brands. Guess there's been some problems
back east. Anyways, we got a new man who don't
reckon how we do business out here in Montana.''

''You talked to him yet, Sheriff?''

'' 'Deed I ain't. Figured you'd want to do that direct.
Always means more that way.''

Bramwell rubbed his hand over his long, lean face.
He'd shaved that morning but it was hard to tell now.
Damn, he hated to shave. He looked at the sheriff of
Custer county.

''Of course, I'll be in town in a day or two to talk
to him. That reminds me, I haven't made my contri-
bution to your reelection campaign fund yet this
month.''

He reached in his pocket and took out five double
eagle gold pieces. He stacked them in his hand and
then clinked them together as he counted them. Then
he put them in the sheriff's hand.

''Thanks for stopping by. Case there's any talk in
town you can set them straight. I'll see that new brand
agent. What's his name?''

''Iver Ingram. He's staying at the Plainsman Hotel.''

The pair sipped on the whiskey until it was gone,
then the lawman stood.

''Better be getting back. Thanks for the drink.''

''No trouble. See you in a few days.''

Bramwell watched the lawman walk across the front

porch and down to his horse.

Bramwell nodded. That was the way he liked his lawmen, ordered up and paid for. It was the only way to do business.

Chapter
Seven

Buckskin Lee Morgan had forgotten what hard work branding was. The makeshift blanking iron worked well, covering the old brand completely. Blanking irons were used many times when a herd was sold and had to be moved through other ranges where some confusion might take place.

On long drives, Morgan had seen special trail brands used to keep stock identified. He figured there would be no problem with a blanked brand here.

One of the top hands had thrown a loop under the rear hooves of a steer and backed his horse away, pulling the rear legs together and tipping the steer on its side.

Then the men with the branding irons stepped in, blanked out the old brand and put the new one six inches away. This was lots easier than branding the steer on the other hip which now lay flat on the ground.

The animal bellowed when the hot iron hit its skin. The object was to burn through hair and into the thick hide but not too deeply, or it wouldn't heal right. In effect the brand produced scar tissue in the desired shape.

The cowboy eased the pressure on the feet and let the steer scramble to its feet.

The steer stood there a moment, not sure it was free, then bleated when the cowboy herded the animal out to a gathering herd of newly branded cattle.

It was well into the afternoon. They had branded the calves and cows first, since they were easiest. Then they went to work on the steers. They found 15 or 20 animals with the Circle-S brands already in place. These were cut out of the herd and moved to one side.

Morgan was pleased at the way the men worked. Branding is a team operation, and if one man misses his throw or eases up too quickly, the whole process often has to start again.

He rode out and roped another steer, a yearling that would bring top price at the stockyards. The steer followed him, twisting and turning its head until he came near the fire. Some long ago memory flooded the steer's small brain and it remembered pain. It bolted to one side, but Morgan's rope was snubbed around his saddle horn and the larger horse stopped the flight of the frightened steer.

A minute later one of the hands threw a loop around the back feet and the steer toppled over and the branders rushed in.

Heather rode up on a sleek pinto beside Morgan and watched.

"You've thrown a rope before," she said. "I like the way you work. Can I talk you into staying on the Circle-S?"

"It would take some tall talking. I'm supposed to have a ranch up in Idaho, if I ever get back up there and take care of it."

"Men have been known to work two ranches—even own two ranches."

He saw her look up sharply at him, testing the waters. He knew what she was thinking and had felt some of the same tension the first night he was on the spread, but that just couldn't be. She was young and needed a fine young man to work the ranch and raise her children. Hell, he was too old for her.

"Heather, one ranch is even too much for me right now. Let's see what happens here in the next few days. I'm sure Bramwell is going to make some kind of move."

She set her mouth and sighed. "I know you're right, but sometimes I get so impatient. Dad just sits there and watches me with that one good eye. He can't even write down what he wants to say anymore."

"I know it's hard."

He watched her. She had worn a blouse this morning open at the throat and stretched tightly across her full breasts. He'd seen some of the cowboys openly staring at her. She didn't seem to mind, but it was a dangerous way for her to dress. She caught him looking at her and grinned.

"I better be getting back to the ranch house. Looks like you'll be done here in an hour or so. Willy Joe and I talked, and he's going to drive the herd well west and north so the Bar-B riders can't find them. In two

73

months those blotted brand marks will hardly show.''

"You want a hand to ride back with you?"

"No, not unless you want to come."

"Somebody should. I don't like the idea of you riding that far alone."

"Good. We'll leave in about ten minutes. The chuck wagon should be almost back to the house by now."

When they rode, she kept watching him and at last caught his glance.

"Did I tell you I was head-over-applesauce in love with you when I was a skinny thirteen?"

"You mentioned that."

"I'm more grown-up now, Morgan, but you still don't look at me that hungry way that some of the cowboys do."

"Good, I'm trying hard not to."

She laughed. "Maybe I'm making some progress after all."

"You know that Willy Joe would kill for a smile from you," he said.

"I know. We've talked about it. I've kissed him. He's a nice boy."

"He's twenty-two or three."

"Actually, he's twenty-one, but I prefer an older man."

"That kind of talk isn't a good idea, Heather."

"It seems right to me, Lee Morgan. Let's rest up there by the river. I'm getting tired."

They rode under the trees along the Tongue River about a mile above the ranch house. He let both horses drink and found Heather sitting on the grass, her split skirt spread around her.

"Come and sit a minute. There's no rush to get back to the house."

He tied the two horses and sat down facing her.

"Morgan, you know how bitchy a woman can get when she starts ordering men around? It gets awful. I knew a widow who ran a ranch over east a few years ago. She was in her thirties, blonde and pretty with two kids. Then her husband got killed, and a year later she was as tough as a saddle horn. She was tanned like leather and swore worse than the cowhands. A year later her ranch was going nicely, making money. Then one day she met a gambler in town, sold her ranch for half of what it was worth and ran off with him to San Francisco."

"She must have wanted to," Morgan said.

"Lee, I never want to get that hard, that bitchy or that desperate. I want a man to run this ranch. I want you to run it."

He had been chewing on a stem of a red clover plant, and when he looked up Heather had unbuttoned the fasteners on the tight blouse halfway down.

"Heather . . ."

She slid over beside him, caught his face and kissed him. It wasn't a virgin's kiss. She clung to him, pushed hard against his chest, and her mouth opened for his probing tongue. When the kiss ended her eyes were closed, then she popped them open with a look of awe and joy on her pretty face.

"Oh, Lee Morgan, yes, yes, yes!"

She pulled the other buttons open on her blouse, caught one of his hands and pushed it under her thin chemise to her naked flesh.

When his hand covered one of her breasts, he automatically stroked and petted it. Then he pulled his hand away and caught her shoulders.

"Morgan, don't lecture me. Don't tell me a woman isn't supposed to try to win the man she wants. I don't want to hear any of that because I don't think it's true. It sure as hell isn't fair." She reached up and kissed his lips, nibbling at them, then she leaned back.

"Yes, maybe I'm not the greatest beauty in the world or have the best body, but I'm hoping I'm good enough to get some interest from you, Lee Morgan."

She pushed the sides of her blouse apart and lifted the thin white cotton chemise to reveal both her breasts.

"Do you like them? Men seem to go crazy over bare breasts. I'll never know why." She caught his hand and placed it over an orb with it's pink areola and hard, erect nipple.

He pulled his hand away, then gently brought her chemise back over her breasts and pulled the blouse together. Then he put his arm around her and lay down in the grass. They were side by side with his arm around her shoulders, her face on his chest.

"Beautiful little lady, you are a damn tempting package. You're right that most men go crazy over breasts, but it's a dangerous game. I've seen a lot of ladies without their clothes. Each of you make one of the most beautiful sights in the world, but almost always there are consequences, obligations to be paid.

"Right now we're talking about your future. It isn't with me. I'm a rover. You want to make love with me for a month, say, and then I take off and not come back for another five years?"

"I could make you want to stay here, Buckskin Lee Morgan. I could make love to you every day. I could . . ."

"You could do a hell of a lot better. I'll make you a small bet. I bet that when you kissed Willy Joe he didn't try to rip your clothes off, right?"

"No, he didn't try, but I wouldn't have minded."

"He probably didn't even touch your breasts, did he?"

"No, not at first. Not until I picked up his hand and put it there. Then he moved his hand away quickly."

"Why?"

"Why? He said he'd do everything I wanted him to do right after we got married. He's proposed to me three times."

"He's a fine young man. He's your foreman. And don't worry about getting hard and bitchy. It wouldn't work for you."

"But sometimes I want somebody so bad. I get all hot and itchy and I dream about it and once in a while . . . I mean I put my hand down there below and I rub." She looked away. "I know that's just awful, but it makes me feel better."

"That's normal, natural, not a thing to worry about. You don't have a mother to help you with these things. Young boys and young men get the same feelings, usually lots stronger."

She pushed against him and sighed. "Is it true that boys take their hand and . . . you know . . . do it themselves?"

"Yes, true. Makes them feel better. I used to do that now and then."

"Oh, damn, why does it have to be so difficult? Why

do I have to want you so much, but you don't want me?''

"Hey, not true. Wanting to make love to you is one thing, but letting you do it is another matter. Hell, let me be kind and do the right thing here for you. That's more important to me than ripping off your clothes and fucking your brains out.''

Heather giggled like a young girl. "I've never heard that word but once or twice.'' She sighed. "Would you at least kiss me again and maybe feel my breasts?''

He reached over, kissed her and put his hand on her breast. She bit his lip, held him and jammed her tongue into his mouth, and as she did he could feel her jolting into a climax. She shivered and moaned in rapture. He rubbed her breast gently and held the kiss as long as she climaxed. Then he put both arms around her, pulled her over him and held her tight.

It was three or four minutes before she sighed and pushed up so she could see him plainly.

"That was glorious! Marvelous. The very first time I've climaxed when I was actually kissing a man. I'll remember that for just years and years.''

She sat up with the bounce and renewal of youth.

"Now, cowboy, we better get ourselves back to the ranch and get our clothes changed and a bath for me and them some supper. I'm as starved as if I roped half the cattle out there today.''

That night Morgan asked Heather to invite Willy

Joe to eat with them. He was management and could give them a report on the branding.

"You don't give up easy, do you, Morgan?"

"Not when I know something is right. Anyway I don't want you attacking me in my bedroom."

She laughed and stuck out her tongue at him.

Willy Joe was self-conscious that night at the supper table for three. He had taken a pan bath, combed his hair, shaved and put on his best go-to-town shirt.

A wild steer had tried to run when roped and had to be dumped with the catch line. In the process the animal had broken it's neck and had to be shot.

That meant fresh steak for the crew for the next two days—or as long as they could keep the meat fresh in the cool of the well house. After the steaks, vegetables and fresh dinner rolls, they sat back with their coffee.

"What kind of totals did you get today," Morgan asked Willy Joe since he hadn't volunteered more than three words as they ate.

"We branded a hundred and twenty-two cows, ninety-four calves and a hundred and ninety-three steers. We found twelve cows that had Circle-S brands and eight calves with them—a fine day's work—but I figure the Bar-B still owes us another twenty-five hundred head. They've rustled that many over the past two years. We didn't even notice it until the roundup a year ago. We'd missed roundup that fall, and the spring was a real shock." He gulped and looked back down at his plate as if he'd talked too long.

"Four hundred and twenty-nine all together,"

Heather said, "not counting the one we're having for supper. Now that's a good start in getting our cattle back. But will it be so easy the next time?"

"Not easy at all, I'm afraid," Morgan said. "Bramwell will pull most of his stock back from this side of his land. We better do the same thing and leave nothing on the eastern side of the Tongue River for a while. They just might make a retaliatory raid."

"Our guards haven't seen or heard anything the last two nights," Willy Joe said.

"We have to keep the guards on duty until this is settled," Heather said.

Dinner was over, and they sipped their coffee.

A strangled cry came from the other room, and Heather dropped her coffee cup, shattering it on the heavy plank table.

"Daddy!" she cried.

They all rushed into the living room, through the parlor and to his bedroom.

Milburn Scoggins lay on his bed, flopped over forward as if he had tried to get up. His one good eye stared blankly at them. Morgan got there first and held his finger under the man's nose, then he pushed him back on the bed and held his fingers to the frail chest. He touched the man's neck and then looked up at Heather.

"I'm sorry, Heather."

She gave a cry and leaned against Willy Joe. He caught her and held her and walked her out of the room. Morgan reached over and closed the eyelids on the remains of Milburn Scoggins, then pulled the sheet up over his face, went out and closed the door.

He could hear Heather in the parlor, crying softly. Then he heard Willy Joe talking to her calmly and comforting her. Morgan slipped outside. It was time to check and be sure the guards were out.

Chapter
Eight

Parrish Bramwell drove the light buggy into the lane leading to the Circle-S and at once noticed the repainted sign and the gate post that had been straightened. He pondered that as he drove down the half-mile lane until he came to a cowboy on a horse 300 yards from the house. The man carried a rifle across his saddle and held up one gloved hand.

Bramwell stopped the buggy and let the rider come up to him.

"State your name and your business," the guard said as he had been instructed.

"I'm your neighbor, Parrish Bramwell, owner of the Bar-B, and I'm here to see the owner of the Circle-S."

"Don't reckon she'd want to see you this morning," the guard said, blocking his way.

"Now why would that be? Just tell her that I'm here."

"Don't know. We buried her pa this morning."

"Well then, by all means I should see her and pay my respects. I knew the man for over two years."

"I dunno."

"Young man, you tell her or your foreman that I'm here, and let someone in authority decide. Do it at once."

The guard looked at him and shrugged. "You wait right there or you're liable to get shot at. I'll be back."

The guard turned and trotted up to the backdoor of the big ranch house. Bramwell waited. So the old man had died. Good. It put the girl in a harder position. Now the ranch was completely her responsibility. That might work to his advantage.

A short time later the rider came back.

"You're to go to the front porch and wait there. Someone will see you."

"Thank you, my good man."

Bramwell chuckled as he drove up to the front porch and stopped the rig. He stepped down and was at the porch steps when a tall thin man came out the front door. He wore a working cowboy's clothes and no sidearm.

"Bramwell, you're not welcome on this ranch," Willy Joe said.

"I came to pay my respects over your boss," Bramwell said smoothly.

"That's a lie. You couldn't have known until the

84

guard told you. Why are you here, Bramwell?''

"Very well, keep it on a business basis. I came to make an offer to buy the Circle-S. It's next door to my own spread and would be a good addition. I'm prepared to make a substantial offer.''

"The owner is not interested in selling. We are interested, however, in getting back the three thousand head of cattle your men have stolen from us over the past two years.''

"I resent that implication, young man,'' Bramwell said, bristling.

Another man stepped out the front door. He was taller, broader and wore a gun that was tied low. Bramwell knew at once that this man could be trouble.

"Resent it all you want to, Bramwell,'' Morgan said. "We know you rustled the cattle, and we can prove it. What we're more interested in first is your turning over to us the three men who escaped three nights ago when they tried to rustle another two hundred head from the east range.''

"If I was wearing a gun I'd make you back up those words, sir!'' Bramwell shouted. "Ridiculous charges. Outrageous. That's an insult of the most vile kind.''

"You deserve it, Bramwell. Don't try to be modest,'' Morgan said.

"I'm not going to stay here and be insulted,'' Bramwell said.

Morgan's gun came out smoothly, and before Bramwell could even think of drawing the derringer he was covered.

"You'll stay right here until we say you can go, Bramwell. We could trade your carcass for the three rustlers, but if we started hanging rustlers from your spread, you probably would only have the cook and a stable boy left."

"We could ransom Bramwell here for those three thousand head of beef," Willy Joe said. "Think his hands would figure he was worth that much?"

"Doubt it. Don't figure as how this runaway Englishman is worth much to anybody as a hostage." Morgan shook his head. "Now if he'd sent over his foreman, that would be a man we could use as a fair exchange."

Bramwell felt his skin chill. What was happening here? How could they be so outlandish? How could they be so right? He squared his shoulders.

"I'll just put it down to a hard morning on the whiskey bottle for you two. If the owner is here, I'd like to make her an offer on her ranch."

The six-gun in Morgan's hand snarled, and a hot lead slug ripped into the dirt between Bramwell's polished boots. The Englishman jumped two feet backwards, his eyes wide.

"No cause for any gunplay," he said in a stronger voice than he felt.

"Let's talk business, Bramwell," Morgan said. "Over the past two years you've rustled over three thousand head of stock from this ranch, rebranded them and sold them in the Miles City stockyards. Say a third of those were cows that would have produced at ninety percent over two years. So that means there would have been another nine hundred calves a year

86

or eighteen hundred head.

"You owe this ranch four thousand, eight hundred head of stock. We'll expect a thousand head on our border by noon day after tomorrow. If they aren't there, we'll just have to come and get them. Understand?"

"You have a vivid imagination, I certainly won't—"

Another shot slammed into the soft morning. The slug tore through the Englishman's pant leg where it bloused around his boots.

"At noon, day after tomorrow!" Morgan roared. "If you think you're lucky you might try making some additional comment that will upset me. When I get angry my six-gun here just seems to go off."

Bramwell turned stiffly and walked toward his rig. Morgan fired again, and the round slammed into the wooden box that held up the buggy seat. Another round made holes through the black top of the buggy.

Bramwell turned and stared at Morgan.

"The next time I see you—"

"You better have a thousand head of cattle or I'm going to shoot up your right knee. How do you like walking on crutches, Bramwell?"

The Englishman glared at Morgan and Willy Joe, stepped into the rig and drove away. He didn't look back.

Heather slipped out the front door and watched the buggy drive down the lane.

"Thanks, both of you. I don't know what I would have done without you. We're not selling the ranch, that's for sure. Think he'll bring the thousand head day after tomorrow?''

"Not a chance," Morgan said. "So we need to have an alternate plan ready to go.''

"What is it?" Willy Joe asked.

"Not the slightest idea. We'll work up something.''

Two hours after dark that night a rifle fired six shots into the big Circle-S ranch house. Four windows broke. The lights in the house were blown out quickly, and four men rode hard to the east but found no sign of the shooter.

About the same time the two Bar-B riflemen were peppering the Circle-S ranch house, Bramwell stood up and shouted in his den. Elly looked at him in surprise.

"By jove, I've got it. Knew I'd seen that face before—a face I'd seen and a man good with a gun. Bad combination, Elly, but I got the bastard. I've seen him on a wanted poster in the sheriff's office. Know damn well I have.

"How would you like to go to town and buy a new dress tomorrow? We'll leave at daylight. I need to see that sheriff as soon as I can. Without their top gun, the Circle-S will be much easier to deal with.''

Bramwell went to the front door and told the guard there to go find Jed Hackett and have him come into the den. Five minutes later Hackett was there. He looked at Elly who had slipped on a blouse, but she didn't bother buttoning it and the swell of both breasts showed plainly. Hackett looked away quickly, and as he did, Elly swept the sides of the blouse open, then closed.

"Hackett, you know I rode to the Circle-S this morning. They've got out guards, and two men talked to me. One was the foreman, tall and skinny. The other one was also tall but solid and used his gun like a great sharpshooter of yesteryear. He was an artist with it."

He told Hackett about the conversation and the demand for the thousand head.

"We're not taking them back, are we?"

"Absolutely not, but we need to give them something—a surprise, I'd say, that will catch them off guard."

"With their men surrounding the place, that's gonna be hard, Mr. Bramwell."

"True, but that's why I'm paying you so well. And speaking of pay, I think it's time you had a bonus."

"A bonus?"

"Right you are, Hackett. Elly, for instance. You want to throw a good poke into her?"

"Parrish, no!" Elly said quickly.

Bramwell ignored her. "What do you say, Hackett?"

The foreman stood there, looking as if he wondered if the boss was joking with him or not.

"Luv, slip out of that damn blouse and show Mr. Hackett here what twin beauties you have."

She frowned, then saw that he was serious. It took

her half a second to evaluate her situation and know there was little else she could do, so she grinned.

"Hell, why not. One prick is a lot like the next one. Hey, Hackett, you ever see a pair this good before?" She shrugged out of her blouse and stood straight, pushing out her breasts to show them off at their best.

"Holy shit!" Hackett said softly.

"That's putting it a bit crude, old boy, but I think you are rather impressed. Go ahead, get on with it. Been a time since I got to watch one."

Hackett turned toward the owner. "You want to watch? Watch the two of us . . ."

"Yes, quite. Surprising what one can learn about technique in copulation by simple observation this way."

"Where?" Hackett asked.

"Why, on the floor, if you find no better spot."

"Come on, luv," Elly said, "the man is serious. I can tell. He gets a wild hair now and then and won't nothing satisfy him but a good watch. Two or three times and he'll be purring like a kitten again." She took a lap robe from a chair and spread it out on the floor and sat down.

"Come on, luv. You don't even have to take your boots off. Some girls are particular that way, but not me. I'm easy."

Hackett looked at his boss, and Bramwell motioned him forward.

"Come on, come on. The girl could catch cold down there."

When Hackett slid down to the floor, Elly laughed softly and unbuttoned his pants.

"Don't be embarrassed. Just forget he's over there. Just you and me, right, Hackett? Ain't you watched my tits swinging around and wished you could play with them?"

Hackett nodded.

"Here's your big chance, Hackett. Grab them, kiss them, bite them. You've got a license to fuck here, so come on."

She had his pants open by then and had fished out his prick. She giggled.

"You still soft as an old worm." She lifted up and pushed a big breast into his face. "Chew me, darlin'. Chew on me a little, and maybe that'll get your motor running, like on one of them trains. Come on, chug-chug."

Hackett kissed the big breast, then closed his eyes and sucked the nipple into his mouth. She wiggled out of her skirt and wore nothing under it. As she told Bramwell often, no sense wearing a lot of clothes that she would have to take off twice a day to service him. Made it simpler.

Hackett kissed her breasts, and then she pulled him down toward her stomach and then further down, his head in a grip that he didn't try to break.

A minute later his face pushed into the blonde fuzz around her crotch, and he moaned in amazement.

"Just a few licks, little darlin', and you'll be hot and ready to poke."

She grabbed his shaft, and this time he was erect and ready. Elly went on her hands and knees on the floor and pushed her round little bottom at him.

"Think you can find a hole in there somewhere, sweetheart? Take a shot and see what you can do. Just don't trip over your pants."

Hackett came up behind her and probed.

"Lower down, you fucker, lower down."

He poked at her again, and then she grinned and giggled and nodded and began pushing backward with every stroke he made. Soon they set up a motion that suited both of them, his hips pounding harder and harder until he bellowed and fell forward, pushing the girl flat on the floor on her big breasts.

"G'damn, I think he made it." Elly looked over at Bramwell and laughed. He had his back to them, and now he turned and finished buttoning the front of his trousers.

"Was it real good for you, Bram? Good as before? Damn but you are a corker. I'm just glad we don't have a big bitch dog or you'd be on her."

Hackett stopped heaving and rolled away from her. Quickly he adjusted his clothes and buttoned his fly. When he looked at Elly sitting there naked on the lap robe beside him, he shook his head.

"Tomorrow I won't never believe it happened. All them tits and that hole and a poke I won't never forget. Goddamn!" He leaned in and kissed her surging breasts again and licked her nipples.

"Hey, you getting ready for another one, Hackett?" She looked at Bramwell. "You said to do him once or twice, or are you too tired for a second go-around?" She laughed when Bramwell shook his head.

"Sorry, luv," she said touching Hackett. "Only once. Maybe another night when the topper there is feeling like a real strange person. Y'all come asking once in a while, hear?''

Hackett stood up, took another long look at Elly in her naked glory and then hurried out.

Elly shook her head. "That poor jackass, Hackett. Now he's gonna have a hard on all night.''

Chapter Nine

When the four shots slammed into the Circle-S ranch house, Buckskin Morgan had been in the parlor talking with Heather. They were trying to lay out a course of action against Bramwell.

One round shattered a window in the parlor, missing the pair by six feet. Morgan grabbed Heather and pushed her flat on the floor. Then he crawled to the window and looked east, but he saw nothing that would show new rounds being fired. Smart. Hit and run.

"It's probably over, I'm sure Willy Joe will send some men out, but they won't find anyone. Fire and move. Those men are on their horses and riding hard for the Bar-B by now."

"Why?"

"Harassment. Paying back. Tit for tat. Pride. Now more than ever we need a plan."

"I don't like the idea of stealing our stock back from Bramwell," Heather said.

"It's practical, quick and sure. The only thing is it's also illegal. How is the sheriff in this county?"

"Mostly a joke. He's bought and paid for by the big ranchers, especially Bramwell. I don't give him a cent. He has a campaign fund he says he uses to spend on his electioneering. He's a fraud, but he's in his second term. My guess is that Bramwell pays him monthly."

"So we could be at risk with the law." Morgan scratched his head in frustration. "I don't see any other way. The man stole almost eighty thousand dollars from you. He has to pay it back."

"But we can't prove it."

"Not in a court of law. But just maybe the jurisprudence of fear can help us out a little."

"What?"

"Never mind, just some law talk an old friend of mine used to do." Morgan stood there and watched her for a minute.

"Willy Joe Dawson is a good man. You remember that, young lady. Right now it's time for another night ride."

For a moment Heather looked young, small and vulnerable. "Are you going to tell me what you're going to do?"

"Not sure yet. I'm picking two men and going for a night ride to see what we can turn up."

"Going to the Bar-B?"

"Heading in that direction."

She jumped off the couch and ran to him, hugging him tightly. "Buckskin Lee Morgan, you be careful.

96

I don't know what we'd do around here without you.''

He gave her a hug and set her down. "Won't have to worry about that. Be back in time for some breakfast.''

Morgan got a light jacket and headed for the bunkhouse. The four riders who had investigated the shots were back, but they had found nothing in the darkness. He took Willy Joe aside.

"I need three good men who can shoot and have a little living experience.''

"You going on a ride east?''

"Yep. Going to try to find one or two of the Bar-B hands.''

"And then?'' Willy Boy asked.

"Hell, I'm not sure. Try to talk to them, reason with them. Who can tell?''

"Want me to go along?''

"No. Need you here in case they make another attack even though I don't think they will. Let's keep our guards out, maybe put on a couple more.''

Willy Joe picked out the three men he thought would be best. Two of them were the oldest in the group, the other one a young redhead but with lots of range savvy and good with a rope.

"You men bring a jacket, a rifle, a six-gun, your best rope and we'll go on a ride.''

Two hours later they moved up quietly through Bar-B land toward the buildings that they couldn't see yet. Morgan told them what he wanted them to do. They spread out just so they could see each other in the dark and began walking their mounts forward. The horses' muzzles were tied shut with bandanas so they couldn't whinny and give them away.

They moved slowly that way until one man held up his hand and they all stopped. Morgan moved over to the rider who had signaled. The redhead pointed forward.

"Saw what has to be a cigarette burning up there. Guy takes a drag every so often, glows red as hell."

Morgan nodded and dismounted soundlessly, handing the reins to the redhead. "Move everyone back for five minutes and wait," he said.

Morgan lifted his six-gun and walked forward slowly, being sure he didn't make any noise. He moved to the side for 20 yards, then forward again.

He squatted and watched the spot where he guessed the sentry would be. Soon he saw the glow of a cigarette. The redhead had been right. Morgan moved again until he was even with where the glow had been. Now he could see that the man was on the sloping bank of a little stream.

Morgan eased down into the now dry stream bed and paused. He saw another cigarette glowing. Two men? He edged forward slowly, then saw the cigarette move suddenly. The man had spotted him.

He stood and growled. "What the fuck you guys doing smoking? You ain't supposed to be smoking out here." By then he was on them, one man scrambling down the bank, the other one stamping on his smoke and trying to stand up at the same time.

Morgan clubbed the closest one with the butt of his .45 and grabbed the other one by the shirt front, pushing the big revolver barrel against his throat.

"Easy, no noise or you're dead and in hell. Agreed?"
The man nodded.

Morgan stripped the six-guns from the two, then picked up one rifle. "Anybody check on you, make rounds?"

The man shook his head.

"When you due to be relieved?"

"Daylight."

"Perfect. Haul your buddy up the bank now. I don't want any talk or noise. You try to run and you're dead."

The frightened cowhand lifted his partner and pushed him up the bank, then climbed up himself.

Morgan jumped up beside them.

"Now carry him," Morgan said.

"Can't. He's too heavy."

"Wake him up then. Slap his face. Get him conscious right now or I slit his throat."

The cowboy knelt by his friend and got him to regain consciousness.

"We got caught, and he's got our guns," he told his buddy. "We got to do as he says, you understand, Wally?"

The man nodded and stood up. Slowly they walked due west. It was ten minutes before they found the three men and the horses.

"Jackpot," Morgan said. "We needed jacks or better to open, and it went around three deals and look what we got. I didn't find any horses. We tie their wrists together in front of a rider. Mount up."

He helped the two Bar-B men mount, then the redhead came up.

"Want me to go look for their horses? Must be a pair back there in that gully you told us about."

Morgan nodded.

The redhead was back in ten minutes with the two Bar-B horses. They had the Bar-B guards mount, tied their wrists to the saddle horns and led the horses. They rode back toward the Circle-S covering about a mile before they found the dry creek and followed it down a half mile to a stream with water in it and two good-sized cottonwoods.

Morgan stared at the two Bar-B men, then at the cottonwoods. He rode up close to them and looked each man in the eye until they glanced down.

"Both you men know that the Bar-B has been stealing cattle from the Circle-S ranch, isn't that so?"

"We heard about it," the taller of the two said. He was the one captured without being knocked out. Now he was angry and surly. "You'll have to talk to the owner about that."

"Not true," Morgan said quickly. "Both of you have been on raids into Circle-S land, isn't that right?"

"Yeah. We were told to go, ordered to go," the smaller one said this time.

"But you knew that was illegal. You knew you were rustling cattle. Both of you know what the penalty is in Montana for rustling cattle?"

"Yeah, sure, but a court would have to decide if we was guilty," the taller one said.

"We've got a court right here—a qualified judge, a jury of your peers. What could be more legal?"

"You . . . you wouldn't do that," the smaller man said.

"Why not? The Bar-B has stolen more than four thousand eight hundred head of cattle from the Circle-S. You want to pay forty dollars a head for each one you've helped steal?"

"God, I couldn't do that."

"I figured." Morgan turned to the three Circle-S riders who sat there watching, not sure what would happen. "Members of the jury, have you reached a verdict in the case of these two Bar-B riders and the rustling charges."

"We have your honor," the redhead said quickly. "We find both guilty of rustling."

"What's your verdict?"

"That they be hanged by the neck until they are dead," the oldest of the three riders said.

"The court concurs. One of you men throw your rope over the big branch on that cottonwood. Might as well get this over with."

"You're not really gonna do this," the larger of the men said, but his words were tinged with fear.

"Do it? Of course. You rustled Circle-S cows, calves and steers. You admitted it, so you both die."

"We were following orders."

"That's no excuse. If my boss tells me to kill everyone on his ranch, you expect me to do it? You follow an order when it's lawful, not to rustle cattle."

The redhead threw his lariat over the cottonwood. The rope was too short to double down so it could be tied off.

"Put a loop in the end and snake it up there tight," Morgan said. "We don't have to take the rope down."

A few minutes later the rope was in place.

"Can't tie a proper hangman's knot in a lariat," the redhead said.

"What's your name?" Morgan asked him.

"Fletcher. Dan Fletcher, Mr. Morgan."

Morgan took the rope from him in the dim light

and tied a slip knot with a big loop. He pointed at the tallest of the two rustlers. "Bring that one over here. Untie his hands from the horn and tie them behind his back, then lift up the stirrups so he can't get his feet in them."

"Still don't think you're gonna do this," the taller cowboy said. "This would be cold-blooded murder!"

"The way the Bar-B men did to the young Scoggins boy when they shot him through the head? That was murder. This isn't at all the same. More like the way the three rustlers two nights ago got shot while trying to steal more Circle-S cattle."

"You guys did that?"

"Some of us. Man's got a right to defend his property, protect what's his. Rustler is a damn bad word around here, in case you're a stranger to Montana."

The man flinched as Morgan dropped the loop over his head and double-checked the knot. He left a foot of slack but didn't think the drop off the horse would be enough to break the cowboy's neck, not without a proper heavy knot to snap his head to the side.

Morgan rode close to the man. "You got any last words to say, rustler?"

"Ain't no rustler. Just followed orders. I didn't know . . ."

He stopped. "Like hell you didn't know," Morgan shouted. "I'll bet everyone in the bunkhouse was talking and joking about how easy it was to rustle cattle off the Circle-S, especially with the son dead and the old man laid up in bed and about ready to die."

Morgan rode around him and faced the other way, checked his tied hands, then the knot against his throat.

"You have a name?"

"Carlyle, Ken Carlyle."

"You have anything else to say, Carlyle?"

He looked at the other men. The three Circle-S riders were lined up about ten feet away. Two of them were grinning as if they didn't think it would happen. It was a big scare for this pair. They'd send them back to the Bar-B so scared they probably would never stop riding until they got all the way to Miles City.

Dan Fletcher wasn't grinning. He sucked in a quick breath and watched, his face serious, his eyes squinting just a little. He took off his hat and wiped out some sweat, then fit it back on carefully.

"You can't kill us this way," Carlyle said. "Just ain't right—sure as hell ain't legal."

"All depends," Morgan said. He pounded his fist on the hindside of the Bar-B horse, and it jolted forward. Carlyle moved forward six feet, then slipped out of the saddle and off the hind quarters of the mount. He fell to the end of the rope. There was a sharp snap as the body stretched the rope as far as it would go and the knot jolted Carlyle's head to one side.

Carlyle's feet swung a foot from the ground. His tongue lolled out of his mouth. His whole body jerked and spasmed, his arms twitching as he swung back and forth.

"Holy shit!" one of the Circle-S riders breathed softly.

"Damn!" the other older one said.

"I knew it," Dan Fletcher said, a gleam in his eyes. "I just knew he was gonna hang that son of a bitch."

The second Bar-B rider suddenly kicked his heels into the sides of his mount and it shot forward. Dan

Fletcher was closest to him and surged his mount out in pursuit, glad for the action. He caught the other horse 30 feet ahead and led him back to the hanging tree.

Morgan took a pad of paper from his jacket pocket and wrote one word on the cardboard backing. He ripped off the paper and pushed it back in his pocket, then took his pocket knife and cut an inch long slice in the middle of the cardboard.

By now the body that had been Ken Carlyle had stopped swinging and twitching.

Morgan rode up to the body and pushed a shirt button through the cut in the cardboard which stuck in place on Carlyle's chest. The word showed plainly in the partial moonlight: "RUSTLER."

Morgan rode up to the second Bar-B rider and stared at him.

"You ready to die, cowboy?"

"A man's never ready, is he?"

"True. You're getting a reprieve." Morgan turned to the closest Circle-S cowboy. "Untie his hands."

As the Bar-B rider's hands came free, Morgan held the mount's reins. "In exchange for your life, you have a small duty to perform. You ride back to your boss and tell him exactly what happened here tonight. You tell him and all the hands what happened.

"You warn every man on the Bar-B payroll that they all are guilty of rustling Circle-S cattle, and any caught will be hanged as the rustlers they are. You make it damn clear this will happen. Then you draw your pay and ride into Miles City and right on out of Montana, if you want to go on working cattle for a living. Do you understand me?"

"Yes, sir!" He looked at Morgan. "Don't worry none. Bramwell will want to know what happened, and I'll flat out tell him. Then I'll tell everyone else and ride out of there before daylight. You can count on that!"

"You have a name?"

"No sir, no name. If I did I just forgot it and I'll get me a new one."

Morgan nodded. "Good thinking. Now ride out of here like the hangman is right on your critter's tail." Morgan handed the man the reins to his mount and slapped it on the rear, and it surged away.

Morgan watched him go.

"Goddamn!" one of the cowboys said.

Neither of them would look at Morgan. Only the redhead, Fletcher, watched him as they turned and rode slowly back toward the Circle-S.

"Now that is what I'd call a good night's work," Fletcher said as they rode away. "We dropped a rustler into hell and sent his buddy back to spread the word to the rest."

Morgan looked at the redhead.

"I hung that man, but I didn't enjoy it. There's a difference. We'll play as tough and rough as we have to because the Bar-B players are still far, far ahead of us in dirty dealings."

"You're the boss," Fletcher said.

Morgan stared at the young cowboy. He wasn't sure he liked all of what he saw. "Close enough," Morgan said and spurred the horse to a canter across the flat landscape.

He would watch this young man, Dan Fletcher. Morgan was not sure about him. So far Fletcher was doing fine, but somewhere Morgan had a raw gut feeling that didn't set well. He was afraid that Dan Fletcher would prove troublesome in the future.

Chapter
Ten

Young Wolf stood in the open door of his lodge and thought about what the man from the Circle-S ranch had told him. Thieves and rustlers now controlled the other nearby ranch, the Bar-B. Yes, he would help his friends at the Circle-S. It was for the good of his people.

For several years there had been no buffalo within two weeks' ride of his small band's lair. His people must eat, and the buffalo had been the staple. Now, over the years, they had learned to use other food.

Young Wolf was Mandan and proud of it. Each person in the band knew of the terrible fate of their tribe. Few of them understood history or the passage of the years, but Young Wolf had been able to study about his people.

It had been in 1837, 46 years ago, when the Mandan

people had been a force in the upper Missouri River area. There had been over 1600 of them, scattered among loosely associated villages in semipermanent settlements.

Their warriors were some of the fiercest in the plains, their arrows the straightest, and their ceremonies widely imitated by other plains Indians. One, the *o-kee-pa,* was often copied and altered into the ritual called the sundance that was used by almost all of the plains Indians.

The Mandans built sturdy shelters they called lodges that were sometimes 40 feet across and could house whole families and their favorite horses as well. They had solid walls and roofs so thick and sturdy that the children often sat on them to watch the rituals and dances the elders performed.

Then in 1837 the powerful illness came to one of the Montana camps, and runners hurried to the other villages and warned them of the pestilence, not realizing that they were spreading it. Within two months the Mandan people as a force in the land were gone. Of the 1600 men, women and children, only 31 survived the deadly 1837 smallpox epidemic.

The lucky ones who survived may have had some natural immunity to the disease. Some had been on long hunting trips or visiting their tribes at the time of the devastation.

The survivors had gathered together, fled the villages and found a retreat in the mountains, far from everyone, both white and Indian.

Slowly they returned to the old ways. They had always been a tribe of planters and harvesters. Once again they began to plant corn and beans, squash and pumpkins. Slowly they became a strong band once more, small but self-sustaining. But they were short on women. So they made a raid on a Sioux tribe and came back with six young Sioux girls who became wives.

Now, after two generations, almost no one remembered the dreaded smallpox. It was behind them, but they knew of it in stories and songs. Whenever possible they would stay with their own kind and avoid all contact with both white and Indian, so the smallpox could never again destroy them.

Young Wolf was the only one of the Mandan tribe ever to go out into the white world and return. His father had watched the whites invade the Indian lands, watched them take over the best fields, use up the rivers and destroy the buffalo. He knew change was coming, that the Mandan people could not stand if they maintained the old ways.

When his eldest son was 12, Lonesome Wolf had taken his best horse and ridden with Young Wolf into the land faraway where the white eye lived. Many years before, Lonesome Wolf had saved a white eye from dying on the scorched summer land. The white eye had become a blood brother and visited the tribe from time to time. Now the time had come for the white eye to repay the favor.

The white eye was a medical doctor to the people of Billings. He trained the young Indian boy to read and write English, tutored him until he was ahead of the students in the local school, then put him into the school so he could learn to become as white eye as the white eye students.

After seven years of study and training, the medical

doctor had enrolled his protege at the University of Nebraska in Lincoln.

It was different, strange and unusual, but Young Wolf had his seven years with the white eyes in Billings to prepare him. His white-eye name had been Will Young, and he studied history and education and won his degree and his Phi Beta Kappa key. Then, just as planned, Will Young vanished and returned to his people. His father had told him to do all of this when he was 12. Now he was 24 and ready to help lead his people.

When he first returned he found many ways to assist them. He improved the water supply and insisted that portable outhouses be used and the holes filled in and the houses moved often to be downstream of their water supply.

He returned with 20 new kinds of seeds to plant and to cultivate, everything from potatoes and yams to peanuts and cabbage. He brought with him two dozen fruit trees to be planted in their village.

That had been six years ago. Now they had several kinds of fruits and various vegetables. He also had returned with six baby chickens from Billings, and now the entire band was overrun with chickens. They soon learned to eat the chicken eggs as well as the chickens.

Yes, he had helped his people, but there was so much more he wanted to do. They were still afraid of the outside, still wary of strangers and still living in their primitive lodges with dirt floors. It would take time and resources, but resources, especially money, the Mandan Indians didn't have. There was no way they could produce anything that would bring them the white man's dollars.

Then an idea struck him. Why not beef? Why didn't the Mandan Indian clan go into the ranching business? There were hundreds of thousands of unclaimed acres in the mountains and some of the valleys to the west that would support beef cattle.

He knew a steer when sold at the railroad stockyards turned into $40. What better way to utilize the native lands of the native Americans?

True, the Mandans had no tribal lands that they could bargain with the government for. Yes, he would talk with the tall man from the Circle S.

His people would go on gathering wild fruits in the summer from wild persimmons to choke cherries. They would gather all sorts of roots and stalks to eat. He especially liked the young thistle stalks that were peeled and tasted like bananas.

Yes, they would still make jerky from whatever meat they could get, from beef to bear to venison. As long as they could, they would store the fall harvest in jug-shaped holes dug into the ground, a kind of elaborate root cellar that would keep many of the vegetables from spoiling for several months.

Drying was still the best way they had to preserve the fruits and vegetables.

Young Wolf walked around his lodge. The Mandan had constructed permanent dwellings for more than 100 years. But he wanted so much more for his people. It was his dream to combine the best of the Mandan and the white eye, but that would take hard money. Until now he'd had no idea how to accomplish that. Now he had.

He walked to the central lodge they had built at the center of the village. It was kept for special functions and for the daily lessons. He had been to Billings once and came back with enough tablets and pencils to last for two years.

He had also found some first readers, but they would have to wait. Now he was concentrating on teaching the children to speak English. That he must give them. He could live out his days in this valley with only an occasional contact with the white men, but for his children and their children, they would have to learn to mix and compete with the white men.

That meant they must know how to read and write English, at least to the eighth grade level. He had sent a bright young girl to school in Billings at the good Doctor Lewis's house. She had been gone two years. In another three years she would be back to take over the teaching duties in the new Mandan school. He had it all worked out.

Until then, he was the teacher. The children sat on logs across one end of the lodge, 16 of them, all from five to 16 years of age. All were making progress. Some had been working at the language lessons for three years now, every day of the month.

Only English was spoken in the learning lodge. Today Young Wolf told the students what it had been like his first day in the white eye school in Billings.

"At first I was afraid, but after the first day I felt better." He stopped and asked them if there were any words they did not understand."

"Afraid," one small boy said.

Young Wolf told him what it meant, then had each of the students repeat the sentence as best he or she could remember it. About halfway around the 16 boys and girls he stopped them. His original sentence had grown and changed in the telling. He told them again and then continued around the circle with each one repeating the sentence in English.

He talked and instructed them for two hours. When he let them go, they hurried off to their work places in the small fields and along the stream that was diverted to water the crops. There had been a heavy snow last year, so there would be runoff water for most of the growing season this year. They would have plentiful crops.

A rider rushed in from the north end of the small valley, and Young Wolf watched him. By the way the man rode he knew it was Falling Tree. The rider came quickly, guiding the mount by his knees as he had been trained, so he would have his hands free for fighting.

He saw Young Wolf, rode directly up to him and leaped off the war pony, his eyes angry.

"We have trouble," he said in his native language. "We rode far to the east and north chasing a pair of deer. They got away, and we scared some of the beef cattle high on the slope. They ran away from us.

"Three white eyes rode up and screamed at us, they yelled something about rustling cattle and fired their rifles at us. We both rushed away for the timber, but One Coyote was hit. He yelled at me to go on, and he fell from his horse. The cowboys kept firing at me and him, and at last I leaned off the side of my mount and galloped for the trees."

Falling Tree walked with Young Wolf as they took his horse to the small pasture.

"I hid behind a tree and watched. They rode up to One Coyote and kicked him, then made him stand up and run for the trees. The three white eyes made One Coyote a target. They shot him ten times, then laughed and rode off after the cattle.

"I went back to look at One Coyote. He was dead. I brought his body on his pony well into the trees, then rode like the wind to tell you."

"Did you see the brand on the hip of any of the horses the cowboys rode?" Young Wolf asked.

"Yes." The young warrior knelt in the dust and drew the brand. It was a B with a bar in front of it.

"The Bar-B," Young Wolf said. "We'll go bring back One Coyote."

Young Wolf caught his favorite riding pony, and they rode through the timber and dry land to the point where the dead man lay over his pony's back. Slowly they led him back to the camp.

There would be much wailing and crying, but the Mandan women no longer slashed their arms or their breasts in their grief. Tonight they would hold the ceremony of the lost warrior, and tomorrow at dawn they would hold his funeral high on the peak of their mountain, where his spirit would be able to lift to the heavens and be at one with the Great Spirit.

That night after the ceremony in his own lodge, Young Wolf talked with his wife, Running Fawn. She was five years younger than he was but had been promised to him the day he was sent away to school. When he returned he found Running Fawn the prettiest girl in the whole village, and they were married.

She had been 19 at the time and already had been called an old maid. Young Wolf had laughed at that and taken her to his lodge where the marriage ceremony was held.

Now Running Fawn looked at him as he lay down in the bed beside her. He had built up a bed two feet off the floor as he had gotten used to in the white-eye world. She had grown used to it. She rubbed his brow and kissed his cheek.

"It is bad?"

"Yes, bad. We haven't had anyone in the village killed in nearly ten years. The young men were warned not to go that far, but the thrill of the chase and the hunt made them forget."

"His wife and two children?"

"One Coyote has a brother. He has agreed to take a second wife and support the children."

"But you don't allow two wives."

"It is better than to make them beg for food, to let them die in the winter with no man to care for them. They will go with Deer Killer."

The matter was closed.

Much of the night Young Wolf struggled to sleep. The problem of One Coyote scalded his mind and kept him awake until he could solve the problem. What should he do? How should the Mandans react to this murder?

He could ride to the Bar-B headquarters and protest and demand payment for the slain man's family—$500 or 20 head of beef. But if the Bar-B riders were a hint of what the owner was like, Young Wolf might never return from such a ride.

Should he take six warriors and kill one of the Bar-B cowboys in retaliation? That could start a small war with the cowboys searching out the Mandan's village and burning it to the ground, killing everyone who did not flee.

There must be another answer.

By morning, Young Wolf did not have the answer. He took the long walk to the top of the mountain where they had left the body of their young warrior to ascend to the gods. He struggled with his anger and his desire for a quick retaliation against the killers, but he didn't know who the cowboys were. He had no way to identify them.

At last he decided he would talk with Morgan, the man from the Circle-S. Now he had two problems to talk about with this man who he trusted. He was a good man who could be hard when he had to be, but soft as a woman's kiss when the situation demanded.

That morning he rode to the lightning-scarred pine tree at the second fork in the river. He was about to put a message there in a small wrapper when he saw a glass jar with a top on it. He opened the jar and took out a message, written with pencil on white paper.

"Young Wolf. Could we meet? It has been two days since we last talked. If you can meet with me, ride two hours south to the big curve in the creek, make a fire and allow a continual trail of smoke to rise in the air just at midday. One of our people will see your smoke, and I will meet with you three hours later at the lightning-scarred pine. Your neighbor and friend, Lee Buckskin Morgan."

Young Wolf smiled. It was three hours before midday. He rode his pony down the tributary of the Tongue to the big curve and at noon made the fire, using green branches to make more smoke. After it had burned for a half hour with a continuous column of smoke, he put out the fire and rode back to where he could see the downslope of land that led up to the scarred pine.

In the time before Morgan came, Young Wolf decided that he had to make some Indian response to the owners of the Bar-B ranch. It simply had to be done. It was a matter of pride as well as a matter of common sense. Let a bully push you around once and he would do it again and again until it became a habit. Push the bully back harder than he pushed you, and he would take a new look at you and probably never touch you again. Most bullies don't like a fair fight.

It was nearly 2:30 that afternoon when Lee Buckskin rode up. He swung down from his horse and took a long drink from the creek, then sprawled on the grass to wait for the Indian.

Young Wolf stepped out from the fringe of brush where he had waited.

"You are most prompt, I appreciate that. I only put out that jar message this morning. Surprised that you found it so quick."

"Actually, Mr. Morgan, I was trying to contact you. I am of the Mandan tribe. Do you know our history?"

"One of the smallpox tribes, yes."

"Those of us left are few, and that makes life precious to us. Yesterday the men of the Bar-B used one of my young men for target practice and killed him."

Young Wolf went on to explain the circumstances. "I wanted you to know. I have decided that I must make a measured response, not too extreme, but punishing enough so the man who owns the Bar-B will understand."

"Damn, Young Wolf, the way you think and the

smooth way you talk, you should be a diplomat.''

Young Wolf grinned and threw a stone into the water. "I'd like to be an ambassador for my people, but we don't have diplomatic recognition as a separate nation."

"So what are you going to do to the Bar-B?"

"I wanted some advice and consent from you on that matter. I had thought of finding a cowboy and killing him in the old way, with his head slowly cooking over a controlled fire as he hung from his heels."

"Why did you reject that?"

"It would not be just. If I killed anyone it should be the three men who shot my warrior."

"Hard task."

"Impossible task. So I have decided to burn down the ranch house at the Bar-B and leave a note explaining to the owner why I have done it, demanding that the three men who killed One Coyote be discharged at once."

"But you know he won't do that."

"I realize that. He'll never find out who killed my friend. The cowboys won't talk."

"The death of the big ranch house will satisfy you?"

"For now, until I can help you in your task of routing this rattlesnake from our land."

"Good, I had some ideas I wanted to talk to you about, but figure now I should wait for you to have your bonfire."

"It will be tonight. Now a separate matter. There are only fifty-one Mandan Indians left in the whole United States. We were a dying tribe, but recently we have grown slightly. I am trying to bring my people peacefully into the white man's world, and it is a tough job.

"We are a settled people, not nomads as most of the other tribes. I want you to come and visit my village, today if you have time. We plant crops and harvest. We can feed ourselves on this land, but we need yankee dollars to learn how to live with the white men. My village is little more than a two hour ride from here. Can you come?"

Morgan nodded.

On the way to the village, Young Wolf told Morgan of his dream to raise cattle, not just enough to see them through winter, but to raise cattle for sale at the railroad stockyard.

"There are more than a hundred square miles back in here where I can raise cattle, and no white man will think to come back here for another fifty years. By that time we can buy our own land from the government or establish our own reservation and become self-supporting."

"It's a great idea, Young Wolf. That's what's wrong with it. It's so good that the Indian Commission, or whoever's in charge, won't like it. It's reasonable, logical and practical, so they'll try to stop you."

Morgan rode along thinking about it. At last he nodded. "Yeah, Young Wolf, give it a try. I'm sure that we can get you say fifty head of good breeding stock and about three range bulls to give you a start. Hell, make it a hundred cows. Say you get a ninety percent drop the first year. Then you should have about forty-five bulls to cut and sell and forty-five more cows to add to your brood stock."

"We have no money to buy cattle."

"Hell, you don't need none. Don't you see? Mr. Bramwell, the owner of the Bar-B, is going to contribute these animals to you in compensation for his men killing One Coyote. He just doesn't know he's going to do it."

Young Wolf smiled. "Buckskin Morgan, I like your logic and the slant of your mind. You and I are going to get along fine!"

Chapter
Eleven

Wally Pendier, the cowboy who had just seen his friend hung to a cottonwood tree, rode toward the Bar-B ranch, not exactly sure what to do. He had to tell the foreman what had happened. Jed Hackett would be furious and would probably make him tell his story to Mr. Bramwell.

Hell, maybe he should just circle around the ranch and head for Miles City. For damn sure he wasn't working for this outfit anymore. Sure, he knew the hands had rounded up cattle with the Circle-S brand. Happened all the time. The problem was the Circle-S stock wasn't driven back to the other ranch. They were all rebranded. That was rustling. He knew it, and the foreman knew it. Hell, what a mess. At least he was still alive. He thought of Ken Carlyle and shivered.

Damn! The expression on Carlyle's face when his horse jumped forward and Carlyle knew damn sure that he was gonna die. That was a look of terror that Wally would never forget.

The Circle-S men had untied Wally's hands from the saddle horn before they let him go. He didn't have his gun, but at least he was alive.

For now he had to keep riding. It was still the middle of the night, just past midnight he guessed. The foreman, Hackett, would probably slap him around a little. Guess he deserved it letting that guy slip up on them. He'd told Carlyle to keep low when he puffed on his smoke, but the guy wouldn't do it. Said it hadn't hurt anything before.

Wally knew he should wait for sunup before he rode back to the ranch, but something urged him forward. Loyalty to the Bar-B? Hell no. He'd only been here six months. He knew he could find the way back to that cottonwood tree even in the dark since there were not many of them up in this section of the range.

He shrugged and lifted the gait of his mount. He had decided. He'd tell Hackett as soon as he got in. Wally rode straight for the bunkhouse to wake up Hackett. Nothing could be worse than what he had just gone through tonight.

It was only a little after 1:00 A.M. when Wally knocked on the outside door to the foreman's quarters. He had a special room on the end of the bunkhouse with a separate door, and Wally had to bang six times before he heard a bellow from inside.

Hackett came to the door in his long johns, his six-gun in his hand.

"What the hell you want?" Hackett snarled. He was still half-asleep.

"Wally Pendier, Hackett. Got some bad news. Some Circle-S guys grabbed Carlyle and me when we was on guard at the outer circle."

"Pendier, what the hell you talking about? Get in here. I'll light a lamp and then you can say your piece."

Inside the foreman's room, Hackett lit a coal oil lamp, set on the glass chimney and turned up the wick. He squinted at the other man.

"Pendier, you better have a damn good reason why you're in here and not on guard."

"Circle-S riders hung Carlyle about five miles out."

Hackett stared at him. "What?"

Pendier went through the whole thing right up to the time the Circle-S riders slapped his horse on the hindside and Wally rode for the ranch buildings.

"Oh shit!" Hackett said, staring at Pendier. "You bunk down right in here for the rest of the night. You don't say a word about this to anybody, you hear? I'm going up to talk to Mr. Bramwell right now. He'll probably want to see you. If you say one word about this to any of the other hands before I get back, I'll gut shoot you and laugh while you die real slow."

Hackett pulled on his clothes and glared at Wally, then headed for the main ranch house.

Bramwell hadn't gone to sleep yet. He left Elly in his rumpled bed, pulled on a robe and went into his den where he listened to the story. His eyes glittered with anger.

"Bring this man, Pendier, up here right now. We

can't have him telling his story to the crew. Then you and one man you can trust ride out there, cut the man down and bury him deep right there. No marker. Give the hand twenty dollars to keep quiet. Move now, Hackett!''

By the time Hackett got back to his quarters he found it empty. He knew that Wally Pendier had jumped on his horse and ridden hell bent for Miles City. Hackett raced around to the bunkhouse where three lamps burned and half the men were awake.

''Hackett, is it true what Pendier told us about Carlyle getting lynched by some Circle-S men?'' one of the cowhands asked.

Hackett slammed his big fist into the man's jaw, knocking him off his bunk where he had been sitting. Hackett stared around a minute. ''Not a word of truth of it. Pendier got sacked so he's telling wild stories. Utley, need you to replace Pendier in the guard. Get your clothes on and come with me. I'll show you where his guard spot was.''

Seven hours later, Parrish Bramwell rolled out of the Bar-B ranch in a light buggy and headed for town. He was grim-faced and angry. If he found Wally Pendier he would shoot him down like a dog. The whole crew knew about the hanging. Bramwell figured he would lose at least five more hands by the time he got back. Men had no sense of adventure anymore. What was so threatening about being hung? People had been trying to kill him for years.

Bramwell drove the 15 miles into Miles City stewing all the way. This damn Lee Morgan was the key. Once the sheriff arrested the bastard it would all settle back down. Kill the leader of the opposition and the woman and her hired hands wouldn't have the guts for a good old-fashioned range war. It took him almost four hours to get to town, then he made his first stop at the sheriff's office.

Sheriff Straud stood up as soon as he saw the Englishman march into his domain.

"Well, Mr. Bramwell, didn't expect to see you so soon in town. Any problems?"

"Damn right I've got problems. Let's see your wanted posters. I was going through them last time I was here, and I spotted a man who's wanted. I need to prove it to you."

Sheriff Straud pulled a two-inch stack of flyers from his drawer. Bramwell spread them out on the desk, going through them one at a time. He was halfway through the stack when he grunted.

"Yeah, he's using the same name and everything. Here he is, Sheriff, Buckskin Lee Morgan. Wanted for murder in Arizona with a two thousand dollar reward. I'm willing to share that half and half with you."

"You seen this gent, for sure?"

"Absolutely. Yesterday as a matter of fact. I offered to buy the Circle-S, and they threw me off the place. He's a bad one, a gunman who likes to shoot."

"First time he comes into town, I'll arrest him," Sheriff Straud said.

"Not at all correct, my good man. You'll raise a posse, go out there right now and arrest him or gun him down. I don't care which. Night before last he also rustled over a thousand head of my cattle. I won't press you to settle that, if you bring him in today on this wanted poster.''

"Mr. Bramwell, you know a wanted poster ain't what it used to be. I've heard of unscrupulous men sending out spurious wanted posters just so they could get an enemy killed or jailed.''

"That may be true, but look at this one. It's got the Tombstone, Arizona district attorney's name and the sheriff's name on it. That one certainly isn't a fraud. Now I insist that you arrest this man.''

The sheriff stood, walked around his office and looked out the window. "Only got one deputy right now.''

"I'll be glad to go along. Swear me in.''

"No, no need for that. I guess I can go out and talk to him. Have to use a buggy, though. My hip's been bothering me lately.''

Bramwell stood, his anger coming through plainly now. He caught the sheriff by the shirt front and lifted him up on his toes.

"Sheriff Straud, you get out there and arrest that man, or you'll never be elected in this county again. I'll spread stories that you demanded bribe money from me and half the store owners in town. I'll even file charges against you with the circuit judge. Before this is over you won't have a pot to piss in. Now get six deputies and ride out there and arrest him. Then we split the reward, and you get elected again.''

"All right, Bramwell," the sheriff said. He stared hard at the man for a moment, then sighed. "I was hoping it wouldn't come to this, but if you start stories about me, I'll spread a few about you, too. I'll tell everyone what happened out in Bozeman when that fifteen-year-old girl turned up raped and dead in the valley, and then again in Lincoln. You got a few dead skunks in your closet, too, you know.''

''Sir, those are rumors, and you can't prove a thing. You just do your job, Sheriff, and things will be fine.''

It was an hour later before Sheriff Straud and one deputy left Miles City in a buggy and headed south along the Tongue River road toward the Circle-S ranch. Straud had been there before several times. He just wondered who this new hand was. Straud had the wanted poster folded in his pocket. Probably just a mistake. The Englishman tended to get over-excited now and then.

It was a three hour drive to the ranch, and it went smoothly but slow. Straud much preferred to stay in the little town. He noticed the new paint job on the Circle-S sign and that the whole gate had been straightened.

A half mile from the ranch house they came to an armed guard with a rifle resting across his saddle.

The rider held up his hand. ''Gents, who are you and what's your business at the Circle-S ranch?'' the cowboy asked.

''I'm Sheriff Straud, coming to see Miss Scoggins and her father.''

''She know you're coming?''

''No, I'm afraid not. Why the guard?''

''We've had some trouble with someone shooting out our windows. We don't like that. The other man your deputy?''

''He is.''

''All right. Move ahead.''

Once they were down the lane, the guard took out

127

a six-inch square mirror and sun-flashed the house a dozen times, aiming at the windows in the front. It would be enough to alert Miss Scoggins that company was on the way.

The sheriff's buggy came to a stop at the front porch, and as Straud got down, he saw Heather Scoggins come out to welcome him. It almost always happened that way. There are not many visitors at a ranch, and when one came usually there was a welcoming committee waiting to say hello.

Straud walked toward her with a grin. She had grown into a right pretty woman in the past four years.

"Afternoon, Miss Scoggins."

"Afternoon yourself, Sheriff. What brings you way down here from town?"

"A little business. How's your pa?"

"You didn't hear. My father died two days ago. We buried him up on the hill. His heart just gave out, I guess. He'd suffered long enough. More'n a dozen times he asked me to bring him his six-gun so he could end it sudden. I wouldn't do it."

"I'm sorry for your loss, Miss Scoggins. That means you're running the ranch then?"

"I have been for the past year, Sheriff. What's your business?"

"Need to talk to one of your hands, this Lee Morgan."

Heather looked up sharply. "Talk to Lee? Why?"

"Business, Miss Scoggins. Where can I find Morgan?"

"He's out on the range working. Should be in with the rest of the crew in about an hour." She hesitated.

"You . . . you want to wait up here on the porch out of the sun?"

"That would be right neighborly of you, Miss Scoggins. I hear you hired some new hands and paid cash for groceries. Things picking up for you here at the ranch?"

"You might say that, Sheriff. You sit down over there in the rocker, and I'll bring a pitcher of lemonade."

The deputy stayed in the buggy.

By the time the crew rode in about five that afternoon, the lemonade pitcher was empty. Heather met the crew, motioned to Willy Joe and Morgan and told them about the sheriff.

"He called you by name and said he had some business with you," Heather said.

"He shouldn't know my name."

"But he does," Willy Joe said.

"Oh, damn. On my way here a few days ago a couple of guys bushwhacked me. They had seen a wanted poster on me. It's an old one, never was any good. Some crazy sheriff in Arizona."

"But it's still out there, and somebody saw it and told the sheriff," Heather said.

"Probably our good friend Parrish Bramwell. He had a good look at me yesterday when he came calling."

"What do we do now?" Heather asked in a small voice.

"I talk to him, and you don't get worried. If he's a fair man we can reason with him."

All three of them walked around the house to the

front porch.

The sheriff stood when he saw them coming, looked at both men, then nodded at Morgan.

"Mr. Morgan, I need a word with you."

"Speak up. These are my friends and we have no secrets. You must be here concerning that Arizona wanted poster."

"That's right, Morgan. You admit it's you the poster is talking about?"

"Of course, but the poster is five years old. It's been withdrawn and never should have been printed in the first place."

"Easy for you to say, Morgan. Just the same I have to take you in."

"Have you sent a telegram to Arizona to check on the paper? I'll pay for the wire. You're going to save yourself a lot of trouble if you contact them first."

Sheriff Straud frowned. "You mean that, about sending a wire?" He walked around in a small circle. "Tell me about the paper. Why was it printed?"

"I had an argument with a gentleman in a saloon. I thought it was all settled, then the man pulled his gun. He drew first. I had twenty witnesses who agreed to that, including the sheriff of the county who was on the scene. It was reported and written off as self-defense.

"A month later, after I had moved on, the district attorney for Tombstone came back to town from a trip. The dead man was his brother. He overrode the sheriff and the witnesses and issued the wanted poster on his own. The paper is no good, Sheriff. Check Tombstone, Arizona."

"Be glad to do that, Morgan, but I want you in my

jail cell while I wait for the reply. You come along easy now with no trouble, and we'll have this settled in a day or two.''

"I can't do that, Sheriff. I've got work to do here. Who told you about this paper? It's been in your desk for at least five years."

"I just noticed it. I was going through . . ."

"I haven't been in town for over five years, Sheriff. There's no way you could have known I was here unless somebody told you. It was Parrish Bramwell, wasn't it?''

"No, why would he . . . ?" The sheriff shrugged. "Hell, no law against a citizen pointing out a wanted poster.''

"No law at all, but it is peculiar—especially when that citizen has been looting the Circle-S ranch for the past three years and has rustled over four thousand head of stock.''

The sheriff looked up sharply. "Now rustling is something I don't tolerate. Used to run some cattle myself. Can you prove any rustling? If you can you come in and file a complaint, and I'll do my duty and arrest anyone.''

"You'd even arrest Bramwell?"

"If you can prove he rustled. You'll need eye-witnesses and rebranded stock on his land. Best to catch the rustler rebranding with a running iron or a blanker. Either way you got them good.''

"Hard to prove that way, Sheriff."

"Then get your horse and let's ride. We can be back to town in time for a late supper at the Plainsman Hotel.''

"Can't do that, Sheriff." Morgan drew his six-gun

so fast the sheriff's mouth fell open.

"Be damned," the sheriff said softly.

"Tell your deputy to put down that rifle he's holding, or you're a dead man."

The deputy stood the rifle on the ground with the muzzle on the side of the rig.

"Good. Now, Sheriff, draw your weapon easy and push out the five rounds into the dust. We don't want anyone to get hurt here."

"This isn't a good thing to do, Morgan. I'll just have to come back with a posse."

"Good, Sheriff, you do that. But as you raise your posse, you tell them they're going up against twenty-five men with Spencer repeating rifles. Last I knew it was hard to find five men for a posse in Miles City even to chase a bank robber.

"You try to find some men in town who want to go to war. That's what it'll be. You take the easy way out and send that wire. By now there's a new sheriff and a new district atttorney in Tombstone, and they'll tell you the wanted poster was withdrawn about four years ago."

The sheriff spilled the rounds out of his weapon and slowly holstered it.

"No cause for this, Morgan. What's a day or two in jail for you? If it's as you say it is, I'd have to let you go."

"No cause for me to go to jail, Sheriff. You get word from Arizona. Then if you have a local warrant from a circuit judge, I'll be glad to come to jail. But you won't I'm saving us both some time and worry and expense.

132

"Now, you ready to move against Bramwell for us about those rustled cattle?"

"Like I said, Morgan, you get me proof and a warrant, and I'll be glad to arrest him and his whole crew."

"Maybe I'll just go into town and have a wanted poster printed with a five thousand dollar reward for Bramwell. That seems to be all you need for arresting people." Morgan holstered his pistol. "Relax, deputy, you aren't going to get shot today."

They saw the back of the buggy move as the deputy evidently shifted his position.

"Sheriff," Heather said, "usually I'd invite you to stay for supper, but under these conditions . . ."

Sheriff Straud tipped his brown hat. "Miss Scoggins, no apologies needed. Couldn't sit down with a man like Morgan, anyway."

Morgan grinned. "Well now, Sheriff Straud, I might just have to look into your background and your sheriffing. I've heard tales that you are taking bribes from half the merchants in town and from most of the big cattle ranchers. Now, that's the kind of behavior that could get you put into your own jail."

The sheriff turned and walked away, his back stiff, his fist halfway to his weapon before he remembered it was unloaded. He got in the buggy, and it pulled away.

The three on the porch went inside and watched the rig roll down the lane until it was almost out of sight.

"Will he come back with a posse," Willy Joe asked.

Heather shook her head. "I doubt it. A posse is hard to put together in Miles City. Three years ago when we had a bank robbery a posse went out and five of the ten men were killed. It hit the town hard. Since then I don't think there's been a posse moved out of town."

Morgan took off his hat and worked on the crease. "Heather, I'm sorry my personal problems came up this way."

"It doesn't matter. My problems became yours, so now your problems are ours. It has to be Bramwell who told the sheriff. How did you know about our sheriff taking money? Most folks know about it but are afraid to accuse him to his face. He almost turned purple when you told him. He came to see Daddy two years ago and talked about his reelection fund. Daddy said he didn't bribe sheriffs. He said a good sheriff wouldn't need to do any money spending to get reelected. Made Sheriff Straud really mad."

"So we won't worry about Straud," Morgan said. "What's Bramwell going to do next in response to last night? And what is Young Fox going to do in retaliation for his dead warrior?"

"We could use more guards out," Willy Joe said. "My bet is that Bramwell will do something tonight. Maybe try to burn down a building or a barn."

Morgan nodded. "Which means we need more men. Tomorrow, Willy Joe, you go into town and hire fifteen more men. We're going to need them. We have to do guard duty, army duty, and at the same time get about three hundred steers ready to drive to the stockyards."

"Isn't there something we should do about Daddy?" Heather asked. "Do we file a death notice in the paper and get the property transferred?"

Morgan nodded. "Yes, you're right, Heather. I

should have thought about that. You and I and a driver better go into town tomorrow and get that done. Then you and the hand can come back to the buggy, and I'll stay on and hire some new men.''

"But the sheriff . . ."

"He won't even know that I'm in town. If he does, he won't make a move until he hears from Arizona.''

"Was that right about new lawmen being there and throwing out that wanted poster on you?'' Willy Joe asked.

"Yes. First thing a new sheriff does when he takes over is clean out the old local cases. Mine must have been thrown out three or four years ago.''

"If you're sure, Lee,'' Heather said. "We can't get along without you here right now.''

Just then the dinner bell rang as the cook hit the triangle with an iron bar. All three headed for the kitchen and their supper. Willy Joe had been taking supper with them regularly now, and Morgan watched the growing relationship between the two young people. Good, it was right.

Chapter
Twelve

Young Wolf wore his town clothes, a battered wide-brimmed hat, faded blue work shirt, jeans and cowboy boots. He had the saddle bags packed and two cans of coal oil tied to the back of the saddle.

He left the Mandan village well before dusk because he had a 20-mile ride to get to the big ranch with the Bar-B brand. He had figured out exactly what he would do. It would be a measured response to the murder of One Coyote.

Young Wolf had written a logical but strongly worded letter to Parrish Bramwell, explaining what he would do and why he was doing it, and that the responsibility rested with the Mandan Indians who would avenge any further deaths of its tribesmen on a two for one basis.

Young Wolf did not want the rancher to blame the

people at the Circle-S spread for the attack tonight.

The darkness closed in as Young Wolf crossed into the lands of the Bar-B ranch. He watched for lookouts and guards but found none until he was within three miles of the ranch. That's when he left his horse, slung the cans over one shoulder and carried the saddlebags over the other.

Young Wolf went around the pair of guards near a small clump of trees so easily he thought they must be sleeping, but soon he realized they were talking, laughing and not watching where they were supposed to be. They seemed to take this whole guarding routine as a lark.

The Mandan Indian leader went past them and on toward the buildings he knew were ahead on the Pumpkin River. It was a target almost impossible to miss.

Once more he heard guards ahead and waited and watched until he figured out where they were. Then he came up behind them silently, knocked one out with the butt of his .45 pistol and caught the other one around the throat and cut off his air until he fainted.

Then he tied up both with strips of rawhide and left them there.

The buildings now loomed ahead of him in the darkness. He stopped and opened his kit of materials. He had cut dynamite into half-stick lengths before he left his lodge. The dynamite came from a box he had brought back with him from Billings to blow apart some rocks.

Each half-stick had been pierced with a pointed stick so it would be easy to push in the detonating cap. He had fixed the caps with six-inch fuses and pushed the fuse into the hollow end of the copper tube. Now he pushed the detonators with their attached six-inch fuses into the dynamite half-sticks and put them with their fuses pointing up in the front saddle bag.

He turned his back to the buildings and lit a cigar, puffing on it until it glowed bright red, then held the burning end to the rear and walked forward. He didn't think he would meet anyone, but in his cowboy clothes he could bluff his way with some angry talk about guard duty.

He saw no one as he moved to the back of the big ranch house. It was a well-built structure and he hated burning it down, but a price had to be paid. This time the price would be short of taking a human life, but this soft response was a one time only alternative.

He found what he wanted. The back side of the ranch house had been built off the ground to establish it on the level. He worked under the floor and gathered leaves and twigs and some old furniture that had been stored in the two-foot crawlspace. These he soaked with kerosene. The floor above seemed to be half-inch boards, which would burn through quickly and be too hot to stop with buckets of water.

He got everything ready and carwled out without lighting the fire. He looked for his second attack point. Several lights showed in the big house. About halfway along the rear of the house he found a window with no light. At his touch it slid upward without a sound.

Young Wolf parted the curtains and looked inside. It was a bedroom. He slipped inside with the second can of coal oil and splashed it generously on the bed next to the inside wall. When he had it ready, he pushed the can under the bed, struck a match and lit the oil-soaked bedding. It flamed up at once.

The Mandan slid through the window and hurried to the crawlspace. There he lit the second fire, then ran into the darkness where he circled around the yard toward the big corral at the far side.

He was almost there before he heard the first cry of "Fire!" from the house. He couldn't see any flames and hoped that the blaze had not been discovered too quickly. Young Wolf knew that the well was about 40 yards from the front of the house. He quickly planted four of the half-sticks of dynamite under posts on the corral and lit the fuses from his cigar.

Then he ran to one side where he would have a good view of the well. The six-inch fuses on the half-sticks of dynamite should burn about 30 seconds. Young Wolf counted the first one down as he ran behind a wagon 40 feet from the well and about 100 feet from the corral.

When he got down to one in his count, he looked at the corral. The thundering dynamite explosions went off with an outrageous roar, and then at four second intervals the other three blasts shattered the night sky.

Men screamed at each other as the explosions trailed off. In the corral the 50 or 60 horses milled around a moment, then charged past the destroyed corral fences and scattered into the blackness.

"Fire! Save the house," someone shouted. "Don't worry about the damn horses!"

A dozen men turned up with buckets at the well, and just as the first container of water got filled by the man working the pump handle, Young Wolf shot into the air over the man's head.

The men flattened behind the wall. Somebody fired a round toward the wagon, the lead thudding into the heavy wooden side. Just then the fire broke out one of the front windows of the house. Young Wolf took the written letter from his pocket and pinned it to the wooden side of the wagon box with a small folding knife.

Two more shots slammed into the wagon box. Young Wolf pulled a half-stick dynamite bomb from his saddle bag and lit the fuse. He held it for ten seconds, then threw it almost to the well.

The roar of the explosion drove the men back. By the time one had gone off, Young Wolf had lit and thrown two more of the small bombs, one all the way to the well and one past it.

When all three explosions went off, the men who had come to fill water buckets charged away from the well.

"What the hell is going on?" a strong voice bellowed from near the house. "Who has the dynamite? Go out there and kill the son of a bitch!"

Two more rounds were fired at the wagon, but now they were out of range. The fire broke through another window, and then flames roared through the second story roof.

Young Wolf faded away directly behind the wagon toward the edge of the yard. Then in the heavy darkness, he turned and trotted back toward the spot where he had left his horse.

A half mile off, he stopped and looked back at the

141

ranch house. The whole thing was laced with fire, creating a soft glow around it like a halo. There was no way now that they could put it out.

He found his horse, placed the saddle bags on the mount and stepped into the leather. Now, he had a three hour ride to get back into the mountains and his lodge.

From a mile away he could still see the fire burning. It had been a good night's work. They would find the note with the coming of daylight. Then they would know who burned the house and blew up the corral.

"Evaluation," Young Wolf said out loud. It was a word his logics professor back at college often used. "What will Bramwell's reaction be, and what will his retaliation be, if any?"

Young Wolf rode a mile thinking through the question. Bramwell would be furious, but he would also find out that three of his men killed an Indian. Would he believe that the score was even? No, Bramwell wouldn't. He wouldn't believe that one Indian life carried the same value as his 14-room ranch house.

Bramwell was a white eye. He was also a bullheaded Englishman. For the first time in several years, Young Wolf thought about weapons. They had only two rifles in the Mandan camp. Both had been used only for hunting. They had one bow-and-arrow-maker, but most of their hunting prowess was limited to the rifles. Few of his men could shoot a bow and arrow with anything nearing accuracy.

He freely admitted he thought it more valuable to learn to plant crops, to raise food and to help his people learn to read and write English, than to teach the young boys how to be warriors. Now that kind of thinking might come back to haunt him.

Quickly his mind considered alternatives. Yes, there were some defenses they could use. He would establish a set of lookouts, young boys who could practice their bow and arrow skill while watching the trails from the Bar-B ranch.

Any attack by the rancher's men would be spotted while ten miles away and give them ample warning. All of the women and children would leave and rush into the hills, scattering and hiding.

He had come to the end of a small valley where it sloped up into a ridge. The only trail up was along a narrow path that had been kept open and free of rocks by his people, but on three sides of it were jagged rocks and boulders. He would send four of his men to this area tomorrow to prepare rocks and boulders that could be moved to advantageous points. If they were needed, the rocks could be rained down on the attacking line of riders with devastating results.

As he rode up the rest of the trails and through the woods, he devised more defensive moves that his people could make. They would put these first on their work list tomorrow, and stay at it until he was satisfied that they had enough defenses ready. They could not rely on strength of weapons. They would have to use their ingenuity.

Satisfied with his plans, Young Wolf rode on home, thinking what he could do with the rest of the box of dynamite that he had brought back from Billings. He could make up more half-stick bombs, but with these next ones he would tape large roofing nails to the dynamite.

With the nails on the dynamite they would become deadly shrapnel explosives if it came to a killing situation. Yes, they could make 20 or 30 such bombs.

"What in hell is going on?" Parrish Bramwell roared, watching the last of the second floor of his ranch house fall into the first floor with a roar of flames and sparks further lighting up the night sky.

Hackett came up wiping at soot and black streaks on his face.

"We got what we could, Mr. Bramwell. Everything from your den except the big desk. Got out the drawers and all the boxes of records. We didn't have time to save much else."

"Damnit! Who the hell did this? Has to be that bastard, Lee Morgan. Somebody hid behind the wagon you said. Take a lantern out there and look around, maybe we got lucky and shot the son of a bitch."

Hackett ran to the barn to find a lantern.

Elly came running up wearing only a thin white nightgown with one breast showing.

"You get into the far end of the bunkhouse. It's where Hackett usually stays. We'll boot him out of there. Run along now before you catch a tit cold."

She looked down, pulled the nightgown over her breast and walked toward the bunkhouse.

A dozen men stood around watching the house burn.

Bramwell paced up and down in front of the fire. He had to do something. He couldn't let Morgan get away with this. He had to strike back fast, tonight. What time was it? He pulled his watch from his pocket. Not yet eight o'clock. They could ride to the Circle-

S while it was still dark, wipe out the guards and set the house, barn and bunkhouse all on fire. Yes, goddamnit!

Hackett came back with the lantern. He held something in his hand.

"Found a letter pinned to the wagon box where the bastard shot from, Mr. Bramwell," Hackett said, holding out the paper.

Bramwell snatched it from him, unfolded it and held it so he could read it by the light of the lantern.

He read it quickly, snorted and then bellowed in rage. He screamed words that made no sense and balled up the paper and threw it at the fire. When he came back he grabbed Hackett by the front of his shirt and pulled him up close to his face.

"You said something about three of our men shooting at a renegade Indian yesterday."

"Yes sir, they said they killed him. He was just a damn Indian. I don't even know what tribe there is around here."

"This damn Indian, as you call him, is what cost me my ranch house and corral tonight. The letter laced into me about an eye for an eye, but he said he wouldn't take a life this time. That renegade Indian writes better English than you or I do. He said his tribe is the Mandan, and he won't attack us any more if we leave him and his people in peace.

"It wasn't that damn Morgan who did this to me, it was some blathering, savage, Mandan Indian who did it. Now just what the hell do you have to say about that, Mr. Hackett?"

"The boys didn't know who the Indian was. So they

145

got out of line a little. I might have done the same thing. The Mandans, yeah, a little splinter group of Indians. I heard about them living back up there in the hills somewhere. Never saw one. They stay way back in there twenty or thirty miles away.''

''The ones here tonight weren't any damn thirty miles away. And the bloody savage also writes excellent English, so he must be educated. What do you say about that?''

''Lived here ten years and I've never seen one of them Indians. Don't know why they came down to the far range. Maybe they were chasing a deer or something.''

Bramwell shook his head. ''Or something? Why is it all falling apart? First the house gets shot, the barn burns down, I lose four hundred head of cattle and three men are killed. Then one of my guards gets hung. Now my ranch house is burned to the ground, the corral is blown apart, and the horses have run off.''

''I can take ten men and ride up in the hills and find that Injun camp and blow them apart with rifle fire,'' Hackett said. ''Kill all the bucks, then they won't bother us no more.''

''No, Hackett, you're an imbecile. We'll not go after the Indians. We could all get massacred, for God's sakes. Now get out there and try to round up our horses, if we have enough left to saddle. I've got some planning to do. Mr. Morgan is still our main problem. The Indians will stay away from us. Now we have to deal with Morgan and the Circle-S. I owe them a special bit of hell for hanging that cowboy of mine. We have to hit them so hard they will never forget it and never be able to strike back. It's going to take some planning.

"I saw the sheriff and one deputy ride out of town heading for the Circle-S ranch, but I don't know what happened over there. Tomorrow I'll have to find out. If Morgan is out of the way, it will make it that much easier."

Bramwell turned toward the bunkhouse. "Oh, Hackett, I'm taking over your room in the bunkhouse. You'll be in with the other men. Get those horses rounded up before they run all the way to the Circle-S."

Hackett stared at his boss as the Englishman walked toward the bunkhouse. Then he turned and went to look at the corral. There were ten horses left, crowded against the rear. He grabbed men as he found them, told them to go to the corral and hold the mounts there. They would be going out riding as soon as he could get enough men together.

Hackett looked around in wonder. No barn, no ranch house, the owner sleeping in the bunkhouse. What in hell could happen next? They had a devil-man neighbor hanging their riders, and now the Indians were coming down on them. Hackett shrugged. Hell, it wasn't his money. He could ride out tomorrow and get a good job at any spread in Montana. He had a good name in the cattle business.

"Get off your ass, Warner. We've got some riding to do," Hackett yelled at a man looking at the fire. "Get your pants and your boots on and saddle up any horse you can find. Do it now!"

* * *

Fifty yards away in the bunkhouse, Elly huddled in the chilly night air in the foreman's room. It was rough and dirty and had cracked boards on the floor and no wallpaper.

Her eyes were still wide with shock and fright. She had almost been trapped on the second floor of the burning house. How could the big house burn down that way?

She shivered under the old blanket she had found and wrapped around her. In the morning she would go into town. She had to buy some clothes. All of her clothes were gone.

No, she remembered she had washed out a few everyday things and hung them on the clothesline yesterday afternoon. At least she would be decent. She would need to buy a whole new wardrobe, and she would insist on staying in town until Bramwell had a new ranch house built out there.

He might object to that, so she would have to convince him. As soon as he got in the room she would begin. He said something about protecting the records and the cashbox. She knew where he kept the cash-box—at least she used to. A girl had to look out for herself.

Elly frowned at the one coal oil lamp that burned on a small table. Was Bramwell losing his power? Should she look for another man to take care of her?

She remembered one of the girls in Denver who had said that by the time a girl was 30 it was all over. She pointed out that right there in their house the younger girls always got the most business, and the slim younger ones did the best of all.

"So stay pretty, and don't get fat or old," the cute little whore had always said.

Staying slim and pretty was the easiest part. Elly' was 23. She was getting old so fast! There was no way to slow that down. At least she had saved some gold. It was in a safe spot out by the well. Nobody knew about it but her. She had almost $200 in gold double eagles.

Yes, tomorrow she would go to town and buy some clothes and beg to stay for a week while they got things straightened up here at the ranch. Who knows what might happen by then?

When Parrish Bramwell came into the room an hour later, Elly had fallen asleep. She heard him and saw him lock the door. Then Elly pulled off the blanket and the thin nightgown and walked to him slowly, shaking her naked breasts at him.

"Elly I'm not in the mood. We just lost the ranch house and probably a lot of horses."

"That's why it's the right time. You need to stop worrying for a while and let Elly relax you and make you think sexy things for a while. It'll be real good, you'll see. You're all worked up anyway."

She knelt before him and hugged his waist, then unbuttoned his fly and worked her hands inside.

"See! See! Already he's perked up and is wanting me. You can't deny your good friend here a poke or two. He needs them."

Bramwell put his hands down on her generous breasts and toyed with them. He was getting hard without really thinking about it.

A minute later he growled at her. "Woman, I never

could fuck standing up. When the hell are you going to get on your back and spread those pretty little white thighs of yours?''

Elly yelped and scrambled for the wide bunk. Just about in the middle of doing him she would talk him into taking her to town tomorrow. He'd have to go in and get supplies and order lumber and all sorts of things. Yes, it would work out just fine!

Chapter Thirteen

At breakfast in the ranch house at the Circle-S, foreman Willy Joe Dawson reported that the guards had discovered no movement during the night, and that there would be the usual day shift watching the ranch.

"Good, because Mr. Morgan and I will be gone most of the day," Heather said. "I need to go into town and take care of the death certificate for Daddy and to sign over the property in my name with the county clerk."

"I'll be picking up a few more hands, some more rifles and some saddle boots for the weapons," Morgan said. "I'll be coming back later on tonight or in the morning. Depends how many good hands I can find."

"How many more you getting?" Willy Joe asked.

"I'm figuring on ten or fifteen."

"That many more?" Heather asked, looking up quickly.

"Don't worry about paying them," Morgan said. "You know that's all taken care of." Morgan turned back to the foreman.

"Willy Joe, I'd say we have some steers ready for market. Why don't you cut out the lot and put them in a pasture near the barn? Might find two or three hundred. We'll get them ready for a trail drive to the stockyards in Miles City. I'll check on prices while I'm in there. We might as well harvest those steers ready for the supper table."

"Yes, I agree," Heather said. "We need some income for a change."

"Who should we have for a buggy driver, Willy Joe?" Morgan asked. "Since he'll be bringing back Heather alone we need a mature man who can use his gun if he has to."

"I'll get somebody and hitch up the rig," Willy Joe said. He finished his breakfast and hurried out the door.

Twenty minutes later they were on the road with Royce Olson driving for Heather. Olson was one of the old hands who had been with the Circle-S for a long time. Morgan guessed him to be about 35, and he carried a Colt .45 on his right hip. Before they left, Morgan pushed a Spencer repeating carbine in the back of the rig along with a box of .52 caliber rounds.

A mile down the road, Heather motioned Morgan over closer so they could talk.

"You thought Bramwell would retaliate last night, but he didn't," Heather said. "Why not?"

"No idea. He might have some other problems to deal with. Did I tell you that Willy Joe and I ran into Young Wolf upstream at the rear hills. We agreed to continue to let him harvest a steer now and then when his people run short on meat—the way your father said they could."

"Yes, that's fine. I've often thought about Young Wolf. Isn't he the one who went away to college?"

"He sure did and graduated with honors. He's teaching his people to speak English and read and write. He says he's trying to get them ready to join the white man's world."

"That's a good plan. Sooner or later all the Indians left will have to learn to live with the rest of us. There's so many of us and so few of them."

He told her about Young Wolf wanting to start raising beef cattle to sell at Miles City.

"What a wonderful idea! I'd heard that the Mandan was a settled tribe, that they plant and cultivate crops. Raising cattle is perfect."

"I said I'd talk to you about getting him started. Way I see it is we could have six or eight of his young men come down here and live for three or four months. We'd train them how to rope and cut and how to go about branding—the whole works. What do you think?"

"Yes, absolutely. They can live with our men and learn more about white men and how we raise cattle."

"Once they get the know-how, I'd hope we could stake them to a hundred head of brood stock."

Heather looked up. "That's mighty generous of you with four thousand dollars worth of cattle."

"Oh, not from our stock—from the Bar-B. I figure we'll have enough of theirs pretty soon to swing it."

"Morgan, you know this scares me, this fighting with Bramwell. Isn't there some other way we can do it?"

"Sure, let him steal the rest of your cattle and then your land and buildings. You want that?"

"No."

"Good. So let's just hang in there for a while and see what happens. For all we know, Bramwell might just turn his little English tail and run away."

"I'll keep hoping."

They got to town a little before noon and went directly to Dr. Logan's office. Morgan waited in the buggy and told Olson to go enjoy himself for two hours. He should be back at the courthouse at two o'clock.

Ten minutes later, Heather came out of the doctor's office with a white envelope.

"It's all set here. He said we should go to the county clerk's office and file this and then do the deed transfer."

At the county clerk's, the tall thin man with glasses pinched on his nose read the death certificate and nodded.

"Yes, I'll record this. Now what about the ranch property?"

"I'm the only heir. You know my brother was killed about a year ago."

"So it goes in your name?"

"That's right," Morgan said sternly. "Any ob-

154

jections?''

The clerk looked up quickly, shook his head and seemed to shrivel a little. He drew up the papers, had Heather sign them and then he shook her hand.

"You're now the legal owner of the Circle-S ranch and all its property and cattle. Congratulations.''

They went outside, and Heather held his arm.

"I guess now I really understand that Daddy is gone. He was so sick for so long. Now with signing the grant deed . . .''

Morgan led her down to a store and pointed. "What you need now is a new dress and a jacket and maybe a brand new hat. That will make you feel better and will knock Willy Joe's eyes out. Get in there and buy a new outfit.''

"Oh, no, I couldn't.''

"How long has it been since you've bought any clothes for yourself?''

"Oh, a year or so.''

"Go—now. Olson won't be back until two o'clock, and I have to roust up some good cowhands.''

She hesitated.

"Go on. I can boss you around in town. Wouldn't it be nice to have a nice new dress and some under-things?''

"Oh, yes.''

"Then go.'' He fished in his pocket and came up with a $20 gold piece. "Here, the new duds are on me. A birthday present.''

"It's not my birthday.''

"It's for the last one I missed. Now scoot.''

She took the coin, smiled and then vanished inside the woman's wear shop.

Morgan waited until she closed the door, then he headed for the closest saloon. He had a draft beer for a nickel and looked over the men. He didn't like any of them. Maybe after he'd made the rounds of the drinking spots he wouldn't be so choosy.

He went out the door and toward the next saloon across the alley. There was no boardwalk past the alley, so the wagons and delivery rigs could get to the back of the store. Morgan stepped down into the dust and heard a woman's call. He looked down the alley in time to see a hand clamp over a woman's mouth. She was in the dirt of the alley next to a clapboard building.

He stopped and stared that way. Surprise washed over his face as he realized the woman lay on the ground. He saw pure white legs hoisted toward the sky and a man dropped between them on his knees. The woman's voice came again, a strangled scream.

Morgan ran down the alley and slammed his big fist into the back of the man's neck who was trying to rape the woman. The man tumbled off her and lay on his back in the alley with his head halfway in a fresh cow pie that hadn't hardened yet.

"What the hell you doing!" the man roared. He grabbed at his hip for a six-gun. Morgan kicked his wrist, snapping the bones and bringing a scream of pain from the man.

"Bastard! I'll kill you for sure now!"

Morgan slanted the side of his boot at the man's head, slamming him over on his stomach and knocking him out.

The woman sat up moaning. She had pushed her

skirt between her legs but still most of them showed, milk white and slender. The top of her dress was torn almost to the waist showing half of a chemise and one pink tipped breast that poked out where the other half of the cloth had been torn away.

"Oh, God!" she said as a grown seeped from her lips. She shook her head. "Animal hit me three times. I was so groggy." She shook her head again and looked down at her chest. "Oh, damn!"

Morgan pulled the front of her dress up so she could hold it over her breasts.

"He won't bother you any more, Miss."

She smiled. "That's nice. Ain't been called that in some time. I don't mind being . . . I mean I ain't no virgin, but I ain't never been poked in public in an alley this way. Virgil there was too drunk to get up the stairs, he said. I told him I warn't working no more."

She was small, with long blonde hair and big breasts on a slender body.

"You heading somewhere?" Morgan asked her.

"Yes, I just come in town from the ranch. Planning to stay a few days, I got me a room at the hotel. This warthog," she pointed at the man still unconscious in the dirt, "said he knew me and grabbed me off the street and carried me in here."

"Maybe I better help you get back to your hotel," Morgan said. He bent and grabbed the six-gun from the holster as the man on the ground made a grab for it with his left hand. Morgan slapped the man's broken right wrist, and he wailed in pain.

As Morgan walked away with the girl, the man in

the dirt screamed at them in fury. "I'm gonna find out who you are, big man, and I'm gonna cut your balls off and then kill you dead!"

Morgan ignored him. They went down the side street, up an alley and in the back door of the hotel.

"I don't want anyone to see me this way," she said. On the second floor she took a key from a small reticule that she had tied to her wrist. She opened room 211 and stepped inside.

"Come in. I haven't thanked you yet for saving my life. I'm sure he would have killed me—afterwards."

Morgan stepped into the room. She closed the door, let the flap of dress fall down, turned and smiled.

"My name is Elly. What's yours?"

"Lee," he said.

She shook his hand formally, then she went to the big crockery bowl, poured water from the pitcher into it and used a towel to wash her face and arms. With that done she turned again and combed some minor tangles out of her long blonde hair.

She still hadn't covered her one breast that was exposed, but she sat down on the edge of the bed and patted a place beside her.

"Lee, come over here and sit down. I want to thank you for helping me back there in about the only way I can."

"No thanks needed, Miss Elly. Glad I was there when I could be of some assistance."

"Me, too." She undid the rest of the dress and let it fall to her waist with the ruined chemise. Her breasts danced as she moved her shoulders, and he grinned.

"Nothing as beautiful as a woman's fine breasts," he said.

"Then sit down and enjoy them," she said. "I want you to enjoy them and the rest of me just any way you want to. I told you I'm no virgin. Yes, I sold my little bottom for a time, but lately I've been with just one man. Easier that way. Come on, you're not bashful, are you?"

Morgan laughed and sat beside her, then bent and sucked one of her orbs into his mouth and chewed delicately.

Elly sighed. "Yes, I thought you might like a bite of me. I like it too, you know. Makes me feel all warm and gets my blood to racing."

She reached in and unbuttoned his leather vest, and then his blue shirt. Her hands feathered through the thick hair on his chest.

"What do you do, Lee? You a cowboy?"

He came off her breasts and massaged them tenderly with both hands.

"Sometimes I cowboy, sometimes I ride the trains. Whatever is handy."

"Good, I'm handy. I want you to ride me. Please?" She unfastened his belt, then undid the buttons down his fly. She pushed him backwards on the bed and pulled at his pants, then at some short underwear until she found what she searched for.

"Oh, damn, he's not hard yet."

"Maybe you can encourage the old fella to get going."

She played with him, then bent and kissed his limp tool and slowly it began to rise. She yelped in pleasure and kissed more and more until he was stiff and purple-tipped.

"Oh, Aunt Mary's cunt! Look at that dandy!" She

stood and slipped the ruined dress off over her head, then kicked out of some silky underthings and stood beside him naked.

"I need to get the feel of the goods before I can pass it," Morgan said.

Elly yelped and jumped on top of him, pushing him down on the bed again. Her breasts pressed against his chest, her crotch pumped at his erection, and her legs spread over him.

"Easy, easy, I haven't even kissed you yet."

"I don't like kissing much," Elly said. "Besides, you know that whores never kiss."

"You aren't a whore. I've never fucked a whore in my life. When you're with me you're one grand lady, and don't you forget it. You deserve to be seduced at the very least. Now lay down here like a prim virgin and let me have my way with you."

Elly grinned. "Hey, nobody ever said that to me before. Well, one kid did when I was fourteen and getting my tits and he was fifteen with a continual hard on. I mean I could see it bulging out his pants in school and on the street. He said nice things and was polite, right up to getting my dress off. Then he wouldn't stop when I told him to."

"I'll stop if you tell me to," Morgan said with a lecherous grin.

"You do and I'll kick you right in your balls." She smiled. "I do like it better this way. No more fast wham, bang, thank you Sam."

She sank down on the quilts and let him do as he would, thinking again about that very first time behind her dad's barn back in Iowa.

"That's so nice, so soft. When you caress my breasts it feels so good—gentle and pure and nice."

His hand came up her leg, and she trembled. "I don't know when I've felt so much like a . . . like a virgin . . . or maybe a bride. It's terrific."

He reached up and held his face in both her hands. "You always make love this way, so tenderly?"

"Is it good?"

"Wonderful."

"You said you're with one man now, a rancher. Who is it?"

"You wouldn't know him. I'll tell you later. Don't spoil this."

His hand came to the top of her leg, probed gently through the forest of blonde hairs and touched her treasured wetness.

"Oh!"

His fingers brushed over her clit, but she didn't react. He brushed it again, then twanged it a dozen times, but she had no response.

"Now, Lee, right now before I pop, come in me, please, Lee, right this instant."

He kicked off his boots and his pants and hovered over her a moment, then probed and found the slot and slid into her.

Tears brimmed her eyes, and she lay perfectly still. Then as he began to stroke slowly, she lifted her legs around his back and squeezed him so tight he yelled.

She never heard him. Elly was in a special place of her own, where he couldn't follow. Then the pressure built, and he stroked faster and faster until

he was rutting her higher in the bed. He couldn't stop.
The dam broke, and the hot fluid spurted six, seven,
then eight times. He gave a great sigh and rush of air,
and he eased down on her.

She blinked and looked up at him.

As she did, he found her node again and began to
rub.

"It won't do any good. It's not your fault, but I just
never really climax. I try, but it isn't something I can
do."

He kept working the clit. "Have you ever?"

"Just the first time with Harvey. I don't know why.
My mother told me I had sinned and threw me out
of the house. Maybe that's why. I never could after
that, not even by myself."

"It's something you should do." He strummed
again and again, and for a moment she began to
breathe faster but then her heart returned to normal
and the chance was gone.

He stopped and kissed her. "Maybe next time. Just
think good thoughts and tell yourself that you can.
You'll make it yet."

A half hour later they were dressed and sitting on
the side of the bed.

"Oh, you asked me who I was with. I don't know
if I'm going back. He's having some trouble. You
probably don't know him. Last night the ranch house
burned down and half the horses ran away when somebody dynamited the corral."

"That sounds like trouble. What spread is it?"

"The Bar-B."

Morgan looked at her quickly. "You're joking.

Parrish Bramwell's outfit?''

"Yes.'' She frowned. "You said your name was Lee. Parrish was worried about somebody named Lee. I can't remember the last name.''

"Does he know who burned down the ranch house?''

"Oh, yes, he left a note—an Indian by the name of Young Wolf. He signed it and everything. Said some of the Bar-B riders had killed one of his young braves.''

"I'll be damned.''

"You seem pleased over another man's misfortune.'' Elly looked at him in surprise, then a touch of anger. "I really don't understand you, Lee.''

"You mentioned that Bramwell said something about a man called Lee. Was the last name Morgan?''

Her brow shot up, and she grinned. "Yes, Buckskin Lee Morgan. Bramwell said he had a wanted poster on him. How in the world did you know?''

"That's me—Lee Morgan.''

Elly's eyes went wide, then she giggled. "You mean I just fucked the enemy, the one man in town Bramwell wants to kill more than any other man in the universe?''

She turned to him, and tears rolled down her cheeks. He put his arm around her. "What's the trouble?''

"What the hell can I do now? I was thinking about dumping Bramwell and staying with you. You treat

163

me like a lady, not just a whore you picked out of the dirty alley.''

"You said you were going to stay in town. Was that until he got a new ranch house built?"

"We talked about that.''

"It might take him six months to build a new one.''

"He said maybe four months.''

"So stay in town.''

"But he'll come and want me. If he touches me again, I think I'd scream.''

"So tell him. I'll pay for your room.''

"You'd do that?''

"Of course. Nothing wrong with honest compensation for a good day's work.''

She grinned. "Or an afternoon's or evening's work.'' Her eyes went wide again. "Oh God, Bramwell is in town with two men. They're buying things for the ranch. He'll kill you if he sees you.''

"He would at least try, so I won't let him see me. He'll be at the hardware store and general store. I'll watch for him. I have some work to do but I won't do it until after he leaves.''

"When your work is through you'll come back here for tonight?''

"You bet.'' He looked at his pocket watch. It was almost two. He stood up and kissed her on the cheek. "I have to see a friend of mine gets off for the ranch. Then I'll check on Bramwell and come back here. You'll need a new dress.''

"I bought some and paid for them this morning. I'm to pick them up tomorrow.''

He touched her nose. "Don't go away. There are

164

some more things I want to ask you about Mr. Bram-well.''

''More than glad to tell you,'' she said.

Chapter Fourteen

Morgan pulled his wide-brimmed hat down low as he walked toward the court house. The rig was parked where they had left it, and Royce Olson sat on the front seat. A cardboard box and three packages showed in the back seat.

"Looks like Heather has been here," Morgan said.

Olson roused himself from a small nap and nodded. "Yes, Mr. Morgan, she said she wanted to look around in the general store for a few minutes."

They waited. "Any talk around town about the Circle-S?" Morgan asked.

Olson hesitated. He was a big blond man who worked hard and had been loyal to the Scoggins ranch. "Just that we and the Bar-B might be close to a range war."

"That could bring in some gun hands. I hear that

Bramwell is in town buying some supplies, so be watchful.''

Olson sat up straighter. When Morgan saw Heather coming along the boardwalk, he met her and carried a paper sack for her.

''Looks like you found a couple of things you needed,'' he said.

She looked at him and smiled. ''Indeed I did. Even some clothes, but some of them I won't show you. The dress I will. Thanks for making me shop. It's fun to come into town now and then.''

He handed her up into the buggy, and Olson untied the horse from the rail.

''I'll be back tonight with some hands and some more rifles, if the store has any. Bramwell's in town so keep alert. We don't want any trouble between you and him.''

Olson adjusted his six-gun so it was more available as he sat on the front buggy seat.

''We'll watch sharp, Mr. Morgan.''

''Come see me when you get in,'' Heather said. She smiled at him, and Morgan was reminded what a pretty little thing she really was. ''I want to know how you did recruiting new hands.''

She waved, and the rig rolled down the street away from the general store and toward the Circle-S ranch.

Morgan turned back toward the general store and crossed the street. He sat in a chair outside the hardware store and watched across the street. A wagon had pulled in front of the store, and two men were carrying out boxes. Morgan saw a big square of canvas and some tent poles.

He saw a pair of six-foot crosscut saws, two six-foot rip saws and a variety of other woodworking tools. Looked like some of the Bar-B cowboys would be working the woods to bring down enough logs to build a new ranch house—maybe just two or three rooms this summer.

Morgan soon found a saloon half a block down the street where he could sit by the front window and still see the wagon. About an hour later the rig pulled out, came directly past the saloon, and Morgan could see Bramwell himself sitting on the high seat beside the wagon driver. They were heading home.

Morgan took his beer outside and watched the rig until it was out of sight to the south. It was moving slowly. Might make the Bar-B before dark if it moved right along.

It was recruiting time. He went back into the bar and got the men's attention and made his announcement.

"Men, I'm looking for cowboys. I want people who can ride and aren't afraid of a little work. I'm paying thirty dollars a month. You ride in on a horse, you ride out on a horse. We'll be leaving town today. Be glad to talk to anybody interested at that back table."

By the time he got there he had four men lined up to talk to him. The wages were five dollars over the going rate, and he figured that might attract some attention. It had the last time. He signed three of the four and told them where to be at five o'clock with all their gear and ready to ride.

In the next three saloons he found enough men to make up his 15, then he checked with the general store.

He bought three Spencer repeating carbines and three Henry repeating .44's. He'd always liked the Henry, but it was a pound heavier and almost five inches longer than the Spencer. Of course with the Henry you could fire 13 times before reloading the magazine. He bought 200 rounds for each kind of rifle.

Morgan picked out three saddle boots, all the man had, and told the store clerk he'd be back for all the goods just before five o'clock.

That left Buckskin Morgan more than an hour. He went back to the Plainsman Hotel and up to room 211. One knock brought a quick opening of the door.

"Saw you come across the street," she said. Elly twirled for him after closing the door. She had on a new dress that fit her like a tight stocking. It plainly showed her thrusting breasts and her tiny waist.

"Like it?" she asked.

"Prettiest dress and the prettiest lady I've seen in a month of Tuesdays," he said.

She ran and hugged him, then kissed him.

"I put it on special so you could take it off me. You got time? You staying all night?"

"Can't this time. Next time I will. Bramwell come back to see you?"

"No, but I'll tell him next time he comes to town that I ain't gonna be with him no more." She rubbed Lee's crotch. "Morgan, you marvelous cock, get me out of this dress before I explode!"

He helped her out of it, not sure it wouldn't tear in the process, but they made it. He had been right. Elly didn't have a thing on under the pretty red dress. She stretched and put his hands on her big breasts.

"Yes, yes, I love that. Play with them, and make them all warm and ready. That just makes me feel so delicious."

She pulled him to the bed. "I don't want you to undress," she said. "I like it scratchy and rough sometimes." She rubbed his crotch and felt his erection.

"Oh good, I am exciting you this time. I like that." She undid his pants and pulled out his long, hard tool and kissed it. "I really want him inside of me, right now!"

"I wouldn't be a gentleman if I ignored a beautiful lady's wishes, would I?"

Elly squealed in delight as he thrust into her. She panted and brayed with wonder and joy, and thens he threw her legs all the way to his shoulders as he stroked into her responding crotch.

It was over too soon, and this time she wouldn't let him touch her clit.

"Maybe next time. I want us to be just this way, close and warm and resting."

Morgan rested so much he was five minutes late meeting his men outside the general store.

He picked up the rifles and boots, gave the rifles to six of the men, and they headed for the ranch. Each of the riders also had a six-gun on his hip. Morgan wasn't enthusiastic about any of the men, but they were adequate and could provide numbers if nothing else in a showdown with the Bar-B, which he was sure was going to come sooner or later.

They each had a horse, and while not prime cow ponies, they would do. The Circle-S had no large remuda such as would be needed for a long cattle drive, but since their drive would be no more than 20 or 25 miles from any part of the ranch to Miles City and the stockyards, one horse would do the job.

Morgan began to think what next they should do to take the fight to the Bar-B. He was surprised that Bramwell hadn't responded to the hanging, but he suddenly had had other problems—Indian problems. He knew that even a bluffing attack by 15 mounted Indians would scare hell out of the Bar-B riders. It could send four or five more riding for town and a new job. The more cowboys they could frighten away from the Bar-B the better.

An hour later Lee Morgan began to get some ideas to surprise Bramwell with. He worked on them as the men rode south to the Circle-S.

It was well after dark when Jed Hackett led five riders across the high valley of the Tongue River and crossed into Circle-S land. They moved slowly, intent on keeping far from any of the ranch buildings and the guards. They had swung far south before driving west. Soon they came on stock, and when they were sure they were well inside the Circle-S ranges, Hackett called the men together.

"This is the place. What we're doing is killing twenty head of stock. Pick the cows if you can find them. Shoot them in the head with your six-gun at close range. That should do the job. Any questions?"

Nobody had any. The men didn't like the job, but the boss said to do it, so they did.

The six men fanned out across the grassland and found cows bedded down for the night. They leaned down from their mounts and shot them in the heads.

Hackett tried to count the shots, but some came too close together.

"Each man do four," he shouted. He waited and slowly the men came riding back to where he sat.

"Well?" he asked.

They responded sourly that the job was done. One man said he got five by mistake. Hackett told them to stay there and took a quick ride around the area. He counted at least 20. Then the six men turned and rode back to the Bar-B. It was well after midnight when they got to the bunkhouse.

Hackett went to the new tent that the men had put up late that afternoon. It was a wall tent and sported a folding cot inside, two chairs and a rack with some new clothes that Bramwell had bought in town.

"Mr. Bramwell?"

"Come in, Hackett. How did it go?"

"Smooth, Mr. Bramwell. At least twenty, mostly cows, dead."

"Good. That will give the Circle-S something to think about. Now get to bed. We've got to get a small herd of steers ready to take to the pens in Miles City. Say three hundred steers. I'm in need of some ready cash to help get this new ranch house built. How do you like my new accommodations?"

"Bigger than I thought it was. Should do fine until winter comes."

"Yes, quite."

When Hackett left, Bramwell sat there thinking

about his ranch house and how he had never appreciated it. Now he was reduced to living in a damned tent like some servant! He railed at the Indians, but he knew he was in no position to fight with them. Indians were warriors. He couldn't fight on two fronts. For now the Circle-S was the main target. After he had reduced it to a cipher, he would turn his anger at the Indians and this Young Wolf, the crazy white Indian who wrote English better than Bramwell did.

Just at dawn the next morning, Morgan rode out from the Circle-S. He had a big breakfast inside him, two of the new Spencer rifles and 100 rounds of the .52 caliber ammunition. He also had good news for the Mandan tribe.

He rode quickly, pushing the mount to a five-mile-an-hour pace with alternate trotting and walking. He passed the scarred pine but found no message from Young Wolf, so he rode on south following the trail Young Wolf had shown him. He wasn't sure just where the Mandan camp was, but if he rode up this way far enough, he was sure they would find him.

With the strike at the ranch house on the Bar-B, Young Wolf should be expecting some kind of retaliation, which meant he would have lookouts watching the back trail.

Morgan had ridden an hour into the hills, found a trail of sorts but no recent tracks. He walked his mount forward and around a bend in a small valley which seemed to lead to a rocky ledge ahead.

Sitting on his horse 20 yards in front of Morgan was Young Wolf. He raised his hand in greeting.

"My lookouts saw you coming. I figured Bramwell wouldn't send out one man to raid our village, so it had to be you."

Morgan rode up and motioned to some shade where they both dismounted. Morgan offered a drink from his canteen to Young Wolf who declined. After Morgan took a drink and put the canteen back on the horse, he grinned at Young Wolf.

"Good news from Heather Scoggins. She's agreed to helping your people raise cattle. We suggest that you pick out four of your best young men who can ride well and speak English and send them to live on the Circle-S for three or four months to learn the cattle business. You can be one of them, of course, if you want to."

"Good. That's a wise young woman for one so young. I had anticipated such a plan and have three men and myself all ready to come. When?"

"Anytime. We'll be doing some branding and cutting and a minor roundup soon so the men will learn all about the business."

"Clothes. My men will need cowboy clothes," Young Wolf said.

"Three pairs of jeans and three good shirts and boots. We can take care of that once they get on the place. How are you fixed for horses?"

"We have about twenty head. We've kept them and they breed well."

"Good, you're almost in the ranching business.

With the brand inspectors at the railroad yards, we figure that you better use the Circle-S brand. We'll use an ear notch to separate your stock from ours. That way there won't be any problem with the brand inspector.''

"Yes, that's good planning. Do you want to come and see my camp?''

"Just don't think I should right now, Young Wolf. Bunch of things to do back at the ranch. You come down whenever you're ready. I'll find some clothes for your men to wear until we can get them measured and send somebody to town. Just talk to the first guard you see out about three miles from the house, and then come on in. Better make it in daylight so you don't scare anybody.''

Young Wolf grinned. "I'll try to be on my best behavior. I will go back to the village one day a week to check up on things.''

"No problem with that. You can keep your men there as long as you think you need to, a week or a month. They'll learn how to be cowboys mostly by doing it.''

Morgan hesitated. "I hear you started a bonfire the other night.''

"True, a modest payback, but with a good threat of a two-to-one kill ratio if any more of my people get hurt.''

"Bramwell was in town yesterday buying supplies to start rebuilding. You'll probably be seeing him up in the timber around here for new logs.''

"Fine, as long as he keeps away from my people.''

"Be sure your men understand that the Bramwell

white eyes will be up this way.'' Morgan stood. ''I better be moving. As soon as you think your cowboys are ready, we'll cut out a hundred head of Bar-B cows and run them up into your pasture. We'll make sure it's where nobody can find them.''

''Easy, we know every trail and canyon in these mountains.''

They shook hands.

''Whenever you come, we'll be ready for you,'' Morgan said and rode off toward the valley.

On his trip back to the ranch, Lee Morgan tried to get the whole situation into perspective. He listed what had happened since he came to the Circle-S and what had happened on the Bar-B. The scales were still tipped heavily in favor of the robbers. The pivotal problem was getting back the 4000 head of cattle that the Bar-B owed them.

Bramwell for damn sure wasn't going to drive them to the river and say help yourself. Morgan had to decide the best way to get them back, and it wasn't a hard decision.

No one respects action and a bold move as much as the man who has been making such moves. A rustler would certainly understand another man rustling back his own stock. He wouldn't like it, but neither would he head to the sheriff and demand an accounting brand by brand, especially since his own pastures were going to be hip deep in rebranded cattle with lots of blanked spots on the steers' hides.

So they needed to make a big sweep and pull in a big batch of cattle, from 1000 to 2000. Cut down the deficit and then see what the reaction was from

Bramwell.

Morgan realized the original cattle stolen from the Circle-S were probably long since mixed in with the herd or sold to some buyer in Miles City and already on some supper table in Chicago. Substitute beef tasted just the same.

As for the Young Wolf cattle ranch, he could see no problems. The same brand and an ear clip would keep them separate or make them easy to divide. They would make a count on Circle-S land and drive a mixed herd to the railroad or a whole herd from the Indians.

Concerning that damn Arizona paper, he had no idea how to get them to withdraw the wanted poster. Maybe the sheriff's wire to Tombstone would get some results. Maybe it wouldn't even be answered. The law was usually a little unsettled in Tombstone.

Heather could be a problem if he didn't handle her right. He would—hands off! Not even a kiss on the cheek. Willy Joe was the man for her, and she would realize it sooner or later.

No argument that she was as cute as a dewdrop on a honeysuckle petal, but he had too much respect for Milburn Scoggins to bundle his daughter into bed for a month and then leave her crying at the gate. Not a chance. He had to promote the match with Willy Joe.

Morgan's breakfast was starting to wear off. He was hungry by the time he could see the ranch buildings. Thank goodness there was no plume of smoke from burned out buildings. He didn't know if Bramwell would go that far or not. He just might consider it fair play to burn out the Circle-S ranch house as well.

Morgan pointed his horse at one of the new hands and told him to unsaddle her, feed her and rub her down. Then Morgan headed for the kitchen. He could eat half a steer right then whether the critter had been cooked or not.

Chapter
Fifteen

After a big dinner that noon, Morgan laid out the sketches he had made of the Bar-B spread when he had ridden through on the grub line. He had noted where the most cattle seemed to be grazing. There were a lot due north of the ranch, but if they moved in that far they would be less than six miles from the Bar-B buildings.

He didn't mind coming within eight miles, and ten would be better, but six was too close. The Bar-B could respond too quickly, and he was sure they would.

He judged the man he was going up against. By now he was sure there would be no easy cattle for them to grab. Bramwell would have pulled most of his animals back across the Pumpkin River. South of the ranch buildings there was a 35-mile stretch between the Pumpkin and the Powder Rivers, lots of grazing land that was still open.

Morgan figured he would need to take a scouting mission to find out where the most animals were, but that would take another night. He wanted to make a strike in force tonight. He sent the word around that 20 men should catch some sleep this afternoon and left it up to Willy Joe to pick which men.

"We want men who can ride and drive cattle. The more experienced the man the better. We're making another midnight requisition of some Bar-B beef with some of our own mixed in."

Willy Joe grinned and left to pull out the chosen men.

Morgan looked at the maps and sketches he had made. At last he had his war plan. He and his men would ride due north from the Circle-S for 10 miles, then they would turn due east and ride until they hit the Pumpkin River. This should be about ten miles.

They would cross the Pumpkin and ride five miles into Bar-B lands. At that point they should be in some prime beef areas. They would stretch out a half mile to the north and make a sweep to the river, herding everything they found in that line forward.

When they got the cattle across the Pumpkin they would drive them due west, sweeping in everything they could find along the route. There wouldn't be much more in the area between the rivers. When they got the herd to the Tongue, they would drive it across the shallow water and then north to the little holding canyon they used for branding.

That was the plan, keeping back at least nine to guard their ranch.

With that settled he went up to his room for a nap.

They would be up all night and half the morning before they got the critters into the small branding canyon. If everything went well, they would be covering almost 50 miles before they had the critters bedded down.

Just after 7:30 that night when the men assembled, Morgan had Willy Joe pick out his six best shots. Each man was given a rifle boot and a Spencer carbine with four tubes loaded and ready to go. Willy Joe and Morgan also armed themselves accordingly.

They pushed off five minutes later and headed due north. Willy Joe and Morgan led the troops, who were strung out behind them in a disorganized bunch.

''If I had wanted to ride in columns of four, I would have joined the damned cavalry,'' one of the riders growled.

They moved steadily north, trotting for half a mile, then moving at a fast walk. Morgan figured they were making about five and a half miles an hour. By 9:30 they should turn east and then after another two hours should be at the Pumpkin River.

It was just after midnight when they splashed across the Pumpkin and headed deeper into Bar-B lands. There was a moon out that darkened now and then with high, fast moving clouds.

They rode more compactly now, with three of the riflemen in front and three bringing up the rear. Here and there they could see cattle, most of them bedded down but now and then one feeding.

Morgan checked his big pocket watch with a shielded match. When he figured they had ridden for an hour east, he stopped and pulled the men around him. So far they hadn't seen any cowhands or guards.

''We'll spread out both directions north and south

here. Stay about thirty, forty yards apart, just so you can see the next man. We push any cattle we find to the west, right back toward the river. We'll take everything we find except some of the ornery range bulls. Let them go.

"Keep it as quiet as you can. If you find anything unusual, Willy Joe will be at one end of the line and I'll be at the other end. Come see us. Let's go push some beef back where it belongs."

He had told the new men about the rustling of the Bar-B and that this was simply a return of beef to the ranch where they had been bred and raised.

Things got started well when they found a bunch of 50 head in a small draw and moved them out west. They were catching a goodly number as they worked slowly toward the river. After nearly a half hour, one of the men came riding up hard toward Morgan.

"Come take a look at this," the man said. He and Morgan rode toward the north end of the line and soon saw a herd of 500 to 700 head of cattle. A night rider circled them, and to one side they saw a small campfire and a chuck wagon.

"Making a roundup themselves," Morgan said. He evaluated the situation. The small camp was on the west side of the herd. "I'll take care of the night rider. Once I give a yell, I want you to bring up ten men and spook those critters, moving them west. Run them right over that chuck wagon and their camp. They won't know what hit them."

Morgan moved out toward the single rider who was keeping the stock tightly bunched. He rode toward the man as if he was coming to replace him. Ten yards away the man looked up and waved.

"What the hell . . . you ain't due on yet," he said.

Morgan was 15 feet away by then and lifted his six-gun and covered the cowboy.

"Oh, but I am, and so are you. Lift your hands and don't make a sound."

"Who the hell are you?"

"You don't want to know."

Morgan rode up to the man, slammed the big Colt down on the rider's head and caught him as he fell unconscious. He slumped the man forward on his horse. Then, using the man's own lariat, he tied him to the saddle.

When he was satisfied that the rider wouldn't fall off, Morgan took the mount's reins and led it back from the herd. He saw his own men moving up and gave a yell.

Ten men charged at the sleeping bovines, shouting at them, rousting them, galloping into the herd and prodding with rifle barrels.

One of the men had a high voice and began yapping like a coyote. In an instant the whole herd was on its feet and slowly beginning to move west. Then a shot was fired from the Bar-B camp in front of them.

Half a dozen shots came from the Circle-S men as the critters began to go wild and stampede straight west. Within two minutes the cows, calves and steers charged over the small range camp. The chuck wagon was soon knocked over, the fire put out, and half a dozen sleeping cowboys were jumping and dodging cattle, trying to keep from being trampled to death.

Five minutes later the Circle-S riders had swept past the remains of the camp and drove the laggard cattle on west. The other ends of the line of drovers picked up more cattle and pushed them in the same direction.

Soon the cowboys came on some of the stampeding cattle that had tired and slowed to a walk. The men pushed the doggies on toward the river with the rest of the herd.

Morgan worked up and down the line, urging his men not to miss any pockets, to sweep the range free of cattle.

Soon they reached the river which the cattle crossed after a quick drink. Once beyond the Pumpkin, Morgan on one end and Willy Joe on the other end of the long spread began to turn the ends in, bringing the animals toward the center where they could be formed into a more compact cattle drive.

It took them another five miles to get the cattle formed into a long line, maybe ten cows wide. Once they achieved that they spaced the riders out with one rider on each side of the point, two more on each side as swing riders and two more as flankers. Half a dozen were left to sweep up any strays that got away from the other men.

Morgan found four of the riflemen and stationed them 200 yards behind the herd as a rear guard. He wasn't sure if they needed it or not, but he wasn't taking any chances.

They were ten miles from the Pumpkin and probably back on Circle-S land when Morgan heard the first shots from the rear. He raced back and found the four riflemen off their mounts, laying down a concentrated fire at six winking points of light 100 yards to the rear.

Morgan pulled his Spencer out of the boot and slid down beside one of the riflemen.

"How many of them?"

"Five or six, not sure. They came up on us sudden, but we heard them and fired first."

"Any of our men hurt?"

"Don't think so."

Morgan fired at a point of light and rolled to one side. Two rounds blasted into the spot where he had been. The firing tapered off. When they heard one horse move out, two men fired at the sound, and they heard a scream of pain.

A minute later another horse left.

"Want to charge the ones left?" the cowboy asked.

"We're not in that kind of a war," Morgan said. "Just push them out of there." The five Circle-S rifles fired again, and soon the last winking light out in the prairie vanished. The Circle-S men waited for five minutes, and when they heard nothing more, they mounted and rode toward the herd.

"Anybody hit?" Morgan asked the four men.

"Picked up a scratch," one of the men said, his voice sounding a little haggard. Morgan moved over by him and got there just before the man fell to one side. Morgan caught him and looked at his shoulder, a red, sticky mess.

They stopped, and Morgan took a shirt out of his saddlebag, cutting it into strips with his knife. He used his handkerchief as a compress over the bullet wound and then tied the square of cloth firmly in place with the cloth strips. He gave the man a drink of water.

"Can you ride?" Morgan asked.

"Hell, yes. Just got a little dizzy there for a minute."

"Some scratch."

"Yeah. Not so bad. I been shot before."

They helped the man back on his horse and started off. Soon they caught up with the herd and reorganized a rear guard.

Morgan searched out Willy Joe who was out in front of the lead steers.

"What was the shooting?" Willy Joe asked.

"Six mad Bar-B cowboys on roundup, I'd guess," Morgan said. "We pushed them back. One of our men took a round in the shoulder. How far to the Tongue?"

"I figured we'd cut off the corner so we're slanting northwest. Should be within five miles of the river, then another eight or nine miles to Branding Valley."

"Sounds good. The critters are slowing down a little. Lucky hitting that herd back there they had already gathered for us."

Willy Joe chuckled. "They're going to be downright pissed when morning comes. Bramwell will shit in his pants."

Both men laughed.

"How many you figure we have here?"

"One damn good downpayment on that four thousand that they owe us. I tried to estimate them as I rode the line. Stretched out for damn near a half mile. They're walking about ten wide. Hell, I'd say we have fourteen hundred. Maybe fifteen hundred."

Morgan laughed. "Not a bad night's work, if we get them all the way. Doubt if the Bar-B has time to launch any kind of an attack. They'd have to go back to the ranch, dig men out of bed, get them mounted, then try to find us. We'll be twenty-five miles from them by the time they can get underway."

"Critters are slowing down, boss. Getting tired."

"They've come over fifteen miles already. I've seen

a herd take all day to make ten miles. We've got to push them another ten before they get to rest. Gonna take some doing.''

''At least we have twice the number of men usually needed for a herd this size,'' Willy Joe said. ''We'll let them move slower, but keep them going.''

Morgan agreed. ''Sounds good. Won't matter if it takes us another two or three hours to get them to Branding Canyon.''

Morgan wanted the Big Dipper moving in it's nightly trip around the north star. The pointer stars on the cup were moving farther and farther down. When they were straight down, pointing upward from a six o'clock position on a clock, it would be four A.M. That time was coming up quickly.

It took the men an hour to get the herd across the shallow Tongue River. They drank, stumbled out on the other side and lay down. A thousand animals had to be prodded back to their feet and jolted on the move again.

By daylight the herd was stretched out close to a mile but moving steadily toward Branding Valley. Morgan figured they had pushed the cattle more than 19 or 20 miles. They were so tired they could hardly walk. If he tried to push them too far they would lose a lot of them.

He rode to the front of the herd and told the point men to start circling the critters. They made a quarter mile circle smaller and smaller until the cattle were massed together. Almost at once they dropped to the ground and rested.

Morgan called the men together and sent out four of them to ride herd to be sure the animals stayed bedded down. They would get a six-hour rest; at noon they would be moved out again toward Branding Canyon.

Morgan called over the six riflemen. He sent them around in pairs to give the herd protection. He and Willy Joe rode on a mile to a small knoll where they could get a longer view of the mostly flat valley.

The rest of the men lay down in the shade of their horses for a quick nap. They would rotate every two hours on riding herd.

Willy Joe and Morgan sat on their mounts and stared back the way they had come. They saw a three month-old calf running forward and bawling like he had lost his mother, which he had. He would find the herd.

"So far, so good," Willy Joe said.

"Right. I haven't looked at the brands, but probably most of them are Bar-B. They probably rebranded and sold the cattle they stole from us. What's the situation with brand inspection here? You have a state man who checks brands at the stock yards?"

"Usually. One we had here for years got transferred. I know he was on the Bar-B payroll. He never even sniffed at the Bar-B animals when they went through. Doubt if he looked at one out of a hundred. I saw him one day. The animals plainly had blocked out brands. The blocks were no more than a week old in some cases. Everyone of those animals should have been challenged. I don't know who is in that spot now since we haven't had anything to sell for almost a year."

"We'll find out soon enough. You probably should go into town and check out the brand man. Find out how he calls them and what he thinks about re-branding.''

A rifle shot boomed from the south where the rifle-men had been stationed. Both Morgan and Willy Joe kicked their mounts into a gallop that way. When they came on the scene one of the guards was on post and the other one was a quarter of a mile east. They heard another shot in that direction.

''What happened?'' Morgan asked.

The cowboy pointed. ''We thought we saw a rider coming, but then he must have hit a swale, and we couldn't see him for a while. When he came back up he was three hundred yards away and we whaled away with three shots. Missed us. Ronnie and I returned fire. He told me to stay here, and that's him out there.''

''Bar-B sent a tracker to be sure who drove off the animals,'' Morgan said. ''Smart. They know where they are, but I don't think they'll come after them. I'd guess that Bramwell is getting short on men. He must have lost six or seven men by now. That could pull him down to about eighteen. With guard duty and range work, that's cutting it thin.''

As they watched the man out in front of them, he sent two more rounds at the evidently retreating rider, then turned and trotted back to where the three of them waited.

''Don't think I hit the son of a bitch, but I scared the hell out of him. He flat out galloped that animal for a half mile.''

''Just one of them?''

''Damn sure. No other rifle fire. This one wasn't too good with his piece. He should have shot both of

191

us off our saddles.''

Morgan nodded. "Keep on post here and sound off if you see anybody else coming. My guess is that one was supposed to trail the herd as far as he could, then report back what he saw.''

"Figures,'' Willy Joe said. Willy and Morgan rode back to the herd and told the men what had happened. The cattle were so tired they had gone to sleep in the middle of the morning but would be ready to walk again by noon.

"No food for you men, but we'll eat good once we get these critters in the canyon. I'm going to head back to the ranch house and get the chuck wagon started out there so chow will be ready when you get there. Also I'll have the branding gear on board.''

He and Willy Joe rode off to the side.

"I'm leaving you to get these beef to the canyon. Once there, bed them down or let them graze, whatever they want to do. We better wait a day before we start branding. I'll put ten bedrolls on the chuck wagon. Pick out the ten men you want to have brand, and send the others back to the ranch. I'll come out with the food and then go back to the ranch tonight.''

"You expect Bramwell to retaliate?''

"He just about has to, otherwise he'll be saying we can come and get his stock anytime we want to. He'll do something. I'm just not sure what.''

Morgan looked at the cattle.

"We pushed them pretty hard. There might be ten, fifteen maybe even twenty of them that won't be able to get up when you roust them out. Just leave the weak ones. They might make it, and if they do, they'll join the rest of the range herd. Now I better get moving.''

He waved and rode off to the north. He wasn't exactly sure where he was, but they were only four miles from the river. He could hit it, move north and get to the ranch.

The first two miles went well, and when he saw the river, he turned further north to save time. For a moment he dozed in the saddle and then shook his head. Wouldn't look good for him to fall off his horse and break his neck.

Morgan began to sing a little tune to keep himself awake. He wanted to evaluate, but his brain felt like mush. How were they doing in the war? Damned if he knew. He was hungry and more sleepy than he figured he would be. It was broad daylight and he was nodding.

It was almost eight o'clock before he spotted the ranch house and buildings. He should have thought about the chuck wagon. It should have been at Branding Canyon waiting for the crew. Maybe the cook could get out there in time, since it would take the herd until four that afternoon to make it.

After loading the bedrolls and branding irons, Morgan instructed the cook.

"Might take them two or three days to do the branding, so take along plenty of food for ten men."

Then he went toward the ranch house. He saw Heather at the backdoor waiting for him. What a pretty, young woman! He scowled. No. She was Willy Joe's woman and Milburn Scoggins daughter. Hands off! He walked up and grinned.

"Got any breakfast left for a hungry cowhand?"

"Yes. How did it go?"

Morgan told her, and Heather laughed softly.

"Now, Mr. Bramwell, you can see how it feels to pay back what you have stolen from us, even though you don't want to. Serves you right."

"Enough of the gloating, pretty woman. Where's my food?"

Chapter
Sixteen

While Morgan was eating breakfast, Heather said, "Some of the hands found twenty-two head of cattle dead about five miles north near the river. The hands came in early this morning."

"How did they die? Poison?"

"Gunshot to the head. All of them. Mostly cows. The hands said some of them even had powder burns."

"Well, we know how Bramwell replied to one of our hits against him. He's getting desperate. We made a good trade-off for the twenty-two head." He finished the stack of hotcakes, eggs, bacon, toast and coffee.

"You look like you better get to a bed before you fall over asleep on the table," Heather said.

"Good idea. Wake me up at noon. I need to get out to the Branding Canyon for some work." He stared at her for a minute. "Wonder if the sheriff ever sent that wire to Tombstone?''

"We'll probably know soon enough. Don't go asking for any more trouble when we got more than we need right on our doorstep.''

Morgan nodded and walked up stairs to his bedroom, peeled off his dusty shirt, flopped on the bed and slept.

He awakened at noon, ate two roast beef sandwiches and rode off for Branding Canyon. Morgan got to the canyon before the herd, so he angled to the southeast to find them, running into them a half hour later.

"Had a hard time getting them on the move,'' Willy Joe said. "Had to boost some of them up with a rope slap on their backs, but we got all but about ten.''

"Good work. We've got chow ready for you when you hit the canyon.''

Two hours later, they swept the last of the critters into the Branding Valley's narrow mouth and put a pair of cowboys there to contain the stock.

The chuck wagon was set up and waiting. Some of the men washed the dust off their hands and faces at the water barrel on the side of the wagon. The rest of them just grabbed tin plates and loaded them with beans and potatoes and gravy and thick steaks that were still sizzling on the grill. The cook had timed their arrival just right.

A half hour later they started branding the cattle. Again it was a process of blocking and rebranding. They found about one animal in eight already had the Circle-S brand and hadn't been redone.

"Those Circle-S brands save us some time,'' Willy Joe said.

They worked until it was so dark they couldn't see. The tally man said they had branded 314 and had found 42 with Circle-S brands. That made a total of 356 for the afternoon.

"Take us another two days," Morgan said. The cook had a beef stew ready for them loaded with onions, carrots and potatoes. After eating, Morgan turned toward the ranch.

"I better keep a line on what's doing back there. If there aren't any problems, I'll be here tomorrow." He grinned. "That is I'll be back if I'm not so sore and stiff that I can't get out of bed."

An hour and a half later, Morgan rode past two alert guards and into the ranch yard. He put his horse away, fed her some oats, then went up to the ranch house.

Heather was reading a book in the big living room. She looked up and smiled.

"Lee Morgan, you look tired."

"Totally wrung out, like a wet towel. All I want to do is find my bed. How did things go here the rest of the day?"

"Fine. No problems. Guards didn't spot any trespassers. I don't expect anything tonight. Bramwell has to collect his forces and decide how to retaliate."

"I can't figure out what he'll try," Morgan said. "He could poison our waterholes, but it's a free flowing river so he can't make that work. He might burn down every building on the place, but that only would be an irritant. He might try an all-out assault, which would come at night. But he knows by now that I hired fifteen more hands, so we must have more hands and guns than he does. That won't sound reasonable to him."

"Maybe that's the point," Heather said. "He might be so angry and pushed so close to the edge that he'll do something irrational."

"Good point. We wait and see." He waved. "I'm going to wash some of my grime off and dive into bed. No, no, that's all right. You don't have to sing me a lullaby—I'll make it just fine—but thanks." He grinned and headed for the stairs.

"Morgan?" Heather called.

He turned. "Yes."

"Sweet dreams."

He grinned and carried the lamp up the stairs and to his room. Inside he put the lamp on the dresser and heaved a long sigh. He wished he would take time for a long hot bath, but knew he wouldn't. Instead he stripped himself naked and washed off most of the dirt from the long day and night, then totally exhausted, fell on the sheets. It was warm enough that he didn't need even a sheet over him.

Buckskin Lee Morgan was sleeping before he could adjust his head on the pillow.

Downstairs in the living room, Heather had watched Morgan walking up the steps with a notion growing in her head. At last she nodded. Yes! She would try it. She opened a drawer in the small stand beside the couch where she had been reading and looked in the very bottom where she found what she wanted.

It was a book of drawings and stories. She had found it in her father's things when she had started looking through his desk only yesterday. She could tell at once that the book was about sexual matters and intercourse. At first she had put it down quickly, but now she looked at it.

The first chapter was about: "The reproductive system of the human male, how it works." She stared at the drawings of a man's penis and scrotum, showing the tubes inside. It was all interesting, but she felt a flush come to her neck and face. What if someone caught her reading this?

Who was there to catch her? Anyway, she was curious. Her mother had not been able to tell her anything about her own body, let alone that of the opposite sex.

She read the first paragraph and understood almost none of it. Heather turned the page, and the drawing there was of the male organ "in erectus." Her eyes widened. It was greatly enlarged, the text explaining that it became extremely rigid and hard.

Heavens! That is what goes inside . . . she couldn't even continue the thought.

As she flipped the pages, she came upon more drawings. One showed a naked woman on her back with a man between her thighs and his penis penetrating halfway into her crotch.

She pulled the book to her chest and looked around. There was no one else there. Slowly she lowered the book and read.

"When the male penis is inserted into the vagina of a woman it remains rigid and stiff until the male ejaculates, usually after a period of stroking or pumping into the woman. This often produces a pleasant sensation for the woman, and if the penis can strike or rub the woman's clitoris, there sometimes can be a mutual climax of the partners."

Heather found that she was breathing hard. She saw

that her legs had spread slightly and that she could detect a dampness between them.

That must be what her best friend in the whole world, Mary Beth, was talking about a year ago after church. They had been in her father's buggy waiting to go back to their ranches. Mary Beth lived on the other side of Miles City about five miles. She had two brothers and knew a lot more about boys than Heather did.

"I heard that girls can do it, too. There's a little hard place just above our slot. It's all hard and can be moved around. I've heard if you take a finger and rub it back and forth that sometimes it will let a girl climax."

Mary Beth was already 18 and had a boyfriend.

She watched Heather. "You ever seen a boy do it? You know, pump off his whanger?"

Heather shook her head. Mary Beth laughed. "No, I guess you couldn't, not having no brothers anymore. I seen my next younger brother one day in the barn. He opened his pants and got out his thing, and it was hard already. Put his hand around it and pumped away, and before long his hips bucked and he panted and his whanger shot out whitish stuff, six or seven times. It was something to see."

After that Heather wished that she still had a brother so she could watch him do that. Now she put her hand down between her legs and under her skirt and touched her crotch. She worked around until she found the hard place and rubbed it twice. Mary Beth had been right. It did feel good.

Six times she rubbed it, and she felt like she was going to explode. Instead she put the book back in the bottom drawer and with a determined expression marched over to the stairs. She took the lamp from the side table and walked up quietly.

Heather was not exactly sure what she was going to do, but she remembered that time under the trees with Morgan, and she was determined to try him again. Maybe this time he would be too tired to resist. She was ready and so curious she could almost cry.

She paused at the door, then turned the knob silently and saw there was no light inside. She pushed the door open and lifted the lamp so she could see.

Glory! He was spread out on the bed, halfway across it, lying on his back and as naked as a newborn puppy! She looked at his crotch but saw only a black swatch of hair. Slowly she eased into the room, walking quietly toward the bed, expecting him at any time to sit up, look at her with displeasure and scold her.

But he didn't. She put the lamp on the dresser and watched him. Now she could see his long, limp penis lying against his scrotum. This was real, not just a picture in a book. Suddenly her crotch was so wet she thought she might drip.

She took two more steps to the bed and stood directly over him, his crotch within reaching distance.

Quickly she unbuttoned her dress top and pulled it down to her waist, then she took off the cotton chemise and dropped it on the floor. Now she would have something to offer. Her hand went out slowly toward his penis, but she touched his leg first, softly, so gently she wasn't sure he could feel it. She did it again and watched him.

He mumbled something. His hand came across his chest and stopped.

She rested her hand on his thigh an inch from his penis. She began to breathe faster, sweat popping out on her forehead. One hand rubbed her breast without realizing it.

Her other hand moved now and touched his limp member. He didn't move. Gradually she began to work with his penis, to lift it and stroke it gently. She grinned when she saw it responding. It grew longer and thicker, and then a moment later it was fully erect and hard. She saw that his scrotum had lifted with the erection, pulling the tender hairy sack up tighter to his body.

Her hand gripped his penis now firmly, and she stroked him, almost wanting him to wake up. When one of his hands reached out toward her, she lifted it to her breasts. His hand caught them and clung there, caressing them tenderly.

She stroked him again, and he groaned. She could hear his breathing quicken, and then his hand caught hers on his penis and he was sitting up, frowning at her.

"What in hell are you trying to do, little girl?" Morgan demanded with more of a snap and bite in his voice than he had intended.

He pushed her hand off his penis and caught both her hands.

"You're really trying to get into trouble, aren't you? Young lady, if you want to get that virgin little pussy of yours poked by a man, you go talk to Willy Joe." He pulled the sheet up to cover his crotch.

He took her hands in his and kissed them, then sat her down on the bed beside him. "Sweet Heather, I told you before that your breasts are beautiful—perfect.

There is nothing the matter with you, but I'm not going to steal your virginity. That is the whole point of this little lecture.

"Leave your maidenhead for your husband. You'll both be a lot happier that way. You're a smart girl, Heather. You can understand that. Have a long talk with Willy Joe. Tell him you want to get married next week. Then when you agree on the date, do a sexy little naked dance for him and you'll find out what sex is all about."

He put his arms around her and hugged her tightly. Then he pulled up her dress top to cover her and kissed her cheek.

"Little Heather, a word of warning. This is absolutely the last time I'm going to see you naked and stay around here. Anything more like this and I'm going to get on my horse and ride for Idaho."

He watched her face but could read nothing there in the soft light. "Heather, you don't understand it yet, do you? You're a grown woman with a woman's body and a woman's desires and needs. So get yourself married. I've got too much respect for a gentleman by the name of Milburn Scoggins to touch one inch of that pretty little body of yours. Now, Heather, do you have the complete picture?"

"Yes," she said with a small voice.

"You know, if you try anything like this again, I'll be gone from here like a jack rabbit with six dogs on his trail?"

"Yes."

"Good, now give me a kiss on the cheek and get yourself out of here and to bed so I can get a few hours of sleep. I don't want to go to sleep branding tomorrow.''

Heather kissed his cheek and stepped back, holding her dress up. "I know you think all of this you're saying is what's best for me, but it would have been just glorious to be with you for the rest of the night." She shook her head, sighed and walked to the door. She took one last look at him, then took the lamp and went down the hall.

When Morgan was sure she was gone, he found a straight-backed chair in the dark, closed his door and slid the top of the chair under the doorknob. Now he could get some sleep.

Chapter Seventeen

Morgan slept until almost nine o'clock the next morning. He hadn't done that for years. By the time he'd had a quick breakfast that a smiling Heather cooked for him, one of the range guards from the south knocked on the ranch house door.

Heather brought him into the kitchen.

He was a short, sturdy young man with intense blue eyes and a smudge of dirt on one cheek.

"Mr. Morgan, I got me a strange bunch. They say they're supposed to be here and one of them speaks good English. They're Indians!"

"Young Wolf?" Morgan asked.

"Yeah, he said that was his name. Got all four of them right outside."

Morgan hurried out the door and grinned when he saw Young Wolf. The tall man had on a pair of full-

205

length blue jeans, a plaid shirt and a dirty old cowboy hat. Beside him were three young Indian men, ages 18 to 20, Morgan guessed.

"Young Wolf, welcome to the Circle-S. Step down and relax. Have your men had any breakfast?" Young Wolf said they had eaten already.

The four Indians dismounted but held on to their horses. None of them had saddles.

Morgan held out his hand, and Young Wolf shook it. He said something swiftly in his own language, and the three braves stepped forward and held out their hands. Each one gave an English name Young Wolf had probably picked out. Lee shook each man by the hand and repeated the names, which were Harry, Walt and Joe.

Each of the men had on blue jeans and looked uncomfortable. They wore no shirts or hats. Morgan grinned when he saw the eagerness, the fire in their eyes. This was a new adventure for them.

"Glad you're here, men," he said to all of them. "We're doing some branding, and it'll be a good time for you to see it."

Young Wolf translated some of the words, and the men all nodded.

"These men know some English, but it will be a learning process for them. I'll have to translate some of the words, but all three are eager and anxious to learn about cattle and English and took forward to raising stock on our own land."

"Those hackamores will serve for now, but we can get proper bridles for you later when you want them. I never tried roping without a saddle. See what your men decide later on.''

Morgan looked at the three Mandan Indians. ''Harry, Joe, Walt, you like coffee?''

''Coffee?'' one of the men said.

When Young Wolf translated, they shook their heads.

''Afraid I'm the only one in my camp who likes the foul stuff, but I sure would like a cup if you can spare one.''

A half hour later they were riding for Branding Canyon.

''We saw tracks of a big herd of cattle that had come from the east to the west,'' Young Wolf said. ''Did you borrow some cattle from the Bar-B last night?''

''Night before last,'' Morgan said. ''About fifteen hundred our first estimate. Bramwell still owes this ranch over two thousand head.''

By the time they had ridden the seven miles to Branding Canyon, Morgan had told Young Wolf and the others exactly what they were doing out there.

''After today your men will see how important a rope is to a cowboy. They'll be given lariats, and some of our men will teach them how to use them. A good cowboy can't get along without his horse or his rope.''

Once at the canyon, the other cowboys stared in amazement at what obviously were four Indians. Morgan rode around explaining to everyone.

''These men are to be treated as equals. They have just as much right here as any of you. They aren't here to take your job. We want them to learn to handle cattle and know all we know about how to raise and breed them.''

He was talking to six men who had been roping and bringing cattle in for branding.

''Now, these men are guest workers on the ranch. If any of you men can't accept that, I want you to speak up right now, draw your wages and get off the Circle-S.''

One man rode up to Morgan. ''My kin was kilt by a bunch of savages just like them four. I won't stay a day on a spread that puts up with savages on the place.''

Morgan punched the man in the jaw, almost knocking him off his horse, then handed the man a gold eagle worth ten dollars. ''You ride, mister. Pick up your gear and the horse you rode in on at the ranch. You take anything don't belong to you, I'll ride you down and slice your balls off. You understand?''

The man growled, took the coin and rode for the ranch.

There was no more trouble. The four Indians rode from one point to another watching what the cowboys did and how they caught and branded the cattle. Morgan explained why they were blanking out the Bar-B brand.

When everyone had seen the Indians and work returned to a normal pace, Young Wolf asked what Morgan wanted him and his men to do.

''You can't rope the critters, and you have no saddles to use to snub them tight. We better get saddles for you for tomorrow. Let's work the brand-ing.''

The five men dismounted, and Morgan showed them exactly what the branders did. He made sure that Young Wolf told them that the branding iron was supposed to singe off the hair and burn only the outer skin. If it burned too deeply it would heal too slowly or perhaps not at all.

They watched a dozen animals being branded, then Young Wolf stepped up and asked to do the next steer. He took the hot iron and put the Circle-S brand on the steer's hip, holding it exactly the right amount of time then removing it. He branded ten more, then chattered with one of his men and gave the iron to him.

The first steer was branded too deeply, and Young Wolf pointed this out quietly to the man. The brave did the next brand correctly and soon had the feel of it.

Young Wolf put all three of his men through the branding operation. The cowboys who had been doing it stood around grinning, glad for the break.

When all four had mastered that skill, Morgan told them to mount up and had two of them guard the growing herd that had been branded or Circle-S cattle that had been weeded out of the herd.

The tally man reported they were working faster today and already had over 300 done before noon. About a third of those had been cut out without branding because they held Circle-S brands.

When the triangle clattered at the chuck wagon, the Indians looked up in alarm. Young Wolf explained to them that the white eyes ate three meals a day.

They would, too, as long as they were with the ranch.

Morgan followed the Indians through the chow line. That noon they had thick steaks, boiled potatoes and brown gravy, carrots and peas, thick slabs of bread and butter and coffee. The three Indians tried the coffee and were undecided. One of the Indians sat cross-legged and ate the steak with relish but only toyed with the carrots and peas.

Only one of the three decided that he liked the coffee. They all ate, then lay down where they were and went to sleep. Young Wolf growled at them, and they came awake, looking surprised.

"Often after a big meal we lay down for a nap," Young Wolf said. "It is a small habit that we will break. It will take us a while to get used to the white eye ways."

"You're doing fine. Your men caught on to the branding fast. Some cowboys just can't get the hang of it." Morgan drew a cow's ear in the dust where he sat near Young Wolf. "What we'll do to identify your animals is to cut a notch in the left ear that will tell us that animal is a Wolf brand animal.

"Oh, you noticed how we blanked out the Bar-B brand. We could vent it with an angled bar brand across it. But then we'd have to show a bill of sale to the brand inspector, and we don't have that. What we're doing here is illegal, Young Wolf—I want you to know that—but we're just getting back what was stolen from us in the first place."

The rest of the day went well. The Indians could ride their ponies, the cowboys gave them that. They could guide the little ponies with their knees and legs and feet, and they were good at cutting out a certain animal from a herd. They seemed to have a sense of where the steer or cow might be heading on the next charge. They ultimately would need a rope to bring the critter up for branding, and learning to rope was going to take more time.

Morgan got four lariats and took the Indians to one side and demonstrated what to do with a rope. They tried and found it was new and different. He had them lasso each other, working in pairs. First one and then the other would throw the rope. At the end of an hour, two of the Indians were getting the hang of it.

"Saddles," he said. He hoisted one of the young men into his saddle and put his feet in the stirrups. Young Wolf was there, translating and encouraging.

"After watching the other men work," Young Wolf said, "it now seems obvious that we're going to need saddles and boots for my men. Roping seems to need a saddle horn sometimes to help control the steer."

"How does this man react to the saddle?" Morgan asked.

Young Wolf and his brave talked back and forth a while and laughed and talked again.

"Harry says the saddle must be used for roping and branding, he can see that. He doesn't know if his pony will like the saddle or not, but he likes the way it gives him more control over the animal he's roping."

Before chow call came at six, all of the Indians had been on a horse with a saddle. Morgan looked over the chuck wagon and found a spare saddle, carried in case of emergency.

Morgan brought it over to the Indians and asked which one wanted to try it on his pony.

"Me," Harry said, stepping forward. It was the first time one of the braves had spoken to Morgan. They both grinned, went to the man's pony and eased the saddle on its back. The smallish horse stepped quickly to one side, then stepped back. He turned and looked at Harry who was soothing him, talking to him all the time. At last the horse settled down. It was another 15 minutes before Harry stepped into the stirrup and swung up on the mount's back.

The Indian pony again turned, looked at Harry and took a few tentative steps. Harry rode him out to the branding site and back. He then swung down from the horse as he had seen the cowboys do and smiled.

"Yes, I like," he said.

They branded cattle again until it was dark. Morgan went to the tally man and learned that they had processed 645 animals that day. The running total was 1001 so far. Almost 300 of those had had the original Circle-S brand on them. One yearling steer had bolted, tripped and fell, breaking his neck. One of the hands had butchered the animal which they would eat tomorrow for the noon meal.

"Figure we have about four or five hundred to do tomorrow," the tally man said. He looked at Morgan. "Them real Indians? That one talks better than I do."

"He should. He's a college graduate. Yes, they're real Indians from the Mandan tribe back up in the hills near here. Any objections?"

"No. Just that I've never seen a real Indian up close before. They sweat just like I do."

"True, and they bleed and cry and laugh the same way. Indians are human beings just like us. Sometimes we forget that. Good work on the tally sheets."

After they had finished the last branding for the day, Morgan found Young Wolf and his men.

"I forgot to bring blankets for your people," Morgan began.

Young Wolf laughed. "You are talking to a Mandan, sir. We never use blankets in the summer, neither inside nor outside. We saw some brush and a few trees at the head of the canyon. We'll go up there to sleep and be back here for breakfast. Already I'm falling into the white man's ways."

Young Wolf looked away a moment, as if he were embarrassed. "Morgan, you are a true friend to the Mandan people. You are giving us a new means of life. The white man's buffalo will now roam our lands deep in the hills, and the Mandans will be able to grow and prosper and train for the day when we must join the white man's world. Every man and woman in our village thanks you."

Morgan gripped the Indian's hand and smiled. "About time around here for a neighbor to help out a neighbor. We may want a small favor later on dealing with the Bar-B, but we won't ask your young men to go to war. Now I better ride back to the ranch house."

He talked with Willy Joe before he left.

"I won't be coming out tomorrow. Finish up and

let the herd drift out here. They should be safe enough. When things settle down a little we'll cut out those prime yearling steers and the two year-olds and take them to the railroad.

"Use Young Wolf and his men however you can. Try to get them experienced in as much as possible. Their roping isn't workable yet, but let them try if it won't hold up things. You should be through early afternoon. We'll see you back the ranch tomorrow."

He was about to turn away when he stopped.

"Oh, understand that Heather is right fond of you. I don't often give advice like this, but that young lady is all ready and primed to get married. You want her, you better move fast, or she's going to marry somebody else just so she can jump in bed with him. She's needing right now. Hate to see her get involved with the wrong man. You're the right one. You get your wits about you, Willy Joe, and we could have a wedding next month. I wouldn't mind giving away the bride, but it'll have to be soon."

He saw the look of surprise and wonder on the foreman's face.

"Oh, I figured that she cottoned to you, Morgan."

"Not a damn sight. I'm way too old for her. The field is clear, but I'd figure you better move damn fast."

Willy Joe watched him for a minute, then his frown was replaced by a big grin and he slapped his hat against his leg. "Yeah, Mr. Morgan, I plan on doing that first thing we get back tomorrow. I thank you."

Morgan waved off the thanks, mounted his sorrel and rode through the gathering darkness toward the ranch house.

When he came up to where he figured the ranch house should be, he found it dark. When someone challenged him with a high nervous voice, he identified himself and rode on in.

Heather came running toward him, threw her arms around him and sobbed into his shoulder.

When she could talk, she looked up at him with tears on her cheeks.

"They've been shooting at the house again. Every time I light a lamp, they shoot again, so I haven't had a light on for hours."

He hugged her tight and walked her toward the house. "They are angry and frustrated. If this is their only response we'll be lucky. Right now, let's put a thick quilt over the window and then light a lamp. They won't be able to see any light at all."

Ten minutes later they had lamps burning in Heather's bedroom and one downstairs that couldn't be seen from the east side of the house.

"Feel better?" he asked.

"Yes, much better." She looked at him with a slight frown. "But when is all this going to end?"

"When you give up, or when he gives up—not before. You knew it wasn't going to be easy when this all started."

"We're really having a war, aren't we?" Heather asked.

"Yes. Not a lot of shooting yet, but a real war. As

with any war, both sides can be battered and bloody and sick of the fighting. The one who wins is the one who can hang on the longest. In this case, that has to be us.''

Parrish Bramwell sat at a small table that had been salvaged from the ranch house fire and stared at the problems he had. He had listed them all on paper.

The main problem came back to one point, one situation, one man—Buckskin Lee Morgan. The damn sheriff should have arrested him already, but the sheriff whined and said the man drew a gun on him and ran him off the ranch.

"You should have roared back out there with a fifty-man posse and wiped out every one who tried to shoot at you," Bramwell had screamed at him. "You should have cut them all down for harboring a fugitive."

Sheriff Straud had said he had sent two telegrams to Tombstone to check on the old wanted poster.

Bramwell paced back and forth. Slowly an idea came forward, and he latched onto it. Yes! That was the answer to his problem. But who should he get? He thought over the men he had known out here and settled on Slade Gelink. He would do exactly as he was told, and he was good enough to get the job done neatly and quickly.

No more fooling around with amateurs. He would go with the man he should have brought along with him in the first place. Slade had demanded $100 a month salary. As it turned out, Slade would have more than saved his salary.

Now it was a different game. Just one quick shoot-out. Slade should be able to get here and do the job in a week, and he'd offer the man $1000. Not even Slade could pass up that much money.

Where the hell would he be now? What if he was tied up on another job?

Bramwell wrote out a telegram, picking out the four most likely spots: Denver, St. Louis, Dodge City and Kansas City. Yes, one of those four should nail him down.

He went out to the yard to look for a messenger and found a lanky Texan who was reliable enough.

He sent the wires to hotels where Slade stayed when visiting those towns. After giving the Texan the message, carefully printed so there could be no mistake, Bramwell watched the rider head out toward town. It wasn't yet noon. The man would get there for the wire to go out today, and it would be delivered today or tonight. Slade would wire back if he got the message.

Bramwell went back inside his tent. During the day it was boiling hot inside, while at night it was cold. Damn that Indian for burning down the ranch house! Bramwell wanted to charge up into the hills, spot the camp of the savages and wipe them out—every man, woman and child—but that was war and he didn't have the troops. He had a hard time getting enough men to stage a small roundup, and now those cattle were gone. The cash he had been counting on from them could be critical.

Damn that man! Lee Morgan would forever be a foul, evil pair of words for Bramwell, but no longer did he have to plot how to eliminate the man. He had been going to send Jed Hackett out with a rifle, letting him creep up to within 100 yards of the ranch house at night along the river. Then when Morgan came out in the morning, he would gun the man down.

Now that wasn't necessary. He had the man on the way who could handle Morgan.

The next order of business was how to get back the cattle the Circle-S had stolen?

He needed more men. Right now he had 15 who could ride. If he kept even six of them for guards around the ranch, that left him only nine men. With Hackett that made ten. How in hell could even an Englishman fight a war with only a ten-man army? He couldn't.

He had sent Hackett into town two days ago to try to hire new men, but there had been a good deal of reluctance when the name of the spread was given. Hackett had offered as much as $30 but only hired two men. Some of the men who had left the Bar-B ranch had done a good job of bad-mouthing it to everyone in town.

Now he would just hold on and wait for that telegram from Rocky. He'd send snipers every other night or so to knock out a few windows from the Circle-S ranch house, but for now any major strike was not possible.

He looked at his bunk, a folding cot he had bought at the store. He shook his head. Damn! He wished that Elly was with him right then. He was missing her little blonde pussy. Damned if she wasn't a handful sometimes, but she was good in bed. He liked that and needed that.

For just a moment he thought about the fat ass of the cook, but he pushed the idea out of his mind. The cook was definitely not the type, and even if he was, Bramwell couldn't allow something like that to get out. In a blink of an eye he'd have only two or three hands left on the ranch.

Bramwell gave a groan and went to lie down for a nap. With his luck he probably wouldn't even have a decent wet dream to help him relax.

Chapter Eighteen

Newton Arlwayer lifted the glass of whiskey and looked out his Plainsman Hotel window. He stood six-one and 240 pounds, a big man who knew his mind, loved his job with the railroad and went where the powers sent him.

Miles City needed a brand inspector for the Northern Pacific, and he had been named to the job. He had done this work before. There was nothing so complicated about it. Just make sure the brand is registered to the man selling the cattle, or be damn sure that he has a bill of sale. Nothing to it.

He did have to be away from home for another three months, but his wife and family were used to it. He'd been a railroad man all his life, mostly in the management end of things and for a time as a conductor when they were short-handed. Now he would fill in here.

Newton loved two things most in life, one being a good brand of Tennessee whiskey. He took another sip of the amber fluid and let it warm a moment in his mouth before he swallowed it. Yes, delicious. The evening clouds had turned a rich blood red and become deeper still until they at last lost the rays of the sun over the far horizon.

"You gonna look out the window all day?"

The woman's voice came from the bed, and Newton turned and looked at the second thing he enjoyed most in life.

"Look out the window as long as I want to, woman!" he said. "I know you can't wait for some more of my body. Don't worry. The next few days you're going to get reamed out regular in all three of your lovely holes."

"Yes, Newton, yes! I like it when a man talks all wild and dirty that way. Hey, I got a surprise for you."

"Woman, there ain't no more surprises for me about a little blonde cunt like you. Hell, I'm fifty-one and been in more pussies than you can count." He turned. "But I'm always ready to say there just might be a chance. You said your name was Elly, right? What kind of a surprise you got for me, Elly?"

He walked to the bed and sat down on the side of it. For five score his body was in good shape, not gone to fat.

Elly knelt on the bed with only a shift over her breasts. Her long blonde hair swirled around her shoulders and halfway down her torso. Her blue eyes sparkled.

"So, Elly, what's your surprise?" He reached out and fondled her breasts under the chemise.

"Bet you've never done it this way before."

"Bet I have. How much you want to bet?"

"Ten dollars."

"You don't have ten dollars."

"I'll owe it to you. Is it a bet?" Elly held out her hand.

"Sure, a bet." They shook.

She jumped off the bed, pulled away the chemise and stood in the center of the room.

"I want you to fuck me standing up."

"What? Standing up? Can't be done. I couldn't even get down there and find your little twat. Not a chance."

"Come on, you're just afraid of losing your ten dollars. Come on over here. I'll show you how. It's not that hard, especially for a big man like you. Come on now, give it a try. You made a bet, so you either pay up right now or give it a try."

"Fuck, for ten dollars I'll try it. Know for certain it can't be done. Tried it with a little Chink girl and just wouldn't work."

"Course not. Their pussies are cut sideways. Everybody knows that. Now get over here."

He stood and moved toward her. She pulled him to the wall, then knelt and worked on his flaccid tool.

"Hey, Newton, are you sure you can come more than once a day? This worm you say you own down here is plum worn-out."

He pumped his hips toward her. "Hell, yes, I can come more than once. Junior there likes mouth-fucking best. Tease him some."

She kissed his tool and massaged it, and soon it grew firm and stiff.

"Now, Newt, that's just a whole lot better. Here's what we do." She put her hands around his neck, jumped up and locked her legs around his waist, then eased back a little.

"Now, big man, you just find my pussy and drive into it. No problem with a wrong angle or anything."

Newton laughed, pushed her hips out a little to let him adjust himself and then grunted as he lanced deeply into her vagina.

"I'll be fucked in church!" Newton brayed. "It *can* be done standing up."

"Told you so. Now move closer to the wall so I can rest my back on it and then you just fuck away."

A minute later she was positioned on the wall, her hands still around his neck as he drove into her with all the delight of a teenager.

"Christ, why didn't somebody tell me about this before? I can really get a head of steam built up this way. Give me a minute and I'm gonna be huffing and puffing and steaming away like a railroad locomotive."

Elly grinned. "And at the same time I just made ten dollars."

"Another ten? Damn, didn't I just buy you that dress and shoes and hat today? Christ! I already gave you ten dollars yesterday and paid for your room for a week."

"So you appreciate a really nice lady when you find one. You told me you didn't want to go over to the sloppy whores. Shut up and fuck." She grinned as she said it, and he laughed and slammed her against the wall.

She thought he was going to knock down the wall

before he roared in jubilation, jammed her six more times and then panted for five minutes. When he could talk again he looked at her.

"What do we do now?" he asked.

Elly erupted with wails of laughter. It was such a dumb question, but one she had been thinking herself. There was no chance they could lay down and rest after this. She unhooked her legs from his back and dropped down to the floor.

"Oh, God!" he roared, then he slipped out of her slot. "You trying to break my prick in half or something?"

"Sorry, I thought you'd be softer by now." They moved to the bed and lay down.

"Where's my ten dollars?" she asked.

"You little whore."

"No, I'm a gentleman's special lady."

"Who told you them fancy words."

"A gentleman."

He laughed. "Hell yes, Elly, you're a gentleman's special lady, my special lady. If I had something like you at home I'd never leave."

"Stay here and fuck me all you want." She leaned in and bit on his nipples."

"I will for a few months, maybe until September, but I should stay at a rooming house and save the cost of the hotel."

"Too many nosy people at a room and board house," Elly said. "They ask too many questions. I like it here."

"We'll stay here. Why not? I got a good bottle of whiskey and a tight little blonde with big tits who loves to fuck. Hell, I'm all set."

* * *

The next day Jed Hackett and his six Bar-B riders brought a herd of 200 steers to the Miles City stock yard just north of town on the railroad siding.

Newton Arlwayer came out of his office and met Hackett.

"Looks like about two hundred head," Newton said.

"Close enough. We're from the Bar-B, and I got Mr. Bramwell's bill of sale here all made out except the number. Charlie W. from Chicago bought the lot."

"Soon as I take a look at them I'll sign them in and you can go get your money from Charlie," Arlwayer said. "Put them in them first two pens, and we'll load them right away. Get them on the eastbound that comes through here about four this afternoon."

They started the loading process. The steers went into the pens, each holding about 50. Each pen had a ramp and a chute that let the cattle walk up the cleated boards that led to the cattle car on the rail siding.

The men used sticks and broom handles to prod the cattle along up the chute. Just as the animals came to the chute there was a place where the brand inspector stood. It was his job to check each brand on every animal.

A year ago the Northern Pacific had lost a lawsuit by a cattleman who claimed somebody stole his herd and sold it, and Northern Pacific had loaded and shipped the animals without proper papers or brand checking.

Now they put on their own man to check brands and bills of sale to be sure they had no more lawsuits.

Ten steers went up the chute, and Hackett held his

breath. They knew nothing about this new brand checker. Some of them were real sons of bitches, rejecting an animal if there was any double branding, unclear trial brand or any irregularity at all. The one who had been here before got $50 a herd from Bramwell and had never cut out a critter in over a year.

This guy was going to be easy.

"What the hell is this?" Arlwayer snapped.

Hackett was beside him with two steps. The steer showed a blanked-out brand, half-grown over with new hair and the Bar-B brand.

"Hell, that's no problem. When we had a joint roundup with three other outfits, one guy with the irons got mixed up some, so we had to blank them out. Remember that joint roundup we had? Covered half of Montana?"

"I wasn't here then. You bring me a paper from the roundup captain, and I'll take the steer. You got any more like this?"

"Oh, hell yes, forty or fifty."

"I'll tell you the same thing about them. I ain't gonna put the company on the spit for no fifty steers at forty dollars a head. Might as well cut out all those blanked-out brands right now and save us both some time."

"Last man here took them blanked-out brands with no questions."

"He damn near got fired, too. Now I'm the one here. Cut them out, or I'll throw them out one at a time."

Hackett's face turned purple. "What the hell's wrong with you? We use blanking brands all over Montana. Decided didn't want to use the vent lines anymore. Where the fuck you been hiding?''

Arlwayer motioned to the railroad man at the head of the chute leading into the car. ''Close it up, Charley, and get them cattle in the car out. This bunch ain't going nowhere, not while I'm on brand inspection.''

''Hell, we can take care of that quick and easy,'' Hackett said. He stepped close to Arlwayer and took a $100 bill from his pocket. He let the inspector see it. The man hesitated, then shook his head.

''No, by damn, I got near thirty years in railroading. I'm not about to throw it down the river for a lousy hundred dollars. Get your bribery money out of here.''

Hackett stepped back as if he had been struck. He turned, took his men and headed for the hotel.

Less than half an hour later, Newton Arlwayer walked back toward the hotel himself. He was looking forward to a nip of that whiskey and a delightful mouth job by Elly. Now there was one classy little whore. He knew she was a whore, no matter what she said.

At least he didn't have to go to the cheap whores over in the houses. He hated that. This was fine. The wife of some local businessman would be better, but hell, these days he took what he could get. He could get Elly three times a day as long as his strength could hold out. Just thinking about her was making him hard. He felt the pressure at his crotch and grinned.

The pair of .44's blasted from the alley just ahead of the brand inspector.

Arlwayer took both rounds in his chest. The force of the lead smashed him backward three feet, sprawling him on the dusty boardwalk planks. One hand was thrown wide, the other lay on his crotch.

Traces of the grin were still on his face as he died.

Two men ran up from the barbershop. One looked at him, then touched his wrist and his throat.

"Nothing pumping through there," the man said. "Looks like this gent is dead as a neck-wrung chicken. Somebody better go get the sheriff."

When Sheriff Straud came five minutes later, he took one look at the man and waved for the undertaker. The mortician, dressed in his usual black suit and black top hat, hired two men to carry the body to his establishment a half block away.

The sheriff looked at the position of the body and then at the gaping mouth of the alley.

"Anyone see what happened?" he asked.

A small man stepped forward. "He was walking in front of me, then I heard the shots and he fell right at my feet. I saw two puffs of blue smoke from the rounds. They was in the far side of the alley, but it was dark shadows in there and I didn't see no men. Heard somebody running away."

The sheriff grumbled, "That's about the end of it. Whoever shot this man is damn long gone by now. Put it down as death at the hands of unknown gunmen."

He looked at the body being carried away.

"Anybody know who he used to be?" the sheriff asked.

"He was new in town, but I heard he was the brand inspector for the Northern Pacific," someone on the boardwalk said.

"Figures," Sheriff Straud said, then went back to his office to fill out the death report.

Hackett toasted his cowboys to two beers at the Yellow Dog Saloon, then sent them back to the ranch with instructions to tell Bramwell what had happened.

"I'll sell the cattle tomorrow. The railroad has to take them, brand inspector or no. Do it the way we did when we didn't have one."

The next day Hackett reported to the station master at the depot. He had a signed statement by the sheriff. The local railroad boss read it and grunted.

The paper was short. "To whom it may concern: The below signed, sheriff of Custer county, state of Montana, does declare that one Jed Hackett, foreman of the Bar-B ranch, is known to me and that the stock he is shipping comes from a large ranch and is properly branded for shipment on any railroad."

The station master scrawled his name on the bottom of the paper under that of the sheriff and handed it back.

"Take this down to the yards. The yardmaster will get your critters loaded and sign off on your bill of sale."

By noon the 200 head of Bar-B steers were on the train. The cattle buyer had been to the bank and paid Hackett $4000 in crisp new, federal greenback $20 bills.

"Thought you were going to have a thousand head for me," the buyer said.

"Soon," Hackett answered. "Having a little trouble with our roundup."

The buyer laughed dryly. "Yeah, I heard you were having some trouble out at the Bar-B."

Hackett spun around and headed for his horse and the ranch.

* * *

Up the street in the Plainsman Hotel, Elly had moved back to her old room. The clerk had come to clean out Newton Arlwayer's things late yesterday afternoon.

He told her flat out that Newton had been bushwhacked and was dead. His personal effects would be sent back to his kin in Chicago.

Elly had sat on her bed for an hour, staring out the window as it got darker. It had happened again. Everytime she got something good going, the man got mad at her or sent her away, or she got feeling bitchy and ran away herself. Nothing lasted.

She hadn't even heard from Bramwell. Hell, she'd live in a tent if he asked her to. That other one, Morgan, was fine. What had happened to him? She fell on the bed and stared at the ceiling until darkness closed in. Then she went to sleep in her clothes. It didn't matter, since there was nobody to see her.

By the morning the next day she had some of her spunk back. She wasn't going to lay down and die. Hell no, she still had her looks and her good tits and her tight little, always-ready pussy. She could make a living anywhere. That first day she was with Newton, she had worked through his suitcase while he was gone and found a secret compartment with four $100 bills in it. She had taken all four and hid them in her room.

Now she looked at the spot where she had peeled back part of the wallpaper behind the curtain. The four bills had slipped behind the wallpaper neatly and were still there. Newton hadn't missed them. The damn sheriff would have stolen them anyway. So she was free and clear, with more money than she had ever seen in her whole life.

231

She should get on the train and ride all the way to San Francisco. She heard that was a wild town. A girl could get up to four dollars for a roll out there.

She kept thinking about Morgan. He said he'd be back. Maybe he would. He said he'd pay for her hotel room. He just might do that. She decided to wait a few more days.

She had heard that Hackett was in town, but he hadn't given her any message. Evidently Parrish Bramwell, big-time ranch owner, had forgotten all about her.

Fine. She would forget about him.

Elly went down to the dining room. It was already midmorning, but she had breakfast, twice as much as she usually ate. Then she went for a walk and bought a new perky little hat at Velda's Woman's Wear shop.

By that time it was noon and she stopped in at the Johnson Family Cafe and had dinner, a small portion of beef stew, a cup of coffee, two slices of bread and a big wedge of cherry pie.

Elly stepped out on the sidewalk and knew she was being stupid. She could eat her way into being fat this way in two months. Then her cunt would only be worth a dollar a throw in the last whore house on the block.

"No, damnit, no," she scolded herself. She took a long walk out to the far edge of town, turned around and walked past the hotel to the last house on Main Street, then back to the hotel.

She would have nothing to eat or drink until tomorrow, when she would have her usual amount of food.

Elly found her book and began to read. She could

read good. She didn't understand all of it, but she could say the words.

Twice she heard footfalls coming down the second floor hallway, but none of them stopped at her room. Elly shrugged and went back to her book. Something would turn up. Something always came along.

She laughed softly. Who cared? She had $400 in cash as her ace in the hole.

Chapter Nineteen

Morgan decided that when it came to cutting a steer out of a herd of cattle, the four Mandan Indians were quickly becoming as good at it as the cowboys who had been cutting steers for years.

The Indians had a feel for the critters that the cowboys never quite attained. A good cutting horse can sense what a steer or a cow or calf is going to do next. They are ready for the move and make it almost at the same time the bovine does. The Indian ponies didn't have that experience, but it seemed to Morgan as if each Mandan brave could sense as well where the steer would head next and quickly communicated the direction to his pony through his legs, feet or knees.

It was a beautiful combination to watch.

Morgan sat on his sorrel and enjoyed the scene. He

grinned at the way Young Wolf brought a reluctant steer to the herd they were forming to take to the railroad. He had planned to take in 1000 head, but they settled on 500, over half being original Circle-S brand and the rest rebranded from the first rescued herd almost two weeks before.

Morgan had no idea what to expect when he got to the loading chutes. He'd heard that the new brand inspector had been ambushed and killed. That was shortly after the Bar-B riders had been refused loading due to brand irregularities. The Bar-B sold and loaded their beef the next day, and no one was charged with the death of the brand inspector.

Brand inspector or not, Morgan figured the railroad wanted the business bad enough to take on a herd of 500 cattle. Their trains were running east nearly empty as it was.

Morgan had seen two cattle buyers in Miles City and expected there were one or two more. One of them would be buying.

They had the 500 cut out and moved into a bedded-down spot a half mile from the ranch house and put six men riding night herd. Another six men stood guard with rifles. Morgan didn't want to have this bunch stolen from them.

He rode back to the ranch house with Willy Joe.

"I see you and Heather have been having some serious discussions these nights," Morgan said.

The young cowhand grinned. "Yeah. It's getting serious. I asked her to marry me last night. She said yes, but she said it has to happen in the next week or two. She wants to be sure you're at the ceremony to give her away. She figures her daddy would have liked that.''

"I'm honored.''

"Don't say anything to her yet. Supposed to be a secret for a while.''

"Why?''

"She didn't say. Hell, if she told me to jump up and turn myself inside out, I'd give it a hell of a try!''

They both laughed. Things had settled down a little around the spread. They even took on two new men who came looking for work. Morgan had paid the crew, and Heather worried about that.

"Why don't we sell some cattle so I'll have some working cash?'' Heather asked one night.

"Good idea,'' Morgan said. "How many?''

"I don't know.''

"Say a steer is still worth forty dollars a head, so if we sell a thousand head that would be forty thousand dollars.''

She stared up at him. "No, that must be wrong. How can it be so much? Maybe four thousand.''

Morgan put it down on paper for her.

"Mercy, so much money! Five thousand head would be worth . . . two hundred thousand dollars! I just can't imagine that much money.''

"It'll be a while before you can sell five thousand head, but a thousand would be a good start.''

Later they found they should let the brands heal more on the new cattle and decided only on 500.

Heather had settled down, too. Now she spent every moment possible with Willy Joe. She rode with him on nearby duties, helped him survey the far pastures, read to him and played cards with him after supper.

Morgan grinned and said nothing. It looked like his

talking to both of them had produced the desired results.

Tonight at the ranch house they had supper from the main cookhouse, plus a dessert that Heather had made.

"It's a lemon meringue pie, and if it isn't good I'm going to burn down the house."

"It's good, mouth-watering good," Morgan said. "I love it."

"You haven't tasted it yet."

"Doesn't matter, same verdict."

"You're crazy."

"In my business it helps."

"What is your business, Morgan?" Willy Joe asked.

"Mostly I don't charge around fighting range wars to save ranches for old friends. Mostly I raise horses in Idaho—when and if I get back out there."

"Sounds interesting." Willy Joe paused. "We're about ready to head out for Miles City in the morning. You figure it'll take us two days all told?"

"Day and a half to drive them to the yards, rest of the day to sell and load them. Overnight in the hotel, and we head out the next morning with the cash."

"It's that day in town that bothers me," Heather said. "What happens if that sheriff didn't hear back from Tombstone or hears back that the paper is still good on Lee Morgan?"

"Then I take my chances with the sheriff."

"He could have ten deputies," Heather said.

"Could, but won't. Don't beg or borrow trouble, my friends. If he calls, I'll answer. Until then, forget him. Remember we'll be up at four A.M. and moving out at four-thirty."

* * *

Two of the Indians went along. The other one and Young Wolf returned to the Indian camp and would be back in four days.

The first half day the trail drive went smooth and easy—no rivers to cross, no dust storms, no lightning, no Indian raiders. Just moving along at two miles an hour with an occasional stop to bring up the strays.

They ate from the chuckwagon and headed out again. An hour before dark they circled the herd and settled them down for the night. There were eight drovers with four more men riding shotgun guard with their rifles.

Morgan had $20,000 worth of beef on the hoof, and he wasn't going to get it rustled right out from under him this close to Miles City.

Morgan figured they made 12 miles the first day. They had another five or so miles on into town, depending whose estimate was right.

Morgan lay with his head on his saddle and looked up at the stars.

Tomorrow would be the turning point for the Circle-S. After the first sale Heather would have enough working cash to do things the way they should be done. She could pay the hands herself, maybe even get some new range bulls or brood stock and begin to build up her herd with breeding. Morgan didn't think they had a count on how many breeding cows they had. That would be a good project once they got back.

A hundred cows would go to Young Wolf, but then the Bar-B still owed them another 2000 to 2500. They'd take whatever they could gather—cows, calves, steers. He hoped they could do it in one sweep, but it might take two. If it took two it could result in a shooting range war. Unless Bramwell was getting ready to sell out, he had to make a response soon.

Morgan went to sleep wondering what Bramwell finally would do.

They started herding the steers into the far end of the Northern Pacific cattle pens an hour before noon. The beef had moved easy and not lost a pound.

Before Willy Joe could get off his horse, two buyers came striding out to talk. Morgan sauntered up and listened.

"Going rate for raw range beef like them steers is thirty-five dollars a head, but I'll give you thirty-seven." The talker was a man in a pure white, high-crowned cowboy hat, a vest with half a pound of silver on it and cowboy boots that had never touched a horse.

The second man's name was Charlie. He grinned when the other man talked. "This is a little game we play, Circle-S. My name is Charlie W. and this polecat is Alonzo P. Jones. He's ornery, but I'm better looking. How many head you pushing?"

Willy Joe introduced himself and Morgan, using only last names, and then pointed at the steers. "We brought five hundred head for starters," he said.

"Good. Alonzo there don't want your beef, that's why he offered you only thirty-seven. Going rate really is forty dollars a head, and that's my offer."

"Sold," Willy Joe said, holding out his hand. Charlie took out a sheet of paper and wrote in the figure 500 and signed it. He handed it to Willy Joe. The Circle-S was already written in on the bill of sale.

"Figured it had to be you coming in," Charlie W. said. "You take this and show it to the yardmaster.

When he's got five hundred head in his cattle cars, he'll sign it off. Then bring it back to me for your money. You want greenbacks or gold?''

"Green money is fine,'' Willy Joe said.

A man rode up on the worst horse any of them had ever seen. It was splay-footed, sway-backed and skiny as a hound dog's bone.

"I'm the yardmaster. You aiming on getting them critters loaded?''

"Yep, sure am,'' Willy Joe said.

"Heard about Mr. Scoggins. A fine gentleman. I respected him. Suppose the boy is running things now.''

"No, sir, he's dead. Mr. Scoggins' daughter, Heather, is boss. I'm foreman.''

"Done,'' the yardmaster said. "No sense talking to the sheriff about brands. I trust the Scoggins clan. Just get them into some cars so we can be ready for the four-thirty. She's late today.''

They loaded four cars at a time, and in two hours the last bawling, kicking steer was prodded into the final cattle car and the door slammed shut.

Willy Joe gave each of the hands a five dollar bill and told them to be ready to ride at ten the next morning at the livery stable.

The two Indians rode up, refused the money and talked to Morgan.

"Ride back village,'' the one called Joe said. He had turned out to be the best of the three with English. "See family. Come again, see you soon.''

Morgan nodded. "Good work. Good cowboys. See you soon.'' The two Mandan Indians grinned, waved and headed back for their village far to the south.

"Next?" Willy Joe asked.

The yardmaster came up, signed the receipted bill of sale and gave it back to Willy Joe. Then the foreman grinned. "Hey, we've got to pick up some cash." He frowned. "What the hell we going to do with all that money?"

"Up to you," Morgan said. "You're the foreman."

"Hell, you help me get it back to the hotel, then I'm taking a third floor room and putting a chair under the door handle and sitting there all night with my six-gun cocked."

"Good thinking," Morgan said. "You might also want to push the dresser in front of the window. That way nobody can get in that way."

Charlie W. was ready with the cash in a small paper sack. He took the bill of sale, saw the signatures and handed over the sack.

"Should I count it?" Willy Joe said.

Charlie W. grinned. "Can if you want to. Might be a good idea. Of course, I've been buying cattle for almost twenty years now, and not a single man has ever counted the money I paid him."

Willy Joe smiled. "No sense in breaking your record." He shook hands with the cattle buyer, and the two Circle-S men left the saloon by the front door.

"Act natural and nobody will think you're rich," Morgan said.

It was an hour later before Morgan had Willy Joe settled in his third floor hotel room. They went down and had an early supper in the dining room with the stacks of bills bulging slightly from inside Willy Joe's shirt.

When they were back upstairs in Willy Joe's room,

Morgan held up his hands.

"Enough of this carousing around. I'm going to get a room and take a nap. All you have to do is lock the door and you'll be as safe as a saint in a Catholic church."

Morgan grinned as he left, walked down the steps and along the hallway to room 211. He hoped that Elly was still staying there.

His knock brought an instant response.

"Who's there?"

"Morgan."

The door burst open, and she rushed into his arms right there in the hall. He picked her up and carried her into her room and closed the door with his foot. Elly peppered his mouth with kisses, a big grin on her lovely face.

"Well, if you don't want to see me . . ." Morgan said.

She shushed him with another kiss. He let her feet slide to the floor, but she was still pressed tightly against him.

"Oh God, but I'm glad to see you. Where have you been? I've been melting in the heat and going crazy here."

"Been busy. Told you I'd be busy. What have you been doing?"

"Nothing, sitting and waiting. Reading. Thinking about going somewhere else, maybe St. Louis or San Francisco."

"Wait a couple of weeks and I might ride along with you, if you head west."

"Now *there* is a proposition. Maybe we could get a private railroad car—or at least one of them newfangled cars with little rooms on it with locked doors and everything!''

"Compartments. You're talking rich here.''

"But other folks would talk if we made love right there in front of them in the coach car.'' Elly giggled. "I almost did one night.''

"Almost did what?''

"Almost got fucked in a train passenger car. This guy had his hands all over me in the dark. Finally we used his blanket and I did him a mouth job. That was one wild night. Right in the middle the conductor came by, and I pretended to be sleeping on his lap.''

"You are crazy—but crazy fun.''

Elly pulled off her blouse. "First we have a good poking on the old mattress, then we figure out what to do next.'' She opened the buttons on his fly and dug through his underwear, squealing when she found his surging erection. Morgan played with her breasts, then bent and kissed both.

"Why am I so crazy about a woman's tits? Doesn't matter if they're a small handful or beautiful or huge and sagging. Tits are just marvelous.''

"Good thing, it gets your old prick hard. I feel the same way about a man's cock. God, it's just beautiful. Guess nature figured out we should think that way.'' She pulled him toward the bed.

"This time I want you all raw and naked, just as sexy as all hell!''

He stripped as she watched. He locked the door and put a chair under the handle.

"Don't you like company when you're fucking?''

"Not so you could notice.'' He dropped down beside her on the bed, and she rolled on top of him.

"Ohhhhhh, you feel so good. So hard and stiff and about ready to poke me. I just got to have me a man poking away in my pussy every day. Don't know what I'd do if I didn't get some fucking every day. Go crazy and attack somebody on the street, I guess."

"All you have to do is crook your finger at a man and wave your hotel key and you'll have them stacked up out in the hall waiting their turn."

"You are naughty."

She kissed him, then moved up and dipped first one breast, then the other into his mouth. As he chewed on her tits, his hands came up to her crotch and he began to massage her and stroke across her pussy. At last he found what he wanted and rubbed her clit.

She frowned and looked at him.

"Today is the day," he said.

Elly lifted her brows, then nodded. "Hell, I'm ready to give it a try."

He rolled her over on her back, spread her legs wide, lifted her knees, then gently began to twang her clit back and forth.

It took a long time, but slowly her desire built. She began to breathe faster and faster, and her hips moved slightly, then again.

Elly began to moan, her hips working back and forth. He kept on target and rubbed her hard clit from side to side with two fingers. Suddenly she gasped and screeched out a cry of wonder, and her whole body began to rattle and shake as the first spasm rolled through her. Then they came again and again and again.

Elly lay there shaking and trembling, tears streaming down her cheeks, her mouth open in a soft wail that became lower and lower until it at last faded out. One more series of spasms shook her, and she closed her eyes and humped up her hips at the same time. Then it passed, and she dropped onto the bed exhausted, still panting from the sudden exertion and the emotional thunderstorm.

It was three or four minutes before she looked up at him.

"Oh God, I didn't remember anything could be so intense, so packed full of wonderful feelings. Can that happen every time?"

"Should happen every time. Make loving the very best it can be."

She reached up, hugged him and pulled him down on top of her.

"Now I want you inside me. Now I want to repay you just a little for making me a whole woman again. I'll never be able to repay you, Lee Morgan, never in a million years."

"Lady, you don't pay anything for a gift. This is my gift to you for the pleasure you've given me. No payment required, permitted or accepted."

Elly grinned. "Okay, now shut up and fuck me."

He did. He couldn't remember her being more animated, more active. Her inner muscles came into play as she milked him. All too quickly he climaxed, and then he was empty and dropped down on her. She wrapped her legs and arms around him, pinning him to her, and they lay there for ten minutes without moving.

She spoke first. "Buckskin Lee Morgan, I hereby make you my love slave for life. You will never be more than an arm's length from my body, and you will service me whenever I demand it."

"Sounds like a good deal to me. When do I start?"

"You signed your lifelong contract twenty minutes ago in the middle of my second-ever climax. I still don't believe all that happened."

"Believe."

"But what do I have to look forward to? I always told myself that if I didn't climax this time, maybe next time. Now what?"

"Now you have that same marvelous climaxing experience to look forward to every time you spread your legs. Tell your lover that this time, you come first, then him. Most men won't mind helping."

"You make it sound so wonderful."

"It can be for a couple of weeks. I have a few more problems to settle out at the ranch."

"Like bankrupting Parrish Bramwell?"

"Part of it. He stole, so he has to pay for it. Nothing personal, just doing a job."

"I understand. I don't worry about Parrish. He'll get by somewhere, somehow. If he don't, he's a big boy."

Morgan pushed off her onto his back. "Right now it's nap time. Then we'll see if you can do an encore before I go down and bring up our supper. We have the rest of the night to invent sexy games and learn how to play them."

"And you . . . you'll help me . . . to come again?"

"Every time. As long as you can hold out."

"Honey, I can hold out for about ninety years!"

Chapter
Twenty

Slade Gelink stepped down from the Northern Pacific westbound train and eyed Miles City. He spat on the station platform, picked up his sleek leather suitcase and headed for the hotel. Not damn much of a town. Probably no decent food or women in this whistle stop.

But $1000 for a job was still $1000. Work like this didn't come along every day. He got a room, then had supper in the dining room. The food was only average, nothing like St. Louis could produce.

Slade stood no taller than five foot seven, but size didn't matter in his business. He had long sideburns that some folks called muttonchops and a matching moustache.

He wore his usual costume—black suit, black silk shirt, black string tie, black leather vest. His hawklike nose dominated his thin face, but the first thing people noticed about Slade Gelink was his eyes. They gleamed unusually bright with a green glint. The way his eyelids were formed left more of the white of his eye showing then most people, and the combination was startling.

Slade glared at the desk clerk at the Plainsman Hotel, stalked out the door and down the steps to the board-walk. There must be something in town to offer amusement. There was no opera, no music hall, no drama troupe. He was sure the whores would be old, fat and ugly.

When a man on the boardwalk turned and stared at Slade, his hand automatically eased down to touch the smooth butt on his Remington .44. The other man saw the hand hovering over the six-gun, and he turned casually and walked away.

Slade knew he looked like a gunman. He knew that his holster tied low and tight to his leg so there would be no movement of the leather when he drew fast was another sign that he was a gunman. He planned it that way. If you can scare a man half to death before you shoot, the advantage is with you, not him. Many times he never had to draw.

If his reputation was enough to cow someone into retreating, he was just as pleased. He was a gambler, and if he didn't have to draw and fire, there was absolutely zero chance that some wild man would be faster and kill him with a lucky shot. Slade played the percentages and always used fear on his side.

Sure, he had a reputation. It was earned. He was as good as the old gunslingers, most of them now dead and gone. Slade was a name known and feared in most of the West. He lived by his gun, and someday he might die by a gun—but not for a long, long time. He was 32 years old and figured he had at least 20 more years before his timing and reactions began to slow down. Then he would pick another kind of work or maybe just quit and live the good life on the considerable bank account he had built up in St. Louis.

Slade moved on down the boardwalk and sauntered into the first saloon he came to. He saw fancy dance hall girls working the tables. Good. At least they had whores here, and he could check them out.

Slade stood at the bar for his first drink, a shot of whiskey. He tossed it down and felt the pleasant warmth as it burned down to his stomach and hit hard. Yeah, he was ready. There had been an envelope of instructions and cash waiting for him at the Plainsman Hotel. He knew his target and had a description of the man and his name. He also knew where the man worked and that he seldom came into town.

Riding a horse was not Slade's favorite method of travel, but if he had to, he did it with skill and patience, knowing that this was simply another part of his job. A quick kill here and he could get on the train and go back to St. Louis and Marlena and his suite of rooms at the St. Louis Grand Hotel.

He watched the men in the saloon. One man who had been standing beside him when he ordered his first drink had slid down the bar to talk to another cowboy. No one else moved in near him. Not a man in the place wanted to bump or get pushed into the man wearing all black.

If one man in the saloon recognized him, everyone

would know within minutes. Slade grinned into the big mirror in back of the bar and put down a silver dollar he always carried.

"A bottle of good whiskey," he said.

The barkeep reached under the bar, found a full bottle with the seal unbroken and held it up for Slade to inspect. Slade grunted, and the barkeep took the silver dollar with a nod.

Slade picked up the whiskey and a shot glass and walked past two tables. He eased into a chair at a small table so his back would be at the wall. He took a shot from the bottle. It was good whiskey. He saw two of the whores whispering at the side of the room, and soon a small redhead came grinding over to his table and stood watching him.

"Need a deck of cards, or a beer, or a naked wrassle upstairs?"

Slade looked up. The kid had guts. He'd remember her for later. "You have a name?"

"Jenny."

"Think you can find a deck of cards?"

"Yeah. You want me to find one?"

"Yeah."

She swished her little bottom as she went behind the bar and brought back a deck of cards, a fresh one with an unbroken seal. The girl had some spunk and style.

"You play cards?"

"Sure, but it costs three dollars an hour."

"More than you make an hour working your backside."

Jenny laughed, and half the men in the place looked

around. "True, so damned true, but I don't like playing cards as much as I like to play with a man. You need playing with?"

"Not at the moment, so let's play cards."

"Money before pleasure."

She took the three paper dollars he offered and pushed them down the front of her dress. Jenny saw him watching where the money went.

"Hell, a little padding on the tits never hurt a bit. What are we playing? Poker or blackjack or old maid?"

They played poker without chips for a half hour. Then Slade patted her breasts and stood up. "You run along and fuck somebody now, Jenny. Be good for you. I need to talk to the barkeep."

"Sure you don't need a fast poking upstairs in my bed? Settle down your gun hand."

He looked down at her sharply. She grinned and he relaxed. "That's always settled down."

"Every man in here knows you're a gunfighter, but then you advertise it, don't you?"

"Yep."

Jenny laughed. "Well, after you kill somebody, you come back and Jenny will give you a ride like you won't forget for months. You'll see."

He grabbed one of her breasts and squeezed. He knew it must hurt, but Jenny just grinned at him. He patted her again and, as he stood, pushed a $20 gold double eagle down her cleavage.

"That gold is still warm from your pocket," she said.

"Keep it that way," he ordered. Slade walked to

the bar, watching everyone ahead of him. Nobody moved. Three men at the bar made room for him, then edged toward tables. Everyone was waiting for something to happen. They must have heard about him; they must know about Slade Gelink.

He pushed his bottle on the bar. "Put the name Slade on this bottle and keep it for me—and don't sell drinks from it."

"Yes sir." The barkeep wrote "Slade" on the label and put it on a special rack behind the bar.

Slade stood at the bar working on a final shot of his whiskey for ten minutes. He was waiting for something to happen as well. He was ready. Tomorrow he'd start hunting his target. Until then it was just time to get mad.

A cowboy came through the front door with a lurch. He should have been under a tree somewhere sleeping off his whiskey. He leaned against the wall just inside, spotted the bar and lunged that way with his shoulders first and his feet scrabbling to keep up.

He lurched off one poker table and a chair and then made the bar. He hung there by one elbow, swinging round, watching the men in the saloon.

"Betcha . . . betcha thought I wouldn't make it," the kid shrilled and giggled.

Then he turned to the bar. "Barkeep, wanta drink. Whiskey. Whiskey on beer, never fear. Yeah, I'll have a shot of whiskey."

"Money?" the barkeep asked.

The kid tossed a silver dollar on the bar. The barkeep poured the kid a shot glass of whiskey, took out ten cents from the dollar and put the change on the bar.

"You drink up this one, kid, then get out of here," the barkeep said. "You're falling down drunk already, and I don't want no trouble here."

"I ain't trouble," the kid said. He grabbed the shot glass and started to drink, then lost his balance toward Slade who hadn't even glanced at the cowhand.

The young man regained his balance for a moment, then tripped sideways again and threw out his hand. It was his right hand that held the whiskey glass, and the contents of it splashed onto Slade Gelink's shoulder and chest.

Everyone in the saloon stopped talking. For a moment there wasn't a sound. Slade turned toward the kid who had caught himself and now clung to the bar.

"Goddamn! Spilled my drink." His bleary eyes looked up at Slade and for a moment his eyes went wide. "Oh, damn. Didn't mean . . ."

Slade's thundering response drowned out whatever the young cowpoke tried to say.

"Bastard!" he bellowed. He spun away from the bar and stood facing the cowboy. "You've got an iron. Draw it or I'll gun you down where you stand."

"Sorry I . . ." The cowboy's eyes seemed to widen as he stared at the black-suited, wet and snarling gunman. He knew at once what kind of man he had doused with his drink.

"Look, I'm drunk. Sorry about the drink. I'll buy you a new jacket."

"I like this jacket. Draw right now and defend yourself, you skinny puke!" Slade waited a minute. "Draw now or I'll shoot you in the knee and you'll be a cripple for life!"

"Oh, damn!" the cowboy said. He let his right hand drop down beside a six-gun on his belt. His hand darted for the gun and got it clear of leather before Slade even started his draw.

Slade's move was so fast few saw his weapon come out and point and fire all in one smooth motion. The cowboy's eyes glazed for a moment in surprise, then the force of the bullet slammed him against the bar and he slumped down to the floor, a bullet through his heart.

Slade stood there a moment, stared at the man, then snorted. "The damn fool drew first. Every man in here saw him. You can tell the sheriff that when he comes. Tell him my name is Slade Gelink and I'm at the Plainsman Hotel if he wants to talk to me about this tomorrow."

Buckskin Lee Morgan stood in the doorway of the saloon. He had just been coming in when the drink had been spilled. He had seen how obviously drunk the young cowpuncher was. Now he stood blocking the doorway as Slade started to leave.

The smaller gunman stopped three feet in front of Morgan who glared down at him.

"You said your name was Slade Gelink?" Morgan asked him evenly.

Slade frowned and looked up puzzled. "That's right. Who wants to know?"

"This kind of cowardly, gutter shooting is exactly what I've heard about you, Slade. A real no-good bastard with a yellow-belly rep twice as long as his shooting ability. Hell, anybody can outdraw a range cowboy who is dead drunk."

Slade hissed, and his face went red with anger. "Who the hell are you?"

"Just a rancher from Idaho who throws up when he runs across rattlesnakes like you, Slade." They still stood toe to toe. Slade's right hand started downward.

Before he could get it near his gun, Morgan's right fist lashed out, smashing into Slade's jaw, slamming him backwards and dumping him on the floor. He clawed for his six-gun, but Morgan's heavy boot hit his wrist.

Morgan bent down and grabbed the weapon, frisked Slade and pulled a hidden derringer from his inside vest pocket and a throwing knife from his fancy leather boot.

"Heard about you in three states, Slade. Always the same story. Little man trying to build a big rep on back shooting and taking on old gunsharps who are over the hill and praying to get a chance to die clean. Figures."

Morgan stabbed the knife into the bar and smashed the six-gun's butt into the blade, snapping it off. He threw the derringer behind the bar and then hefted the gunsharp's six-gun.

"Not a bad Remington, but it don't work any more. The cylinder seems to be jammed." He opened the cylinder and let the four rounds drop out then slammed the weapon against the edge of the bar breaking off the cylinder.

"No good gunslinger in his right mind would walk around with a weapon in that bad a shape, Slade. Damn, but you are one fucking, stupid gunsharp. Maybe you better fess up to the sheriff that you murdered this cowboy here cause he threw a glass of whiskey on you. Either that or you better get on the train first thing in the morning, no matter where it's headed.''

Slade sat on the floor, staring at Morgan. His face grew angrier by the second, and soon it was so red it looked like it might explode.

Morgan turned his back on the man and dropped a paper dollar on the bar. ''That's for the damage to the bar top. Sorry. This next one is for a bottle of good whiskey.''

The bartender grinned when he handed Morgan the bottle and took the two dollars. Morgan accepted the bottle and walked toward Slade who still sat on the floor.

''Hey, you got a lot of trash on the floor here. You best have somebody throw it out into the alley before it rots anymore and the stench is even worse.''

A dozen men hooted and laughed at Morgan's remarks as he turned and walked out the door into the street.

In back of him Slade stood slowly. He touched his bruised jaw where the big fist had hit him, then he went to the barkeep and held out his hand. The barkeep gave him his bottle of whiskey, then picked up his derringer from the floor and handed it to the man.

Not a word was spoken in the bar as everyone watched the drama unfolding. Slade put the derringer away then stared at the barkeep. ''Who was that guy?''

The bartender shrugged.

Somebody from the saloon answered. ''Works for the Circle-S. He was in town last week hiring new hands.''

Another voice piped up. "His name is Morgan, Lee Morgan."

When Slade heard the name, he nodded, and a small smile grew on his face as he walked out of the saloon.

Morgan, Lee Morgan! Now wasn't that just dandy. Morgan was the man he had been paid $1000 to come to Miles City to kill.

When Morgan left the saloon, he had sprinted across the street and into the Plainsman Hotel. He knew the furious gunsharp would come looking for him. He had been shamed, his very manhood challenged, his ability put down, his reputation besmirched. The man would not quit until he found Morgan.

The rancher shrugged. He hated men like Slade who built a reputation on luck and downright dirty shooting and then went around playing the role of gunfighter killing innocents who shouldn't even be armed. Morgan knew that he simply did what he had to do to the man. He'd let the chips fall where they may.

Morgan hurried upstairs to room 211 and knocked, then opened the door and slipped inside.

By now Slade might have found out what his name was. He would know about the Circle-S. Again Morgan shrugged. It couldn't be helped. If the man wanted to find him, he would—but not tonight. He would be nursing his wounded self-esteem and trying to find a new gun that was just right for him. Then it would take him a half day of shooting to burn it in and find out exactly where it fired. It might be an inch high and to the left or low and to the right. There was no way to "sight in" a revolver by adjusting the sights. The sights were fixed, so the user had to compensate for the peculiarities of the weapon.

"Took you long enough," Elly said. "I figured you might be drinking your way back." She sat on the bed with a sheet modestly around her waist letting her breasts swing free. She moved her shoulders so her pink-tipped breasts did a joyous double dance, and he grinned in appreciation.

"Ran into a small problem, a man I've heard about but never seen in action. Now that I have, I've lost any respect for him that I once might have had."

He told her about the confrontation in the saloon.

"So why was he in town?" Elly asked.

"About to ask you the same thing. Had Bramwell ever talked about bringing in a hired gun? Somebody to take me out of the way, perhaps?"

"Once he said that was always an option, but it would be expensive. He said he'd have to offer somebody a thousand dollars."

"Looks like he did. Must be that our friend Slade Gelink didn't know who I was in the saloon or he would have shot me down on sight."

"If he knew you by sight? You said you'd never met."

When Morgan sat down on the edge of the bed, she pulled him over backwards with his head in her lap.

"Now, that's better. We can reason things out a whole lot quicker this way."

"Most beautiful sight in the world," Morgan said, looking upward from her lap at her breasts. "It's a different angle on a marvelous subject."

"You're not thinking about Slade and Bramwell."

"True. Let them think about themselves. I'd rather think about you."

"You never get enough, do you?"

"Not of someone like you. How come you got put together so well, anyway? You do some special exercises or something like that to help out nature?"

She giggled and dropped one breast into his mouth. "No, silly, they just kind of grew. When I turned thirteen I just had little bumps, and when I had my fourteenth birthday, there they were, as big as they are now. I surprised a lot of people."

He came away from her breasts for a moment. "Especially a lot of boys."

"What does this have to do with Slade what's-his-name and him trying to kill you?"

"Not much or maybe a lot. It gives me some time to think it through. He's got some information about me. Knows I'm out at the Circle-S. Now he knows I'm in town. I probably should just meet him on the street and get it over with."

"No!" She bent down and kissed his lips. "He could kill you. I know, I know. You saw him draw and you think you're faster. A lot of gunmen say the same thing. It just takes one little hitch or one small problem, like a runaway horse or a woman screaming. Any little thing can be distracting, and the fastest gun can get killed. Slade could even have a second man in a window with a rifle. Been known to happen."

Morgan sat up and grinned at her. "For a young wench you know quite a lot about the meaner side of life.''

"Either learn it or die. I learned it. That's why you're not even getting your pants off tonight. You are putting your hat back on, saddling up your horse and riding out of here tonight before that bastard Slade finds you. I'll tell your men tomorrow that you had to ride out early.''

"Isn't that just moving my problem out to the ranch?''

"It's not your problem. It's a Circle-S problem. Out there you'll have guards and guns to back you up. Much better odds. Right? What kind of a poker player are you anyway?''

Morgan bent down and kissed each breast, taking his time at it. When he sat up he nodded. "Damn it, woman, you're right. I'll give you my key. You go down to my room, put all my gear in my saddle bags and bring them back here. If anybody follows you, go on down the stairs to the alley. I'll be there by the time you get there.'' He caught her face in his hands. "Scared?''

"Not if you let me dress first. I been close to some shooting before. Once in Dodge City . . .'' She stopped and shook her head. Slowly she pulled on a dress and buttoned up the top. She felt around in a carpetbag and brought out a derringer which she could almost hide in her hand. When she pushed it into a pocket in her dress, it was completely out of sight.

"Now, kind sir, give me your room key, and I'll go pack you for your trip. I'm out of my mind doing this when I could have your hot body bouncing on top of me the rest of the night, but what the hell! There'll be another night—two or three of them, I hope.''

She took the key and went down the hall toward his room at the far end.

Chapter
Twenty-One

An hour after he slipped out of the Plainsman Hotel and got his horse from the livery stable, Lee Buckskin Morgan stepped down from his mount in a stand of brush three miles south of Miles City and rolled out his blanket.

He watched the stars for a while, saw one shooting across the sky in a blaze of light, then closed his eyes. Might as well get some sleep. He felt a little like he had run away from trouble, but it seemed the best way to keep Elly happy. There would be a time to deal with Slade Gelink, but right now wasn't that time.

Willy Joe would take care of the money, and when he rode out this far with the men in the morning, Morgan would join them for the rest of the ride back to the ranch. No big problem.

* * *

It was well after daylight when Morgan woke up, stretched and kicked the kinks out of his legs. He sat up and checked his watch. 6:30. He stretched out again, laced his fingers behind his head and checked the fleecy clouds drifting slowly overhead. It would be a fine, hot summer day, with more sun than anyone knew what to do with and no harsh wind. His luxury was being able to loaf for another three hours. That's about when Willy Joe would have the crew up this far on the trail to the ranch.

He started thinking about his Spade Bit ranch up in Idaho, a half day's ride out of Boise. He wondered what would be left of it, if anything, by the time he got back there. There were two or three people who had tried to steal the land away from him in the past.

He remembered growing up on Spade Bit, then taking off on his own and coming back. He thought of how he had learned to use a gun from his dad, William Buckskin Frank Leslie. His mother was somewhere in the midwest he figured. He couldn't remember her.

Then his dad had been killed in a shootout with another fast gun, Harve Logan. Both men drew, both men fired, and both men died at almost the same instant. It seldom happened, but it certainly had this time.

Then Spade Bit became his responsibility, but still he wandered and rambled. More than once he had retreated to Spade Bit to recuperate and regenerate. He loved horses, but after a while he felt the traveling itch again.

Morgan dozed again. When he woke up the next time he could see the trace of dust downstream where some riders were approaching. From long habit he saddled his sorrel and led her into the brush out of sight.

Long before they arrived he could tell it was Willy Joe in the lead. Morgan rode out and joined them and continued on to the ranch.

"Got a note in my room saying you were on your way back to the ranch," Willy Joe said. "You sure stirred up Miles City. That little gunman, Slade, is tearing the place apart looking for you. He's madder than a dunked setting hen."

"Who?" Morgan said.

The men laughed. "We heard about it," Willy Joe said. "One of our men was in that saloon and saw it all. He told us Slade would either kill you or ride out of town. Looks like he aims to have it out with you sooner or later."

"Let's make it later. That's why I headed out early. We got too many things to get done yet before I talk to Slade Gelink with my Colt. Willy Joe, you still got the cash money?"

"Damn right. If I'd lost that I'd have blown my head off."

Three hours later they rode into the ranch.

Morgan talked with Willy Joe and Heather, sitting around the kitchen table and drinking coffee.

"I think that Young Wolf and his men are ready to take their herd into the mountains," Morgan said, looking at Heather. "Now it's still all right to cut out a hundred head of cows and seven range bulls for them?''

"Yes. Absolutely. Those people need to make a living, too. If they want to move into the white man's world they are going to need some way to earn hard cash. This is it. I couldn't agree more with Young Wolf."

"Good, let's start cutting out the hundred this afternoon. If Young Wolf and his three braves come back, they can help. If not, we'll start driving the herd south, and they'll find us quickly."

That afternoon Morgan and Willy Joe took eight men, went into the southern range below the Branding Canyon and began picking out good brood cows. At first they chose only those with double brands on them, then took Circle-S cows. They selected only those without calves.

When they had 50, they grouped them and began driving them south. As they went through the wide valley with the breaks and clots of brush-filled ravines, they dug out more cows and began to pick out the seven bulls.

Morgan took the best bulls he could find. At the first roundup they would have to thin down the number of range bulls anyway to prevent fighting.

When they gathered 100 brood cows and seven good bulls, they prodded the critters on south toward the big pine with the lightning scar on it.

They had herded the animals for an hour southward and were coming to the rise of the foothills from which the Tongue River emptied. They paused there and looked into the hills. Morgan wasn't sure of the route, but he picked the most likely, as close to the Tongue as they could stay. They began driving the cattle upward.

A half hour later Morgan saw a rider burst from a patch of brush and ride hard toward them. The man was Young Wolf who stared at the beef, his eyes sparkling.

"You should have let us help you," he said. He waved one hand, and eight more riders came out of the brush. Three of them had saddles, as Young Wolf did, and lariats looped from the horn.

"What do you think of your starter herd?" Morgan asked.

Young Wolf looked at the fortune in beef cattle and shook his head. He wiped one hand over his eyes.

"A Mandan warrior does not cry. That is woman's way. I'm simply washing my cheeks with my tears to conserve water."

Morgan grinned. "We weren't sure where to drive this herd, but we figured you'd find us sooner or later. We heading in the right direction?"

"Exactly, but there's a better valley just over the ridge. Let's get them moved over that way. Oh, would you mind if my men try to do the work? You can come along as observers." He laughed. "And if our inexperience means we scatter the herd, we'd appreciate help in gathering them."

Morgan nodded and called to his men. They came in, and the nine Indian riders moved out to drive the cattle over a small ridge and down the other side and then south along a wider valley.

"We're west of where you went up before,"

Morgan said.

"True. This is an easier route for the cattle drive. We'll break back to the east when we get up here another five miles. We'll plan on keeping most of the animals within two or three miles of our village until we learn more about them and their habits and how to care for them."

"Hell, mostly just let them breed and drop calves," Willy Joe said. "Nothing too tough about that."

Young Wolf nodded. "Good. The easier the better. What about disease and other problems? When they happen, may we come riding down to your ranch for some suggestions and advice?"

Willy Joe grinned. "Hell, come anytime."

They drove the cattle southward and gained in altitude all the time. At last they turned east through a gentle pass and came into a wide valley with green grass.

"This will be the home range for a while," Young Wolf said. "If the white men get too close with their trails and their own herds, we'll pull the cattle back more to the east where the mountains rise sharply but where there is enough graze for them."

Morgan reached in his saddlebags and pulled out an ear punch. He handed it to Young Wolf. "Put that v notch in the left ear of every critter you have. That way you'll be able to tell your stock from the Circle-S. As for branding irons, you won't need them until next spring when you get your first crop of calves. Stop down at the ranch and they can make up four irons for you to use."

"What about the winter?" Young Wolf asked. "What will the cattle eat?"

"What do the elk and deer do for graze in the winter?" Morgan asked.

"They go lower in the hills into the timber and paw down through the much lighter snow cover for dry grass."

"Do the same thing with your herd. Move the animals into any kind of timber cover you can find and they'll find something to eat. As a last resort you could cut the tall wild grass along the Tongue, dry it for hay and stack it near your winter range. But that would take some equipment. See how you do the first year, then talk it over with Willy Joe."

On a signal from Young Wolf, the Indian drovers rode back to their leader. They had worked the cattle well, understanding their moods. There was a small stream through the valley that would provide plenty of water for the herd.

Willy Joe looked at the sky. The sun had been down for an hour. "We better get moving so we don't get lost on our way back to the ranch."

"Follow this stream down to the Tongue and you won't have any problems," Young Wolf said.

The Mandan Indian turned toward Morgan. "I would like you to come to my village and meet the rest of my people. I wish to honor you for your help in this matter."

Morgan nodded. "It would be my pleasure."

Morgan waved at Willy Joe and the Circle-S cowboys took off downstream, anxious to be getting back to camp and a late supper.

"The three men you trained, Harry, Joe and Walt, are all excited about being ranchers," Young Wolf said as he and Morgan rode along toward the head of the valley. "They have been named the herders and will spend most of their time with the animals, getting to know them, watching their movements and moods, knowing as much about them as possible. That way they will be able to keep track of where they wander. If they get too far from the others, they'll be driven back so we can keep the herd together, at least at first."

"Good idea," Morgan said. "Remember, you don't have any steers here. When you need meat, send two men back down to the range, find a steer, drive him up here and then butcher him here. That way you'll be able to use all of him the way you used to do with buffalo."

"Yes. But for now we are doing fine with game and our plantings. I try to get to Billings twice a year to buy new seeds. Perhaps I could do the same thing in Miles City if I took one of your hands in with me."

"Yes, I don't see why not. I'll suggest that to Miss Scoggins when I get back." He hesitated. There was so much about Young Wolf that he couldn't read, let alone understand. Morgan just barged ahead.

"Young Wolf, I'm not sure why you invited me to come with you."

"To thank you, to show you to my people. There will be some presents and gifts. I hope you know how to accept gifts."

"I'll try my damnedest." They both laughed.

When they came to the Mandan village, Morgan was surprised. It was situated along a small stream in a heavily wooded section with mostly pines and some oak and brush. The lodges themselves were what interested him the most.

"These are the traditional Mandan lodges. Our tribe was never a wandering people. We built substantial lodges because we stayed in one place for many years at a time. They are strong and good protection, some big enough to shelter our favorite horses in the winter."

Then they saw the people. Nearly 50 men, women and children left the lodges and lined the path they came down. They all called out greetings which Young Wolf translated. Some of the men and children called in English.

At the end of the lane was the largest of the lodges. Morgan guessed it was 30 feet across, and the dome at the top where a smoke hole showed was at least 20 feet off the ground.

Beside the lodge had been placed two tables, built of sawed lumber, with benches attached on both sides. One of the tables was heaped with food.

"A feast for our benefactor," Young Wolf said. Morgan stared at the food. There was cooked meat, soup, straw bowls of fresh fruit, clay bowls of berries and a variety of vegetables including carrots and parsnips and potatoes.

"Our people especially enjoy the carrots," Young Wolf said. "They like the taste and the color. Carrot seeds were some of the first I brought back with me when I finished my schooling."

Morgan was hungry. There was a stack of tin plates which Young Wolf must have brought along with spoons and forks. Morgan took a plate and filled it, then Young Wolf directed him to the end of the second table where he sat down and ate. The roast beef was juicy and flavored with some herbs that he couldn't identify but helped enhance the flavor.

The vegetables were cooked well, and a tin cup filled with fresh water was brought to his place. He looked up at the woman who brought it. She was slender, maybe 16, with snapping black eyes and long dark hair. She wore a white woman's yellow blouse and a traditional Mandan doeskin skirt. She sat down across from him at the table but didn't eat. Instead she watched every move he made.

All of the Mandan people seemed to be watching him. Young Wolf came up with a plate and sat down beside Morgan.

"If you think these folks are staring at you, they are. You're the first white man most of them have ever seen. They are whispering that you look so remarkably like them. I thought it would be good for them to meet you. After we eat and have a campfire, I'll introduce you to each person in the band, even little White Eagle who is only three weeks old."

"Thanks. Now I know a little how you must have felt when you went to the university."

"Right, it was hard at first. Then I earned two good friends and that helped."

When the meal was over, the oldest Indian in the clan stood and motioned toward a clearing where a traditional campfire ring had been built. Around the

sides there were logs placed on the ground for everyone to sit on.

The ancient one, Wandering Elk, who Young Wolf
said was 52, wavered through a traditional song of
the Mandans. Then he led the group in singing the
song.

"We're trying to preserve as much of our heritage
as we can. So much of it has been lost. People forget.
I've got everything written down, but I don't know
music, so we have the words, but the tones and notes
will be gone I'm afraid."

Young Wolf took over then and spoke to them for
a while in English. The younger people listened and
seemed to understand. Some of the older men and
especially the women ignored what he said.

"Today we have a guest, a friend. He comes from
the Circle-S ranch. The owners there are our longtime
friends. Welcome him."

The Mandans gave a series of whoops and shouts,
and then all clapped.

"You are now an honorary Mandan Indian in good
standing," Young Wolf said.

The ceremony went on for another half hour, then
the Indians formed a line and walked past. Young Wolf
introduced each one, and Morgan shook them by the
hand. Even that kind of a greeting was unusual for
the Mandans.

When the line was completed, Morgan looked
around as the people faded into their lodges. Young
Wolf motioned to Morgan. "One Coyote was our
warrior killed by the Bar-B riders. His lodge has been
empty, awaiting a new married couple. You can sleep

there tonight, then stay with us tomorrow if you wish. There's a thick mat on the floor as is our usual custom. If you need anything, let me know.''

He led Morgan down a path to one of the smaller lodges. It was sturdily built with eight feet to the curved roof overhead. Inside there were four solid poles with a frame on the top of the four, binding them together and supporting the curved roof.

A small fire burned in the central fire ring with the smoke going out through the top hole. Beside the mat stood a small table with a gourd of fresh water and some fruit.

Young Wolf waved at the door. "Sleep well. It is a good thing you have done today. The Mandan people will long remember you and this day when our white man's buffalo arrived. Good night, my friend.''

Then he was gone. In the faint, flickering light of the fire, Morgan moved around in the lodge. It was nearly 15 feet across, allowing a lot of room. Unlike a tipi, the side walls were six feet high so all of the space was available for use.

He saw where a horse had once been tied. To the back it was darker, and he saw stacks of baskets and pots. Then something moved. Morgan was alert at once, wondering. The shadow moved again and then came forward.

The shadow became a young woman, and soon in the firelight, he saw that it was the one who had brought him his cup of water at the table and watched him. Her dark eyes glowed, and she smiled as he remembered her.

"I am Spring Fawn," she said in English. "I will

276

help you to sleep well tonight. It is our custom."

Morgan watched her. She was not afraid. She did not seem to be unhappy.

"Who told you to do this?"

"No one." She took his hand and led him back to the mat and urged him to sit down. She looked at his boots and soon figured out how to get them off.

"Spring Fawn. That's a beautiful name."

She looked up at him and then back down quickly. She knelt beside him and unbuttoned his shirt. Before she could take it off, Morgan caught her hands.

"If no one told you to be here and do this, why are you here?"

"It is our custom. Someone must take care of you, fix your food, make your bed, sleep with you?"

"But aren't you married? Don't you have a man?"

"No, we are short of young men in our tribe. I should marry two years ago. Perhaps soon we will decide to have young men take two wives. Young Wolf worry about this many times."

"How many young women like you are unmarried?"

"Three. I talked to them and told them I would take care of you." Gently she moved his hands and took his shirt off. Spring Fawn moved quickly and built up the fire with small wood so it flamed up quickly. She came back and stared at his chest with wonder, then touched the hair and smiled.

That was when he remembered that Indians did not

grow beards, had few face hairs and no chest hair. She ran her hands through it and smiled.

"Good," she said. Then she looked at his belt, figured out how to open it and undid it. She looked at the front and the buttons and soon had his pants undone.

Before she could move to take his pants off, Morgan caught her hands and sat her beside him. He didn't want to hurt her feelings or do something that would make her embarrassed or a laughing stock.

"Spring Fawn. Have you ever slept with a man?"

"Oh, yes, ten times. If Spring Fawn get with child, then she can be married as second wife."

"So you've tried before?"

"Ten, fifteen times."

"But no baby?"

"No small one yet. Think maybe this will be good time. Moon is nearly full, new cattle beasts in valley, everyone happy. Young Wolf happy. Maybe we make baby tonight."

Morgan leaned forward and kissed her cheek. She turned his face to hers and kissed his lips, then her tongue worked into his mouth. She came away and smiled.

"Very good, yes? Young Wolf teach me."

"That old dog, he makes up the rules and then plays by them. No wonder he likes it here." Morgan kissed her again, then unbuttoned the yellow blouse. She pulled it off quickly, and her young breasts thrust out at him.

"Oh, damn," Morgan said, "the things I have to do for friendship. I reckon this is really why Young Wolf brought me back here with him tonight."

"Yes. Spring Fawn ask him to bring her a man. Young Wolf is good friend."

"Relax and enjoy," Morgan whispered. Then he rolled onto the mat with her.

Chapter
Twenty-Two

Spring Fawn kicked out of her soft doeskin skirt and helped him with his pants.

"White man way," she said. "You show me."

Morgan rolled her on top of him and chewed on her delicious small breasts for a time, then lowered her until she was over him just right. He thrust forward, and Spring Fawn yelped in delight.

"It will work this way?" she asked, her face shining in the light from the fire.

He thrust upward again and slid into her until their pelvic bones touched. He moved in and out of her, then showed her how she could move over him, and soon she was riding him like a young steer.

"Oh, good!" she crooned. She went faster and faster and shrieked in joy as she trembled and shivered through a climax. Then he could stand it no longer and he exploded. She fell on top of him, panting and chattering away in some Indian tongue until she remembered and switched to English.

A moment later she slipped from him and built up the fire more. "I want to see you," she said, then came back to the bed. "Many more times," she said. "Must make baby for Spring Fawn."

"Damn tough work, but I'll do my best," Morgan said and grabbed her again.

It was three hours later, and several more additions to the fire, before they at last lay spent and happy.

"Now we sleep," Spring Fawn said. She curled into a ball beside him and was asleep in only a few seconds. Morgan took longer, watching the small child-woman beside him. Perhaps one day she would indeed enter into the white man's world, but more likely it would be her children or her grandchildren who would meet the white man on an equal basis. At last he slept.

With the morning came more surprises. Spring Fawn had been up and had brought him a breakfast of sorts. There was a coffee pot boiling away on the small cooking fire in the center of the lodge. The smell of the fresh coffee had awakened Morgan.

"Coffee," Spring Fawn said proudly. "Young Wolf like coffee, so he bring it for you this morning." She brought a tin cup for him and a tin plate holding three kinds of berries and an apple.

"We have an apple tree," she told him proudly. "White man's apple tree that Young Wolf bring six, seven years ago."

After he had dressed and eaten, he went outside to find a delegation from the village. Three women wearing their best doeskin dresses brought him presents. There was a finely braided rawhide rope that he knew had taken many hours to make.

The second present was a buckskin vest with big brass buttons and a cinch strap in the back. He put it on at once and hugged the woman who had made it. She giggled and hurried off, delighted but embarrassed.

His third gift was a pair of moccasins that fit him exactly, and he realized the woman must have slipped into his lodge last night, made a pattern of his boot and finished making the moccasins during the night. He hugged her, too, and she shrilled with laughter and hurried away.

Young Wolf walked up and motioned for him to sit down in the shade of a large Engelmann spruce.

"You look pleased with your gifts."

"They are too valuable. These women worked many hours to make these gifts."

"It's our way of expressing some of our respect and appreciation to you for what you have done for the last band of the Mandans. With your help we may yet grow and prosper." He watched Morgan for a moment.

"How do you like our quaint customs?"

"Your one custom of making a guest feel at home and well cared for is . . . interesting. I like it. But what can your tribe do when you are short of marriageable young men?"

"A problem. Looks like the only answer will be second wives for some of the more ambitious young men."

"And pray for a good crop of boy babies," Morgan

said.

"At least I have helped end one practice that most of the plains Indians practiced. Most of the mothers nursed their young for three or four years. They were not allowed to have sex with their husbands while nursing. This meant a young woman could have only two or maybe three babies during her fertile period.

"In our agrarian life, we can afford to feed our children without the long nursing, and we have gradually abandoned the practice of abstinence during nursing. I would be delighted if every woman in the band had a baby every year."

"Don't look at me," Morgan said. Both men chuckled.

"I should be starting back," Morgan said.

"First, let's ride out and look at the herd. See what it's done over the night."

The cattle had spread out, but less than Morgan had figured. The graze was better here than lower down on the valley. They could graze here year round and not ruin the grass in the valley. As they multiplied, they would need to move them into some other areas as well.

They watched the cattle for a few more minutes, and then Morgan filled his canteen at a small spring.

The two friends shook hands.

"If you need us to make that bluffing raid on the Bar-B ranch, send up a message," Young Wolf said. "We won't actually attack them, but we can scare them for you."

"We just may need your help one of these days. We have plans for a large gathering of our stolen cattle, and you would be right helpful." Morgan touched the brim of his hat, kicked his sorrel into motion and rode down the valley the way they had driven in the cattle.

There was a wide trail the cattle had made, but in a month or two it would be grown over and rained out. He was pleased with the "seeding" of cattle with the Mandan tribe. He was sure it would pay big future dividends for the native Americans.

As he thought about the whole situation with the Circle-S, it all at last came down to the cattle. Bramwell had stolen over 4000 head of stock, and they had to be returned, which meant one more big raid to recapture the stock. It would be harder this time.

They would need a scout to check where most of the Bar-B cattle now grazed, then start a full roundup force. Perhaps start the roundup late in the afternoon and night drive them. Yes, that had possibilities, especially with the diversion of the Mandans showing up on the Bar-B range at the critical moment.

Morgan was surprised that Bramwell hadn't launched any kind of retaliation against the Circle-S, but slowly he realized that Bramwell had. He had brought in a gunman, hoping to eliminate Morgan, and then Bramwell could rustle back the cattle and squeeze the Circle-S out of business.

"No chance," Morgan said to the sorrel who turned and looked at him from one huge eye. Morgan patted the beast on the neck as they rode on down the river toward the ranch. He considered the threat of the sheriff concerning the wanted poster. If the report came back from Tombstone positive, the lawman would have to make some move against Morgan. He might just wait until he went to town again. Morgan would have to keep close check on that.

When he rode into the Circle-S lands he saw riders working cattle. He wasn't sure what they were doing, but evidently Willy Joe was moving some animals to better graze. Morgan decided that the young man would do well managing the ranch for Heather once they were married.

Morgan took his time and got back to the ranch just before noon. He put his mount away, hung the tack and went up to the house.

Heather was talking to someone in the parlor so he went to the kitchen to see what was for dinner. The cook routinely brought a portion of the meal he cooked for the men to the ranch house for the three of them there. Sometimes he cooked a special dish for them, but usually it was the plain meat and potatoes kind of food that Morgan most enjoyed.

Today's dinner wasn't on hand yet, so he sat reading a week-old newspaper.

In the living room Heather sat on the couch and stared at the young man sitting beside her.

"Dan Fletcher, I told you not to do that."

"I know, but your lips didn't mind at all when I kissed them. I believe in lips more than words." Fletcher leaned forward again, and his lips brushed hers, then pressed harder. She returned the pressure, and her arms came around him gently, then tighter as their lips burned together.

They came apart slowly, Heather breathing deeply, her eyes opening reluctantly. Her fingers touched his cheeks, and then her hands dropped to her lap.

"Dan Fletcher, it's not polite to take advantage of a lady that way. I . . . I told you. Willy Joe and I have talked about getting married, and . . ."

"I don't see no ring on your finger. I ain't heard no announcement about the engagement. I been pining for you for weeks, and now I'm about to have my say."

Fletcher kissed her again. Her arms went around him and pushed her breasts hard against his chest. When his hand worked its way between their bodies, she eased back to give him room.

He held the kiss as he caressed her breasts through the fabric of her dress.

Her lips left his for a moment. "No, no, don't do that," she whispered, but they both knew she didn't mean it. He rubbed her breasts more and worked free a button on her dress, then let his hand slip inside and under her chemise until his fingers closed around her bare breast.

Heather pulled her mouth from his, kept her eyes closed and put her head on his shoulder.

"God, you're so beautiful!" Fletcher whispered. "So beautiful and you feel so wonderful. I don't know what to say, you letting me touch you and rub you so softly, more than I ever expected." He lifted her face and kissed her again, brushing his tongue against her lips. She wouldn't open them. His hand found her other breast, and she moaned softly.

She broke off the kiss. "Don't," she said softly. He took her hand and pushed it down to his crotch where his erection bulged his pants. She let her hand lie there, touching it but not moving.

Heather sighed and reveled in the sweet warm feeling of his hand on her breast. It was so marvelous. Then she gasped as his other hand touched her leg, pushed her dress between her legs, came up and pressed against her crotch.

"No!" she said with force. She pushed away from him, took his hand from her dress top and hastily fastened the button. Heather moved back from him on the couch.

"Mr. Fletcher, I think it's well time that you go outside. I told you that I'm promised. I'm going to marry Willy Joe just as soon as he'll have me. I'll thank you not ever again to touch me or to come to the ranch house. Is that clear?"

"I don't think you mean that, Heather. Let me prove it to you. I'll kiss you again, and if you can tell me to go then, I'll believe you."

As he leaned in toward her, Heather watched him come. Her eyes started to close, but then she jumped back and slapped him.

"Get out of the house, Dan. Right now. Out, and don't come back in here again. Out!" She stood and pointed at the door.

"Well, hell," Dan said. He stood and stared down at her. "I still think I'm the man for you. You spend one night with me and you'll be sure, too. I'd damn like to get your dress off and kiss them twin tits of yours, but guess that won't happen—unless you've changed your mind." He reached down toward her breasts, and she slapped his hand away.

"Out!" she said. "Now."

That evening, after supper, Willy Joe and Heather and Morgan sat at the table planning how they could make one big sweep of the Bar-B and hopefully come up with 2000 head of cattle.

"You're right, we have to scout the range in the daylight and see where they have their stock," Willy Joe said.

"My job," Morgan said. "I knew some Apaches who taught me a few tricks. I'll go out tomorrow, so I better get some sleep tonight." He told them good night and turned in.

Heather watched Willy Joe. She took his hand and led him to the couch in the parlor. She sat down, and when he moved beside her, she pulled him close so their legs touched.

"I really need a kiss," she told him. Willy Joe grinned and kissed her gently, then harder. His arms came around her, and when the kiss ended she nestled his chest and he held her tenderly.

"I had a gentleman caller this afternoon," she said casually. "He told me he was coming courting."

Willy Joe pushed her back and stared at her. "He what?"

"He said since I wasn't promised to nobody, he figured he should come courting."

"Who was it? I'll fire him right now!"

Heather giggled. "You are amazing when you get mad. So strong and rugged. You'll have to get mad more."

"I'm not joking about this, Heather. We've got an understanding about the two of us."

"Oh, an understanding? I don't see any ring on my finger. I don't see any barbed wire fences around me. When did we make the announcement about our upcoming engagement?"

Willy Joe sat down and scowled. "An understanding. Don't need no ring. Who we going to

289

announce it to?''

''The crew and to Morgan and send a note to the newspaper in town for their society page. A woman likes to have these things done.''

''Don't matter none. We're getting married.''

''This young man was very persuasive. He even kissed me.''

Willy Joe jumped to his feet again. ''You let him kiss you? We have an understanding—or don't we?''

''You say we do, but a girl likes to see a ring on her finger. Then every man stays away.''

''Yeah? Okay, next time I'm in town I'll get a ring, an engagement ring, and we'll tell everybody.''

''This young man kissed me twice, Willy Joe. So far you've just kissed me once, tonight.''

He grinned, sat down, and took her in his arms and kissed her properly. He held her close, and her breasts pushed against his chest. When the kiss ended, Heather smiled.

''Yes, that was nice. Did I tell you he touched me—here?'' She pointed to her breasts.

''Willy Joe, after a girl's been kissed sometimes she likes to be touched, caressed.'' She pulled his face to hers and kissed him, then caught his hand and placed it over her breast. His hand trembled for a moment, then he pressed it down and rubbed her breast through the cloth.

She unbuttoned two fasteners on her dress and pushed his hand inside. He looked at her, and she nodded and kissed his lips gently.

''Yes, Willy Joe. Yes, it's time.''

His hand closed around her bare breast, and she trembled, moaning softly.

"Willy Joe, I've been wanting you to do that for so long. Now don't stop. There's two in there you know. Don't say a word. I've been waiting for so long, Willy Joe. Your hand there feels so wonderful to me. Makes me all warm and wanting and loving you. Does it feel good to you?"

"You bet. You know it does." When he kissed her this time, her lips parted. He hesitated, then he pushed his tongue into her mouth. She moaned again, and his hand rubbed faster, harder.

When the kiss ended, Heather stood and caught his hand. She didn't bother buttoning her dress. She led him to the master bedroom and closed the door gently behind them. Willy Joe lit a lamp and turned it low, then she took Willy Joe's hand and they moved to the bed and sat on the edge.

"No more waiting, Willy Joe. We're going to be married next week, and tonight I want you to teach me to make love. You've . . . you've been with a woman before?"

He nodded.

"Good, then show me exactly what to do. I want to please you, Willy Joe, and I want to make love with you."

She began to unbutton the rest of her dress, but his hands caught hers and did it. Then he kissed her, and they lay back on the bed side by side, she on her back.

"You're sure you want this to happen now?" he asked.

"Oh, yes! Oh, yes!" Her hands both moved to his crotch and worked on the buttons at his fly.

It was a small ritual getting undressed. He got her dress off over her head and then her chemise. For a moment he stared at her breasts, then touched them.

She took off his shirt, then he tugged his boots off, and she slid down his pants and shorts.

"Oh, my!" she said in surprise when his erection popped out of his pants. "It's so . . . so huge!"

He laughed. "Not huge, just the right size. Everything will fit. You'll see." He bent and kissed her breasts, and before he realized it, she tore into a climax, shaking and gasping and vibrating as a concentrated series of spasms raced through her.

"Oh my!" she said looking at him. "See what power you have over me."

He pulled down her three petticoats and her cotton drawers, and finally she was as naked as he was.

"Marvelous!" he said. "I don't really believe this is happening."

"What do we do next?" she asked. He kissed her, then pushed her gently onto the bed on her back. His hands caressed her breasts as he kissed her a dozen more times. Then slowly, he touched and rubbed her leg, working his hand higher past her white thighs.

"Yes, sweetheart, I want you to touch me there. Please. I've been waiting so long for a man to do that."

When he found her nether lips they were moist and wet and ready. He stroked her clit a time or two, then pushed his finger into her.

"Ready?" he asked.

She took a deep breath and nodded.

When Willy Joe Dawson took her maidenhead that night it was an act of love, a moment of glory for both of them.

Heather squealed with surprise and joy and rapture,

and they made love three times as quickly as she could bring him back to readiness.

Later they lay on the bed, holding one another.

"I want you to stay right here, naked beside me for at least a week," she said.

"I might find time to visit you in your bedroom tomorrow morning after I get the men out on their assignments."

"You better, or I'll grab a cowhand and rape him." She grinned. "No, I won't. No man but you is ever going to see me naked, let alone ravish me. Just so you make it twice more before morning."

They compromised and made it three more times.

Chapter
Twenty-Three

Sheriff Straud stared at the telegram he held up to the light. He read it again and it said the same damn thing.

"REWARD POSTER ON LEE MORGAN CORRECT. WANTED HERE FOR MURDER. CONTACT ME IF CAPTURED OR KILLED. DISTRICT ATTORNEY CLIVE BARSTOW. TOMBSTONE, AR."

Christ, what did he do now? A citizen had claimed Morgan was a wanted man. The sheriff had talked to him at the Circle-S ranch but had gotten run off by gunfire. Now he was supposed to go out there and have a gun battle to arrest a man wanted in Arizona? Not by a damn sight.

He was in his third term as sheriff, and he'd never

had anything like this come up before. Sure, he'd sent wanted men back to another sheriff or held them for a man to come pick them up—but never anything like this.

Lee Morgan was not your usual kind of man to show up on a wanted poster. Sheriff Straud found a bottle in his bottom drawer and took a pull on it as soon as he got the cork out. Good whiskey helped him think. He corked it and put it back.

What else could he do? Invite Morgan in to see the telegram that cleared him, then have him covered and throw him in jail?

Might work, but probably wouldn't. Morgan would be too smart for that.

Maybe he could catch Morgan the next time he came to town. He had to stay at the Plainsman Hotel, and the clerk there owed the sheriff a favor or two. Yes, he would tell the clerk, Hirum, to be damn sure to tell the sheriff the moment Lee Morgan checked into the hotel or even showed up there. He left the office, spoke to Hirum, then stopped by at the Yellow Dog Saloon.

The barkeep on duty set him up a free mug of beer.

"Afternoon, Sheriff. You keeping the county safe for us law-abiding citizens?"

"Aiming to." He looked around the saloon. "You seen anything of the Bar-B boss or riders today?"

"Nope. Don't think they're in town."

The sheriff nodded. That had been his other plan—to get the Bar-B men to ride out with him to get Morgan. A few extra guns would help. Now even that wouldn't work.

Sheriff Straud gulped his beer. The only way to do

it was to trick the man into coming to town. How could he do that? Morgan was not stupid. It would have to be good. That started him thinking about Slade Gelink.

The man was a backshooting gunslick, not really a gunfighter even though he had a rep. The two of them wanted the same thing, even though for different reasons, and that was Morgan's head in a bucket. So did Parrish Bramwell, but he was too far away right now.

As for Slade Gelink, how could the two of them work together? For two dollars he could hire a messenger to ride out to the Circle-S with a letter for Morgan. Saying what? Sheriff Straud shook his head. He was at a total loss. He finished the beer, thanked the bartender and went back to the Plainsman Hotel.

Hirum looked up from the desk. "Ain't heard a bit about him yet, Sheriff Straud."

"Of course not. I was only here twenty minutes ago. Is Slade staying here?"

"Sure. But I can't give out room numbers."

"I know you can't, Hirum, but you can write it down for your own information."

Hirum wrote 312 on a pad of paper and turned it. "Ever so thoughtful of you, Hirum. You remember about Morgan."

Sheriff Straud walked up the stairs slowly. He wasn't as spry as he was when he was 20 years younger, and he was the first to admit that. He was puffing when he got to the third floor, and he paused at the top a minute.

Room 312 was in the middle of the hallway, and he knocked and stepped to one side of the door—an old habit.

"Yeah?" a voice bellowed from inside.

"Need to talk to you a minute, Slade."

"Who are you?"

"A man who needs to do in Lee Morgan."

The door opened at once. Slade looked down at the star and then at the sheriff.

"You're the law here."

"Right, and you and I both want the same thing. May I come in and talk about how we're going to kill Lee Morgan?"

A half hour and a glass of whiskey later, they still hadn't come up with a plan to get Morgan to town and away from his 35 guns on the ranch.

"If there were just somebody in town he knew we could fake a message from," Sheriff Straud said.

Slade looked up, stroked his mutton chops and then pressed his moustache. "There is," he said. "After he pushed me around, I traced him. It took all the next day, but I found out he stayed most of the night with a woman in the hotel. She's still here."

"Who?"

"A gal named Elly."

The sheriff burst out laughing. "Now that is ironic. Elly is or was Bramwell's lady fair. So what do we say to get Morgan into town?"

"Easy. We send a note in a woman's hand saying that me, Slade Gelink, has been bothering her and that I broke into her room and would have raped her if she hadn't used that little derringer she keeps. He'll believe it. She can plead with Morgan to come into town and take her back to the Circle-S for her own safety. That should do it. She could say come in late in the afternoon or after dark, and she'll have a horse she can ride back to the ranch with him. Then we got him.''

Both men sat back and tipped their whiskey glasses. "I think we've got something here. Now all we need is a woman to write the letter.''

"A small friend of mine will do the letter along with her other duties for a mere two dollar charge,'' Slade said. He grabbed his hat. "I'll meet you in the Yellow Dog Saloon in about a half hour.''

The letter was even better than he had hoped for, Sheriff Straud decided when he read it a short time later. They sealed it in an envelope. The woman had written Morgan's name and the name of the ranch on the envelope for them. Then it was an easy job to find someone to ride out to the Circle-S for a two dollar fee.

The blonde whore who wrote the letter begged the man to ride out to the ranch when she gave him the envelope. She even cried a little so Morgan would have no doubts. The rider swore on his honor he would deliver the letter and took off riding south about two in the afternoon.

Sheriff Straud and Slade watched the rider galloping down Main Street.

"He's off with the best laid plans,'' the sheriff said. "Now all we can do is watch and wait.''

Morgan headed southeast early that same morning to check out the location of the Bar-B cattle. He rode a dark gray dun and wore a gray hat and soft brown pants and shirt so he could blend in with the landscape as well as possible. He wore no spurs and had painted black the bright spots on the bridle and the outside of the bit so there would be nothing for the sun to reflect and give away his position.

He left the house a little after 4:00 A.M. without waking anyone. He rode hard to the southeast for two hours, and it was another hour before he cleared the Pumpkin River. He had seen virtually no cattle on the close side of the Pumpkin. That figured. They had pulled all of their stock back to a more secure area. But where? By now it was daylight and he could see for half a mile in every direction.

He figured he was about ten miles south of the Bar-B ranch buildings, but still he saw few animals. He pushed due east for an hour and ran into some cattle.

Where were the rest of them? After another hour's ride east he ran into more stock. Now he moved more to the south and soon spotted a wood smoke fire about a mile off. It turned out to be a shack of sorts, with a small corral and six horses in it. That could be six riders or two men with three horses each.

He kept in a gully and rode past it another half mile. He was in the edge of the broad Powder River Valley, and here he found the bulk of the Bar-B's remaining cattle. He figured there were about 3000 head, more or less.

It was almost noon. He decided he had found the herd about 30 miles from the Circle-S and more than 37 miles from Branding Canyon.

Trying to move that big herd even 25 miles in one day would be a hell of a job. They would have to go at least 23 miles to get back on Circle-S land. They couldn't do that even if they drove the cattle all night. It might be better to ride in about ten in the morning, round up the critters, push them west and try to be back on Circle-S land before dark.

He'd talk with Willy Joe about it. Morgan looked up in time to see two riders moving across the flat valley, coming almost directly at him. He kept in the gully and galloped the last 50 yards around a small turn just before the riders worked into the gully and checked both ways for stray cattle.

Morgan pulled off his hat and wiped sweat from his forehead, then angled away from the riders and to the west. It would take him most of the afternoon and evening to get home. With a better horse he could average six miles an hour, but he wasn't sure about this dun.

After the first hour he was convinced that he was making his six miles an hour. He heard a rifle shot from across the prairie, but it wasn't anywhere near him.

He ignored it and kept moving behind any cover he could find toward the west. It was nearly three in the afternoon when he crossed the Pumpkin. He turned to the northwest and headed for the Circle-S. He expected no Bar-B riders in this area and found none.

It was almost six in the evening when he walked the tired dun into the barn, pulled off the saddle and put her into the corral.

He'd had a hard day and was looking forward to a big supper and then a bath so hot he would nearly melt. It had been months since he'd ridden 60 miles in a day with almost no break.

Heather came running to meet him as he started toward the ranch house.

"Oh, good, you're back. You'll still have time to get into town."

Morgan stood there half-dead from riding 60 miles.

He blinked, sagged a little and frowned.

"Would you say that again?"

"I said that you're back early enough so you can ride into town. Somebody went to all the trouble of hiring a rider to bring you a letter. It must be important. The rider said the lady who hired him was almost crying."

"Can we continue this in the kitchen over some coffee and food? I'm beat to death, I'm starved and I need a good, long, leisurely hot bath."

"Sure, ignore the letter. Some poor woman is probably dying in Miles City and you can't ride fifteen miles to help her."

"How do you know she's dying?"

"Why else would she spend two dollars to send you a special letter?"

They went into the kitchen. Morgan poured himself a cup of coffee from the big pot usually on the wood-burning kitchen stove, sipped it hot and black and dropped wearily into a chair by the table.

Heather slid the envelope in front of him. It was one of the envelopes the Plainsman Hotel would sell you for a penny. He frowned and turned the letter over. There was no indication who had sent it.

"What did the rider say the woman looked like?"

"I asked. I figured you'd want to know. He said she was pretty and blonde and evidently lived at the hotel."

Morgan ripped the envelope open and read the words in a feminine hand on the pink stationery.

"I don't know if you'll ever get this letter. The rider might take the money and never deliver the envelope.

Even if you get it, you might not be able to get here in time.

"That man you talked about, Slade Gelink, found out that I know you, and he came here and threatened me. He said that I must tell him the next time you come to town. He said if I didn't he would do all sorts of unmentionable things to me.

"He grabbed one of my breasts and squeezed and said he'd cut me if I didn't do what he said. I just know that he's going to come back and tear down the door and rape me and then cut me and probably kill me before he's through.

"I have no one else to appeal to. This Slade evidently is a friend of the sheriff. He gets away with almost anything he wants to in town. I'm not sure what he'll do to me, but I'm afraid to spend the night in my room. I don't know what I'll do. There is no one, absolutely no one, I can trust here in town.

"If you can come, please come quickly. Elly."

Morgan read it through again. It sounded like Elly. She would try to be tough but be scared underneath.

He looked at Heather.

"So who is it? What does she want?"

Morgan dug into the plate of food that Heather had put in front of him. He silently handed the letter to her to read. By the time Heather had read it over, Morgan had finished the food and gulped the last of the coffee. He stood and headed for the door.

"Are you going?"

"Looks like I have to. I met Elly when we were in town with the beef. I'll wash up, change clothes and be ready. Have someone harness me a buggy, and

I want the thickest pillow you have for the seat.''

Morgan left 20 minutes láter. It was three hours to town if he was lucky. Then he'd have to see what was happening. His first thought was Bramwell. It could be a trap Bramwell had set for him. He would know Elly and probably get her to admit they had slept together. Damn!

It was an impossible situation. He had his Colt six-gun and one of the Spencers. If eight shots with the Spencer couldn't do the trick, he would be outgunned anyway. The horse on the buggy was fresh and eager to move, so he let her trot most of the way.

Three hours later when he came toward town, he turned down a side street so he wouldn't come in the usual track from the south. Instead he came up to the Plainsman Hotel by the cross street and parked the rig next to the alley.

After the great Chicago fire, everyone was talking about fire escapes from buildings. The Plainsman had one of sorts, a wooden stairway on the outside at the end of the building that opened into hall windows on the second and third floors.

Morgan took the rifle and Colt with him as he watched the fire escape outside the hotel. He saw no one lurking there. He went to the cross street that came to Main and looked down but saw nothing unusual around the front of the hotel.

He had no idea what to expect, but he had a strong feeling that Elly did not write the note after all. It just didn't quite sound like Elly. Even in a tough situation, he figured that Elly would make do for herself.

Then who had tried to get him to town? He could think of two other possibilities beside Bramwell—

Sheriff Straud and Slade Gelink.

Morgan went back to the outdoor stairway and hid the Spencer rifle near an upright, then he pulled his hat down low to cover more of his face, walked around to the front of the hotel, up the steps and into the lobby. One man read a newspaper, but he clearly wasn't the sheriff or Gelink. There was nobody in the lobby who could be called suspicious. Morgan went to the stairs and walked up casually as if he belonged there, still with his head down. When he came up the steps where he could see into the second floor hall, he paused. There was no one waiting in a chair.

He checked the doors along the hallway. Room 211's door was closed tightly. The one across the hall and one door beyond it were open an inch, providing some watchers a perfect view and a fine field of fire. Two guns, at least. No chance to see Elly that way. He slipped back down the steps and out the front door of the hotel.

Three doors down he found a saloon with two cowboy mounts tied up outside. Both had lariats on them. He reached up, took the longest rope, carried it beside his leg as he walked to the back of the hotel and went up the fire escape. The top supports extended almost to the roof. He shinnied up one, caught a cross brace and pulled himself over the foot-high false front on top of the three story hotel.

He had counted rooms when he had looked down the hallway. Elly was in the fourth room from the far end of the second floor.

Morgan found what he wanted, a sturdy upright at the edge of the front roof directly over the fourth window of the third floor. Elly's room was directly below that. He looked down now and saw that there was a light on in her room.

Morgan tied off the loop end of the lariat around the four by four and let the line play out down the front of the hotel. The line went between the windows. He hoisted himself over the edge and moved down hand over hand on the rope.

He passed the third floor window and a moment later was near the second floor window. He thought of tapping on it but first looked inside to see if Elly had any company. She sat in a chair beside two coal oil lamps reading a book. There was no one else in the room unless they were hiding under the bed.

He checked and saw that the window as not locked, so he held the rope with one hand and slid the window up with the other.

He had it up a foot when Elly looked over his way. She started to cry out, but his voice stopped her.

"Elly, it's Morgan," he said softly. She rushed to the window, pushed it upward and helped him inside her room.

She laughed softly. "You could have just knocked on the door."

"Not really. Did you send me a letter today by a rider who brought it to the Circle-S?"

"What? Of course not. Why would I do that?"

"You wouldn't. It was a way to get me into town. Now I have to see exactly who is playing games with me." She reached up and kissed him.

"When I play games with you, it will be on top of a bed. That's the game where both sides win."

"True. Will you help me?"

"Of course."

"Just down the hall there are two doors that are cracked open so someone inside can see down the hall toward your room and the stairs. Someone is waiting in there for me to come to your door. They have shotguns, I'd guess."

"What do you want me to do?"

"If you could go down the hall and knock on the first door and say you need to borrow a match because your lamp went out—something like that. The light in the hall is dim. I'll follow right behind you, run past you and take on whoever's in the next room."

"Good. I'll take my derringer in case there's any discussion."

"If it's the sheriff, don't shoot him. There probably won't be any lights on in either room. We'll turn yours down as well. Ready?"

Elly took the derringer from a drawer and slipped on her shoes while Morgan turned down the lamp.

She opened the door quickly, and Morgan ducked down as she walked the ten feet to the door across the hall. Morgan followed most of the way, then ran past her and kicked in the other door. There was a light burning low.

When Morgan barged into the room he grabbed a man in the shadows, twisted one arm behind his back and sat on him on the floor.

"Let me up at once. I'm Sheriff Straud."

"Sure, and I'm General Grant. Why are you spying on the lady down the hall."

"None of your business."

A revolver shot thundered through the hallway from next door. Using rawhide thongs from his pockets, Morgan tied the sheriff's hands and feet securely, then raced out of the room. He spotted a man pushing up the window at the end of the hall and going out onto the fire escape.

The man fired a shot into the half-lighted hallway at Morgan, missed and vanished.

Morgan checked the next room. Elly came out, looking rumpled but unhurt.

"Bastard tripped me and got away," she wailed.

"Stay here," Morgan commanded, then ran down the hallway and looked out the raised window. A shot from below shattered the second floor window, showering Morgan with glass but not hurting him. He snapped a shot at the flash of the weapon below, slid through the window and looked downward.

A man in the alley ran forward, a moving dark shadow, then stopped.

Morgan went down the steps in jerks and starts, heard one round fire at him from the alley and pin-pointed the spot. He hit the dirt running and slid into position behind a large wooden crate.

The other shooter was just across from Morgan. There had been no time to stop for the Spencer. Morgan refined the spot where he thought the man was hiding, then fired two shots.

There was a wail of pain, then a man got up and ran down the alley. Morgan fired twice at the sprinting blackness but had no idea if he hit him. Then Morgan was chasing the man. He made it safely to the street and turned away from Main and away from the few lights that remained in the town of Miles City.

Morgan sensed more than saw movement ahead of him. He opened his revolver, shook out the spent rounds and pushed in six fresh ones by feel. Then he jumped sideways and dropped into a crouch just as two rounds slammed through the air where he had been standing. He had his six-gun up and fired twice.

There was no sound of the other man being wounded. Morgan opened his six-gun, thumbed out the two used rounds, fed in two new ones and cocked the hammer. Then he ran forward. He had not seen or heard anything further of the man.

Morgan was halfway to the other man and less than ten yards away when a shotgun boomed ahead of him. He saw the deadly flash of the weapon, and the thought that hammered through his mind was simple: "Oh, God, I'm dead!"

Chapter
Twenty-Four

Morgan had sensed something would happen before he reached the man, and already he had been diving to the left when the shotgun went off and missed him.

He skidded on the ground on one elbow and forearm, rolled on his shoulder and came up shooting twice with his Colt .45. His rounds thudded into the side of the wooden building where the man had taken refuge, but there was no response. He rushed to the building, stopped and listened.

A screen door slammed. A baby cried. A woman called out sharply in pain. Footsteps thudded down the street, and Morgan took off after them.

Every 50 feet or so, Morgan paused and listened as the man continued down the street. Where was he going?

The sound of running stopped when they were past

most of the houses. One loomed directly ahead on the far side of the street. Morgan frowned in the darkness. The man had to be Slade.

"Give it up, Slade," Morgan called then stepped six feet to the side and dropped to the ground. The shotgun blasted again, and this time slugs dug up ground in front of and beside Morgan.

A light came on in the house across the street, and Morgan heard the man running in that direction. A dark shadow burst through the lighted doorway, rushing inside. He heard a cry of protest, then a curse and a six-gun shot.

Morgan sprinted for the back door of the house as more lights flared within.

Morgan eased up on the rear porch, turned the knob to the back door and pushed it open soundlessly. He was in the kitchen and could see a living room ahead. He filled the two empty rounds in his revolver so he had six rounds and cocked the hammer.

He could hear voices ahead, footsteps sounded on the floor above. A small child cried somewhere, and a woman shushed it.

"I'm shot. Get me a doctor," a man's voice said.

"Shut up! You got any shotgun shells?"

So it *was* Slade. Morgan recognized the voice.

"Some in the kitchen," the other man said.

"Go get them. That bastard out there will be coming in the front door, and I want to blow him to hell."

"Just don't hurt my family."

"Get the shells or die."

When the man stepped into the kitchen, Morgan held up his finger to his lips.

"Stay here," Morgan whispered. "Where is he?"

"In the parlor, near the front door."

"Your family upstairs?"

The man nodded as tears welled in his eyes. "Don't let him hurt them."

As Morgan moved toward the parlor, a woman came down the stairs.

"Wilbur? What in heaven's name is going on down here?"

Slade jumped out from from behind a china cabinet and grabbed the woman around the throat from behind. He pulled her against him and laughed.

"I've got your wife, old man," Slade bellowed. "Get out here with those shotgun shells, or I'll blow her head off."

There was a pause, then a quick intake of breath. "I can't find any. I think I shot them up on ducks," the man shouted from the kitchen.

"Too bad. Your wife dies."

"No, no! How about horses? I'll saddle a horse for you and bring it to the front door."

"Yes, only bring it to the back door." Slade laughed. "Yes, that will work better."

Morgan saw Slade loosen his grip on the woman and use the gun barrel to tear the white cotton nightgown from neckline to hem. He peeled it off her, and she huddled, trying to cover herself.

She was about 35, slightly plump, with small breasts and large hips.

"God, you're no beauty, are you, woman?"

She shook her head. "Please, I got a baby to take care of."

"A baby. So you must like to fuck. Good. After I kill that damned Morgan we'll find a nice soft spot and I'll test you out. You better be good.''

"I'm going to get you a horse,'' the man said from the living room, seeing there was nothing he could do to help his wife. "Be just a minute or two to saddle Bluebell.''

Morgan peered helplessly from the living room shadows. He hadn't had a good shot at Slade who kept the woman in front of him. At least Slade thought he was still outside.

Then Slade moved from behind the woman to adjust the lamp.

Morgan had time for only one quick shot, and the round burned a groove through Slade's left side but not enough to knock him down.

He jerked the woman in front of himself and pulled her back into the shadows.

"Bastard! You don't believe me. I said I'd blow her head off. You crazy?''

"You kill her, and you've got no protection—then you die,'' Morgan roared, making sure he was behind one of the big chairs.

Slade fired twice with his six-gun.

"Well, Morgan, it's you. This won't do you any good, Morgan. I might have to kill half a dozen tonight before I get you, but I'll nail you.''

"Sounds about average for a backshooting no-talent who wished he was a gunslinger.''

"I am a gunman, you coward! I got the rep. Ask anybody if they've heard of Slade. Hell yes, they'll say.''

"Then why don't you and me meet right here in the living room ten feet apart? A real live shootout.

314

Best man wins. Guy who comes in second gets buried.''

"Not a chance, Morgan. That damned merchant would shoot me from the side or back. I know all the tricks.''

"And you've used them all. Let the woman go. She hasn't hurt you.''

"Oh, sure, and give you a shot. Not a chance. She's my ticket out of here, away from you. I'll get you later on. Don't worry. I know about your little woman. You're both dead now only you don't know it yet.''

Morgan heard movement. He darted to the end of the living room and looked into the parlor. It was empty. The front door was open.

He rushed outside into the darkness, again letting his ears do his seeing. Around the house toward the back the woman was crying. He got to the small barn in back just as the horse charged past. It carried Slade and the woman, naked now, the nightgown ripped off. She sat astride the horse in front of him on a small saddle blanket, and there was no chance for a shot.

The husband stood by crying. He already had begun saddling the other horse as if he were going after them. Morgan moved in, finished the cinching, stepped into the stirrup and swung up. He nodded to the man and kicked the mount out the door after Slade.

With a load of two Slade's horse would be slower. Slade was on the road going south toward the Circle-S. Did he know where he was going? Twice Morgan stopped to be sure the man was still ahead of him.

"I'm coming after you, Slade!" Morgan bellowed into the night air. Then he set his mount on a gallop

315

and charged straight down the road toward the sound of the other horse.

Morgan quickly closed the gap which he had kept at about 40 yards. Slade turned abruptly to the left toward the river brush and trees, holding onto the woman, knowing that Morgan wouldn't shoot for fear of hitting her.

Morgan almost caught him before he hit the brush, but not quite. He saw Slade unmount, but as he did so, the woman screamed and bit his wrist. When he howled in pain and let go of her, she darted away in the darkness.

Morgan fired, but the round missed as Slade dove to one side. Then he was up and running. Morgan jumped off his mount, knowing he could make better time through the thick brush on foot. Now he had a target.

The moon shone brightly as a cloud scudded past it. Morgan fired and hit Slade in the right leg. He went down but crawled behind a fallen tree, firing twice in return.

Morgan listened again. He saw some weeds and brush move to the left. Slade was working toward the river. The Tongue here was no more than three feet deep and maybe 20 feet wide. Morgan fired a round just over the log about where he figured the gunman lay.

There was no reaction. Then Morgan heard a splash. He was trying the river. Morgan ran that way and saw a head bobbing in the slow current. Slade went underwater and came up at once, screaming and splashing.

''Help me! I can't swim!'' Slade whined.

"Put your feet down. It isn't that deep," Morgan bellowed.

Slade did, and when he stood up the water was well below his shoulders. Morgan lifted his six-gun.

"You wouldn't kill me this way!" Slade pleaded. He walked forward toward Morgan. They were still 20 feet apart.

Slade jerked his six-gun out of the water and fired. Slade's round ripped into Morgan's left shoulder and spun him half around. He turned back and fired before Slade could cock his weapon and fire again.

Morgan's round tore into the back of Slade's right hand, spinning the revolver out of his fingers.

Slade bawled in pain and fury. "You shot my hand, you bastard. How can I be a gunman with a shot up right hand."

Morgan motioned for him to come out of the water. "Get out here and I'll take care of the problem with a round through your worthless skull."

Slade came out of the river slowly. Morgan figured he was waiting for a try with a hidden derringer. And he was right.

Morgan shot him in the left shoulder, spilling the weapon from his left hand.

Slade dropped on his knees.

"Goddamn! Nobody told me you were this good. I'd never heard of you. Where the hell did you come from? I've taken better men than you."

"Sure, from the back, or old men about ready to die. You want to bleed to death or shall we tie up our wounds?"

"Doesn't matter to me."

"I tell you about the gunsharp who got his right hand shot up and let it heal, but all the time he was practicing with his left hand? He came back left-handed and beat the man who busted his right one. I tell you that?"

"No."

"Didn't think so."

Morgan still hadn't holstered his weapon. He was waiting for something.

"You said something about fixing my hand?" Slade asked.

"Stand up," Morgan said.

Slade put his left hand flat on the ground to help push himself up. As soon as his left hand hit the ground, Morgan fired a round through the back of it. Slade screamed.

"Why did you shoot my hand?"

"Remember the left-handed gunman? I don't want you to try to do the same thing. No matter how well your hands heal, you'll never be any good with a gun. I want it that way. That's your price for trying to kill me."

Morgan watched the man and saw him fighting the idea.

"Can you accept that, or do I use up three cents more worth of .45 round and put that one more hole in your skull?"

"Not a chance. I've done my time with iron it looks like. Hell, I know when to quit. Anything is better than dead."

Morgan took out his knife and cut Slade's shirt sleeves off. He cut the cloth into strips and used it to bandage the man's hands and to put a compress on his left shoulder. Then he used his handkerchief and

318

neckerchief to tie up his own shoulder. It was bad, but not too bad.

"Come on, Slade. Now we have to find our horses, and that woman you kidnapped. Both are going to be a problem out here in the dark."

It took them five minutes to find the horses, then Morgan began calling to the woman. After a half hour he decided she must have started back to town. They caught up with her a half mile down the river road. Morgan gave her his shirt to wear, and she sat on the saddle blanket in front of him the rest of the way to her house.

Her husband met them in front of his house.

"Thank God, you're safe, Jenny. Thank God!" Her husband helped her down and hurried her into the house. He came out and thanked Morgan, then turned to Slade. The husband punched Slade twice in the face, knocking him to the ground.

"You bastard! I should kill you."

Morgan nodded. "I agree, you should kill the bastard. You want to use my .45?"

The husband held out his hand, but Morgan shook his head. "First you're taking him to the sheriff and charging him with kidnapping and assault and attempted murder. This one isn't worth killing, but he needs about five years in the Territorial Prison."

Morgan left them, found out where the town's one doctor lived, went there and knocked on the door. When a light came on, the medic looked out and sighed.

"Yep, right this way. This time of night it's got to be a gunshot, right?"

The doctor found that the bullet had gone in and

319

then exited, leaving a slightly larger hole. He put on some ointment and medication and wrapped it up tightly.

"You better get some bed rest, young man. You look plumb beat on your feet."

"Fine idea, doc." When Morgan paid him two dollars, the man seemed surprised to get the money. Morgan walked back to the hotel and up the steps to room 211. The door was open two inches. Inside the light was on, and Elly sat in bed, reading a book.

"I was hoping that you'd come back," she said. "You get him?"

"I always get my man," Morgan said sitting down on the bed heavily.

"Wish I could say the same thing. Can you tell me why I'm waiting in this hotel room day after day?"

"Hoping that I'll come back. Well, I'm here."

She looked at the newly bandaged shoulder.

"Shot up, tired out and almost ready to go to sleep."

"Now, there is a wonderful idea." Morgan struggled to get his boots off, then flopped on the bed. He looked at the girl.

"Sorry, I couldn't even get interested. I've done about six days work today, and I'm slightly on the pooped side."

"Oh, shit!" Elly said. When she looked over, expecting him to laugh, she saw instead that Lee Morgan had dropped off to sleep and was snoring with a soft easy sound. She knew that he wouldn't be awake until morning.

Elly closed the door, slid the straight-backed chair under the doorknob and blew out the lamp.

She watched Morgan a minute, then snuggled up

beside him and closed her eyes.

"Morgan, I'll make you do double duty in the morning before I let you out of bed," she promised herself. Then she slept.

Chapter
Twenty-Five

The next morning it took Morgan an hour to get out of Elly's bed and down to the dining room for breakfast. It had been a most enjoyable hour, but it put him behind in his plan for the day. He left the buggy in town and rode hard for the ranch. He hoped that Bramwell had not launched an attack on the ranch, knowing that Morgan would be away.

He pushed the horse and got to the ranch in a little less than two and a half hours.

Heather poured him a cup of coffee.

"So was the lady in danger?"

"No, it was a forgery and a trap to get me into town. They missed. I didn't. Anything happen here?"

"Dan Fletcher drew his wages and rode out. It's best that way. Willy Joe and I have set the wedding date—a week from Sunday—and I want you to give away the bride.''

"Good, about time. I'll be happy to do the honors in place of your father. Now, what else has happened. Anything heard from Bramwell's bunch?''

"Not even a rifle shot.''

"Good. Where's Willy Joe? We need to make some plans.''

"South range starting to weed out some of the range bulls. He says we have way too many.''

"True. We'll send some to Chicago for pot roast.''

"You going to tell me what happened in town?''

He told her quickly, leaving out the bedroom part. "We'll pick up the buggy next time we're in town. I left it at the livery.''

"Joe Tabler will probably sell it. I'm just glad you didn't get shot up any worse than you did. Want me to look at your shoulder?''

"Should be all right for a couple of days, then we'll look. At least it doesn't bother my riding.''

Heather kissed his cheek. "Lee Morgan, I'll never be able to thank you enough for being here and helping. This whole place would have been lost if it wasn't for you.''

"No matter what I do, I'll still owe your father. Now I better ride.''

He found Willy Joe a half hour later on his way back to the ranch house.

"We need to make some plans,'' Morgan said.

"About a roundup over east?'' Willy asked, grinning.

"About the size of it. We'll leave four men on guard and take the rest for a sweep.''

"You found out where his main herd is?'' Willy

Joe asked.

"About thirty miles from here."

"A two day drive?"

"About the size of it, if we want any of them to stay alive. Heard anything from Young Wolf?"

"Not a thing."

"Way I have it figured, I want to use him and his men in a scare raid."

"We can also use a diversion to pull some of his men down the other way."

"Sounds like a good idea. Let's plan it this afternoon. Then we'll ride out late tonight, do our gathering in the morning and drive them as far as we can before we stop."

"Can we get them off Bar-B land in one day?"

"Maybe, maybe not. Depends how long it takes us to round them up. We'll try for two thousand head."

They ate midday dinner and then planned the raid the first part of the afternoon.

"Do we have any dynamite?" Morgan asked.

Willy Boy frowned. "Oh, yeah, should have about half a case left. We got some to try to blast a well, but it didn't work."

"Been thinking about your diversion idea. If we could send one man north of the Bar-B ranch house about a mile and have him set off a series of three or four dynamite blasts, it would draw some men that way."

"If he tied them on a string and suspended them in the air from trees, they would make one hell of a bang."

"Good. You pick the man who knows powder. If he does that the morning we start our roundup, it

325

would help. Hold some of Bramwell's men at the home place."

"When we gather," Willy Joe said, "Bramwell's gonna know it. He'll have some men in the area."

"As soon as he starts for us with his men and rifles, we'll launch our Indian attack. I'll ride up there this afternoon and set it up with Young Wolf. If we can have them suddenly appear in a long line with guns and bows and lances, it could turn around ten or twelve Bar-B men in a rush."

Willy Boy nodded, grinning. "If they could stall off the Bar-B men long enough, we should have time for that first day's drive and get the critters almost back to the Tongue."

"Sounds about right." Morgan stretched. "You pull in the men and give them some rest. I'll go see Young Wolf. Be sure the men get their gear ready."

They left on their missions. Morgan caught a fresh horse and rode hard to the south. He made dust up the Indian cattle trail, and when he was still four miles from the valley where the stock grazed, Young Wolf met him.

"Figured it was you the way the lookout said you were riding. Must be time for our men to play wild Indians."

Morgan laughed. They dismounted, sat beside the stream and Morgan outlined the raid. "I don't know the area that well, but if you and your men could come out of a draw or over a little rise and block their path, it would be a big surprise and might just turn them around."

"You said they'll have rifles?"

"Probably every long gun they can find."

"So my men and boys could become targets?"

"I'm figuring that you'll know where to appear and what gully or ravine to use to stay out of sight after that."

"It might work. I'll have to look over the land-scape."

"Anywhere between the ranch yard and about ten miles south would work fine. Can you bring twenty riders?"

"By straining the age limit a little. I guess you want us with feathered headbands, war paint, feathered lances and bows and arrows. The whole Wild West Indian Show."

"It would impress the Bar-B riders—unless you've thrown all that stuff away."

"We have it. Ceremonial use now, but I think we can put on a good show. I'll tell the men this is part of their payment for getting the beef."

"How are your cowboys doing?"

"Learning. One of my men discovered that a range bull isn't at all afraid of a man on a horse. He got gored in the leg, but not seriously."

"Some of those old guys can be hell on hooves."

"Timing of our appearance?" Young Wolf asked.

"Anytime after daylight tomorrow morning. We're not sure that anyone will report our roundup, but chances are Bramwell has some guards out or some-body still in that line shack. I guess they'll spot us about eight or nine o'clock. A rider could get to the ranch by ten, and Bramwell will come with all the men he has about eleven. So between ten and eleven would be show time for you."

"Sounds about right. Gives us time to find our spot.

I think I'll bring along all of our rifles and on the first confrontation we'll fire over their heads.''

"Whatever you can do to scare them off."

They shook hands, and Morgan stepped back into the saddle.

"You look tired," Young Wolf said.

Morgan chuckled. "Not as near tired as I'm going to be after two days and nights of getting those beef-steak into Circle-S land."

They both rode away, but now Morgan took it easier, moving back toward the ranch at a slower pace.

The roundup crew left shortly after midnight. Each of the 30 riders had food packed in his saddlebags. There were six chunks of jerky for each man, three apples, four big roast beef sandwiches and a full canteen of water.

"Short rations until we get back," Morgan told them. "After that we'll eat all we can for two days. I promise."

They had 12 rifles with them and had left four men in the usual guard positions around the ranch. They were on duty now and would stay posted for the whole two days. The cook would ride out to them with food three times a day.

The last man stayed at the ranch and wouldn't leave until about 4:00 A.M. when he would ride to the Pumpkin River, work upstream to within a mile of the Bar-B ranch yard and hang his big firecrackers in the trees. They had set his blasts for about 10:00 A.M. or whenever he saw a group of riders get ready to travel south.

Morgan and Willy Joe had been sure to mount the

men on the strongest horses. On a real roundup they would change horses every day, but these mounts would have to do the job of three before they got the beef to Branding Canyon.

They started early so they could walk the horses the first 20 miles. Depending on the time, they would move out faster to get to the cattle just about at daylight.

It was after four when they crossed the Pumpkin River and angled a little more to the east. Now Morgan saw some shadowy landmarks he recognized.

He decided to pay the line shack a surprise call and, taking four men, moved up on it silently. It was just before dawn when they dismounted and pressed against the wall near the front door. It wouldn't be locked.

No one stirred inside, but they had seen four horses in a small corral to one side.

As the sky lightened and they could see better, Morgan eased the door open and stared inside. Two men lay on bunks, snoring soundly. Morgan slipped inside, found their weapons including two rifles and jolted them awake with a bellow.

They came up yelling but were quickly tied up and gagged.

"Somebody will find you in a day or two," Morgan told them.

They left the men, turned loose the four horses and then rode on east, catching up with the crew as they came to the scattered herd of Bar-B cattle.

The Circle-S hands worked through the wide valley, not bothering the animals. When they were on the far side they spread out 20 yards apart and began to sweep the cattle forward to the west.

They drove the cattle a half mile, then bent in the ends and formed the cattle into a compact herd. Four men remained to keep the animals in place, while the other men rode to the north to make another sweep across the green valley.

Willy Joe grinned as they forced a cow out of a brushy spot and chased her forward. A two-month-old calf chased after his mother.

"Looks like a good bunch," Willy Joe said.

"Don't count yet. Just round them up," Morgan said. He was pleased that there had been no reaction from the Bar-B yet. Possibly the two line shack men were the only riders from the other ranch in the area, but he didn't believe that. It was too much to hope for.

Far to the north, Lonnie Jenkins lay in the brush, watching the Bar-B corral. It had been rebuilt and now held about 40 horses.

It was just after 9:00 A.M. when Lonnie spotted a lone rider coming in fast from the south. His horse must be half-dead from the hard gallop. The rider came into the yard and stopped. He ran over to the white tent, and a moment later a man came out.

Lonnie could see the two men talking but heard nothing. Soon the yard was full of men running around and heading for the corral.

Now, Lonnie told himself. He blew on the tip of his cigar and touched the glowing coal to the six-inch fuse of the first dynamite bomb, then ran back 30 feet and covered his ears with his hands.

The ignited sticks of dynamite made a sharp explosive blast. Lonnie looked toward the ranch yard. Men had stopped dead in their tracks and looked around.

Lonnie lit the next six-inch fuse sticking out of the detonator cap, raced over to another and then a third. He dove into the brush and covered his ears as the three more explosions went off, one after another. He set off two more thundering blasts, then got his horse and rode 100 yards north. Soon three riders came galloping toward the blast sites, dismounted and looked over the area.

When Lonnie put the first rifle round over their heads, they dove into the grass and brush. Lonnie kept the three riders pinned down for a half hour. Then one worked around to the side, but Lonnie shot him in the leg and put him down. He wasn't keen on killing anyone, but his job was to keep them there as long as he could.

After another half hour the three riders all managed to get to their horses and ride back to the corral, but by then the men who had saddled up quickly and rode to the south were out of sight. Lonnie wasn't sure just how many had left the Bar-B, but at last count he had seen only six men mounted ready to ride. He had cut the defensive force by one-third!

Young Wolf sat on his bay mare and soothed her neck. She was not exactly a war pony, but he had trained her to answer his commands with his feet and legs. He checked his 21 warriors and older boys in the small ravine. It was shallow enough to hide them but sloped gently upward, so all of them could ride up and come into sight at the same time.

Young Wolf had a lookout on a slope a quarter of a mile to the west. He had a small hand mirror, and the moment the lookout saw any riders coming from the north, he would flash it. There would be one long flash, then a quick flash for each horseman coming.

The sun stood at nearly ten o'clock by Young Wolf's eye, and nothing had happened. He looked at his observer and hoped the young man had not fallen asleep. No, he was reliable.

Just then the long flash came from the sentry. Everyone in the line saw it and now counted the individual flashes. Six.

Young Wolf rode along the line, repeating his instructions. "Remember, when I give the signal, everyone walk your mount to the top of the rise so we can see the Bar-B riders. On my second signal those of you with rifles shoot over their heads."

Young Wolf eased upward on the slope, but even at the top of it he could not see anyone coming. There was a gentle rise here, and a small lift well below them. The cowboys must be in that depression. Even when they came over it they would be 300 yards away.

They would be close enough to see the Indians but far enough so their riflemen would not have good targets if they chose to fire. Young Wolf sat where he was on his bay, watching the landscape. When the first cowboy hat came over the rise, he backed his mount down until he was out of sight.

"Coming. Soon now. We aren't out to kill them. Just bluff them. And be sure to fire over their heads."

The next time Young Wolf eased up to the crest he could see the riders plainly, six of them riding straight at them. He had chosen the spot well.

"Lances up," Young Wolf shouted. "Let's move up the slope slowly."

The mounted Mandan Indians rode up from the depression, and the first Bar-B man who saw them yelled in surprise. Then the others saw them. The Indians stopped. With five yards between them the warriors stretched across a wide swath directly ahead of the riders and looked impressive.

The cowboys stopped and looked at their leader. "Just those pesky Mandans," Jed Hackett shouted. "You gonna let them poor excuses for Indians scare you?"

Just then five rifles fired from the Indian's line, the rounds zipping over the cowboy's heads. Two of the riders turned and galloped back the way they had come.

"Back here, damnit!" Hackett bellowed, but the men kept on going.

"Damn, Jed, four of us against about thirty of them," one of the older hands said. "Not damn good odds. I'm throwing in my hand." He turned and trotted his mount away. Hackett drew his six-gun and aimed at the man, but swore and put it back in leather.

"Hell, we'll pretend to back off, then we'll ride around them and more to the west. Damn Circle-S bastards got to be pushing our beef that way."

Another volley of rifle fire came from the Indians, this time kicking up dust beside the three riders left.

"Get outa here!" Hackett called, and they turned and rode quickly back the way they had come.

Young Wolf gave another signal, and the Indians rode back down into the gully and were gone from sight. If Hackett turned to look back he would have found nothing blocking his way, and he would have been mad as hell.

Young Wolf took his men down the gully to the west, found where he could ride another two miles without being seen, and then waited. If the Bar-B men came back, they would surely come in this direction. Perhaps he and his riders could discourage them again.

Morgan thought he heard some rifle fire at one point, but he couldn't be sure and didn't dwell on it. He had enough to worry about. A cowboy's horse had stepped in a gopher hole and broken a leg. The cowboy put the animal out of its misery but then had to ride double with another cowboy, which made that animal almost useless as well.

They had swept the range three times and decided they had most of the cattle. Now they brought the three herds together and began stringing them out as they moved them to the west. It was grueling, dust-choking work.

He took his turn at drag, catching up any strays or laggards and driving them back to the end of the herd.

The animals were not moving fast. Morgan guessed they were making about two or two and a half miles an hour. At this rate they would need three days to drive the herd to Branding Canyon.

Willy Joe rode up to the side where Morgan was acting as one of the points.

"How many you figure?" Willy Joe called.

"Damned if I know. All I can count is dust in my face."

"That's why you gave up being a cowboy. We got them stretched out damn near two miles now, and we're making a little better time. I figure maybe three miles an hour. Still gonna take us a hell of a long time to get to the Tongue.''

"Won't make it today."

"We'll keep heading straight west to the Pumpkin River, then head northwest for the home range."

"Any sign of the Bar-B men yet?" Morgan asked.

"Not hide nor hair. We'll keep hoping. I've got three riflemen as outriders on the north side. They would make first contact with any Bar-B people."

"How much further to the Pumpkin?" Morgan asked.

"Lead animals should be there in half an hour. Then another hour to get them all across. They'll stop and drink, but we'll yahoo them fast as we can."

Morgan nodded and went back to check on the drag. The men liked to see him back there, eating dust alongside them.

They got across the Pumpkin, less than knee deep this far upstream, and the lead man angled the herd northwest toward home. They still had ten miles of Bar-B range to cover before they would be on their own land.

Morgan left the herd, sat on a small knoll and looked northward. Nowhere did he see any sign of Bar-B riders. He wondered how the Indians had done. That could have been their warning rifle shots a couple of hours ago. He rode back to the herd.

The herd was now stretched out two miles long, five or six cattle wide. That could count up to 2000 head, maybe a few more. If they could get this bunch safely onto Circle-S soil and branded, the debt from the Bar-B would be paid.

Morgan thought that was worth somewhere around $80,000. Good enough. The Bar-B had stolen at least that much, if not more, from the Circle-S. An eye for an eye, he always said.

As the drive moved along, Morgan wished he could urge the critters to walk faster. If they could average three miles an hour for eight hours, they would be back on Circle-S soil. If!

A half hour later, three riders came out of the haze of the midmorning sunshine, surging at the line of cattle, screaming, firing six-guns and waving their hats. The cattle panicked in the line right ahead of the riders. A rifle shot brought one of the stampeders from his saddle, but the other two drove right through the herd, scattering it and taking half a dozen cows and steers with them to the south. They wouldn't see those animals again.

Morgan raced to the spot and began herding the frightened cattle back into the line. It wasn't a real stampede. If the cattle had been bunched and could have seen the men and become frightened at the same time, they all might have stampeded.

As it was, only about 200 scattered, and it took the cowboys an hour to herd them back and get the long line moving.

One of the riders held the Bar-B man who had been shot from his saddle. He brought him up to Willy Joe who took out his six-gun and made the Bar-B man think he was going to execute him. Instead he slammed the iron down across the man's head, driving him to the ground unconscious.

"Drag him back there a hundred yards out of the line of march, and let's keep the critters moving," Willy Joe shouted.

Morgan watched the small drama and smiled. Willy

Joe was going to do just fine running the Circle-S, especially since he would be half-owner.

They worked the animals forward. A half hour later one of the outriders came rushing in, his eyes wide, his horse starting to lather.

"Mr. Morgan, you better come quick. I don't know what to make of this. Up ahead there's about twenty Indians sitting on horses with feathers and lances and rifles and everything. They're just sitting there watching us!"

Chapter
Twenty-Six

Buckskin Lee Morgan laughed deep in his throat. "Don't be afraid of them. They're on our side. That's Young Wolf and his team. They've been shielding us from the Bar-B gunmen. Where are they?"

Morgan followed the outrider a quarter of a mile north and found the Indians lined up on a small rise. Young Wolf came toward them, not touching the reins, using his feet and legs to start, guide and stop the animal.

"Looks like you've made a good roundup," Young Wolf said grinning.

"Caught a few of our rustled stock. You see the Bar-B boys?"

Young Wolf smiled. "We met six of them, fired over their heads, and three of them turned and rode hell bent for Texas. We lost the other three but saw what they did. It could have been worse.''

"A damned lot worse," Morgan said. Cost us about a half hour and ten head. If that's it, we got off lucky. Thanks for your help. Looks like your men and boys did a fine job.''

"Some of the younger ones were eager to play at war, but the older ones told them of the pain and death. It will be a good lesson for them.''

"Thanks for your help. I think we've got the herd well on the way now. We're heading for the Tongue River, and by then we'll be into our own range.''

"Keep in touch with us," Young Wolf said and returned to his men. They followed him to the west where he would go around the head of the column and then far to the south and the Mandan's own range and village.

Morgan watched them go. They had done a good job. Six riflemen bursting in on their flank could have killed three or four of their own men and sent the cattle into a total stampede. He swung west to the head of the column to make sure of the right direction.

Willy Joe was tracking them almost northwest. As the two men rode side by side, Willy Joe looked over.

"Think our troubles are over with his herd?''

"Not a chance. Not as long as Bramwell is still alive and his honcho, Hackett, is still riding. Hackett will figure out that we have to bed down this herd at least once before we get them home. He'll be watching and waiting and try to hit us with all the fire power he has left.''

"Including Bramwell?''

"My guess is yes.''

"So what do we do?"

"Get them doggies as far into Circle-S land as we can before we stop them."

"Night drive? We tried that once, but we didn't have so far to go. We've moved them about thirteen, fourteen miles. That's a good day's drive, only we can't stop. The cows are getting tired. We'll have to slow down before long. It's about three-thirty. Four hours of daylight left.

"What we need to do is find a box canyon, only they don't make them that way out here on the flats. So we push them as far as we can and put every man around the herd on guard duty. Nobody sleeps tonight. Sure, some of them will fall asleep, but most of us will stay awake. Hackett may have just two men left. Those others who turned tail probably are off the ranch by now. He'll go back to pick up the cook and Bramwell for one final attack."

"Sounds like a war," Willy Joe said.

"It *is* a war, and don't forget it. And people get killed in wars. Just make sure it ain't you."

"We could move straight west and get into Circle-S range faster that way," Willy Joe said. Then he shook his head. "Hell, won't matter where we are when Hackett attacks. He'll hit us even if we're in Branding Canyon."

"Figure we have about twenty-two more miles to go to Branding Canyon. Not a chance we can do that without stopping."

"Now!" Willy Joe said. "We stop them right now and give them a five-hour nap, then roust them out when it gets dark. That way we'll be moving them on a night drive, and they won't be bunched up to stampede if and when Hackett drives in on us."

Morgan grinned. "Damned if I don't like it. Start the circle right here."

They bent the lead cows and steers around in a tight circle, and soon the rest of the herd was winding around the center which had stopped. They had the two-mile line tightened up into a good bedded-down herd in a half hour.

The animals were exhausted and dropped down to rest. Morgan went one way around the herd, setting the guards. They had two men riding herd right around the animals. The rest of the men, including Willy Joe and Morgan, either rode guard or stood at fixed guard points. The first ring of six men was 50 yards from the herd. A second ring was 200 yards out with ten men there on the larger circle. The last circle was 500 yards outside the second one and held the last twelve men.

It would take a rattlesnake to get through the guards, especially in the daylight.

Morgan left the circle on a scouting trip and rode a mile toward where he figured the Bar-B interlopers would be. He sat on his horse and looked back through the haze but could see nothing.

He waited.

They would come. He just didn't know how many of them or exactly when. The direction might fool him. If they could keep the Bar-B riders away from the bedded-down herd and get them stretched out again, they would have won.

A full-scale stampede would mean cattle spread out for 20 miles in all directions, and they would never find half of them. All they had to do was prevent a stampede. He had warned the men about not using their weapons while the animals were bedded-down. With a herd this tired, anything from a rattlesnake's hiss to a bolt of lightning could set them off.

Morgan checked his pocket watch. 4:30. Three more hours of daylight. Three more hours of danger.

He scanned the horizon and thought for a moment that he saw something in the distance. He looked away and let his whole face relax with his eyes closed. Then he looked back at the same spot.

Someone was coming. Morgan rode toward the man. He kept to the low lying spots as much as he could, checking to be sure the other rider still was out there. He was three miles away but coming straight for the herd. He could have been following the herd from the dust trail.

Now that it stopped, he moved in to find out why. Then he would report back to Hackett and Bramwell. Morgan knew he couldn't let that happen. The animals would stampede in daylight as easily as after dark.

Morgan checked the Spencer in the boot. Yes, loaded and ready.

He found a small swale and rode down it hard, angling slightly away from the other rider. If he could get behind the man . . .

Morgan came up and saw the other rider less than half a mile away across a flat stretch of land.

Another mile and the scout would see the herd bedded-down, then he would turn and race back to where the Bar-B men were waiting.

Morgan slowly maneuvered himself behind the scout. When the man checked his back trail, he saw Morgan and turned and stared. Then he stood up in his stirrups and looked ahead but couldn't see the herd. He then turned and galloped in an arc around Morgan and to the north where the Bar-B men must be waiting. Morgan swiftly followed.

For ten minutes they thundered across the plains. Morgan came closer, and when he was about 200 yards, he stopped his mount and fired twice with the Spencer. He didn't aim at the man. The scout's horse screamed in pain and terror, then her left front leg snapped as a big .52 caliber slug hit it, and horse and rider went down in a spray of dust and dirt.

Morgan rode up to within 50 yards of the scene. The horse was pawing and screaming. The rider had dropped behind his mount for cover.

Morgan's rifle slug slammed into the dying horse, putting it out of its misery.

"Now, you want the next one?" Morgan called.

"Hell no."

"Then answer some questions. How many men does Bramwell have left?"

"Five or six. Three quit today."

"Make that four, counting you."

"What's that?"

"Bramwell lost four men today, because you just quit. Right? Quit him or die where you lay."

"Right, right. I quit."

"What does Bramwell plan on doing next?"

"Wants to stampede the herd soon as it gets bedded-down for the night."

"What did you see up front there about the herd?"

"Nothing. You think you can find the Bar-B ranch again?"

"Yes sir."

"Without reporting back to Hackett?"

"Yes sir, you bet. Whatever you want."

"Then get on your feet and start walking. You've got a long trail to travel."

The cowboy rose slowly, not sure if he would be shot or not. When he stood up fully he stared at Morgan, touched the brim of his hat and began walking to the northeast. He knew the way home.

Morgan rode back to the outer circle of defense. It was 5:30. The animals had another two hours to rest, then they'd have a long walk.

Nothing happened for the next two hours. Morgan pulled in the defense circles and used the men to start driving the cattle northwest again.

The process of prodding sleeping cattle to their feet is a long and slow one, and half the animals had to be encouraged. A half hour after dusk they had the whole herd up and stringing out to the northwest.

Morgan breathed a sigh of relief, then picked two cowboys to go with him to watch for Hackett and his men. They would come. Even though their scout didn't come back they would figure about where the herd should be and ride to that point.

Then they would swing around and follow the trail. Two thousand head of cattle leaves a trail you can't miss, even in the dark. It's like a huge scar across virgin land. In soft spots the 8000 hooves could pack down the earth six or eight inches.

An hour after dark, Morgan picked up two more riflemen and switched their defensive position a quarter of a mile behind the herd.

It was after 9:00 and cloud dark when Morgan heard the first evidence of someone coming up on them. He warned his four riflemen, and they stopped and spread across the trail at ten-yard intervals.

A white horse showed up first, coming out of the gloom like a ghost. It had to be Bramwell. Beside him were four horsemen, two on each side.

When they were within 30 feet of Morgan, he bellowed at them.

"Hold it right there. You're covered by ten rifles. We all can't miss at this range."

The five horses stopped.

"Bramwell, what the hell you doing out here? You ain't no cowboy."

"No, but I'm an expert shot."

"Not going to help you much with a .52 caliber slug slamming through your brain. You boys are about a herd short and a pound late."

"You're a rustler, Morgan. You'll hang."

"Not true. We're just returning animals to the Circle-S that were stolen by your riders. A cow for a cow, I always say."

"Never get away with it, Morgan. The sheriff is hunting you right now."

"I know. We've already had a discussion about it. He lost." Morgan watched one of the riders edging up a rifle. "Hold it with that rifle or you're a dead man, or you want to get shot full of holes and die an ugly and painful death?"

"I want my cattle back."

"They aren't your cattle. Your men rustled over two thousand, five hundred head of cattle from the Circle-S over two years. The increase in a thousand cows is about nine hundred a year or another eighteen hundred head. We'll settle for about four thousand head, so you're getting a break.

"Turn around now and ride away and you have a chance to gather what's left and build up a herd again. It will take you ten years, but you can do it honestly. Your other choice is to die where you sit."

Bramwell bellowed out an order, and the five men split in all directions. Rifles cracked, and pistols blasted. Two of the Bar-B riders fell off their horses, wounded. One escaped to the rear, riding hell for leather into the darkness.

Morgan raced after Bramwell who had angled to the west and turned, firing his six-gun at Morgan. One round clipped his hat, and another one seared across the horse's right leg. Then the rancher's rounds were gone.

Morgan charged up to him, grabbed Bramwell and jerked him out of the saddle, dumping him between the horses. By the time Morgan got his steed turned around and brought back to the spot, Bramwell lay there on the ground with a derringer pointed at his head.

Morgan had out his six-gun and laughed softly.

"Be my guest, Bramwell. If you blow your brains out, then I won't have to."

"Stay back or I will, I swear."

"Go ahead, no worry for me. Be glad to see you get what you deserve for killing the Scoggins boy."

"I should hate you, Morgan, but I don't. You stopped every plan I tried. You ruined Slade. You got that Indian to burn down my ranch house, then he scared off half of my men. It was your man with the dynamite down by the home place. Damn you, Morgan!"

"Life is tough when you can't cheat and steal, ain't it, Bramwell?"

Morgan stepped down from his mount with his six-gun still covering Bramwell.

"I mean it, Morgan. I'll kill myself, and it'll be on your conscience."

Morgan laughed. As he did Bramwell swung the little gun around and fired once at Morgan. The derringer is notoriously inaccurate past four or five feet, and with Morgan ten feet away, the round spun past, missing him by a foot.

Morgan's right hand reacted automatically. He got his shot off just after the derringer fired. The round cut through Bramwell's chest, splintered a rib and drove half of it deep into the cattleman's heart, killing him instantly.

Morgan stared at the dead man a minute, then lifted his voice in a shout.

"Circle-S riders! Any problems? Call out!" Two of the missing men rode up a minute later. They found the third one with a rifle round in his hip, unable to walk.

It took a while to get the wounded man bandaged up and back on his mount. Once on board, he said he could ride fine. Morgan assigned him to ride with one of the point men, out of the dust, and told the man to watch the wounded cowboy closely.

The trail drive was moving along well. The cows didn't seem to mind the cooler night air once on the move, and Willy Joe came back from the head of the string where he said he figured they were making three miles an hour again.

"At this rate we should be able to move into

Branding Canyon along about daylight."

"Let's hope you're right," Morgan said. He eased into the saddle and felt blood on his left shoulder. Must be that wound he got in town. He put it out of his mind. They were on the home track now with at least $80,000 worth of cattle, and the Circle-S would be back in business on a permanent basis. Morgan grinned.

Chapter
Twenty-Seven

The tired Circle-S cowhands drove the last of the herd into Branding Canyon a little after 7:00 A.M. Willy Joe had two men seal up the mouth of the canyon and remain on guard with rifles.

The rest of the crew rode back to the ranch. The men had their choice of eating first or sleeping. As soon as the cook saw them coming, he cooked up breakfast.

Morgan sat in the kitchen where Heather worked over his shoulder. The wound had broken open, and she undid the bloody bandage, applied some healing ointment and tied it up again with some strips of an old sheet.

"Not a professional job, but it should last for a few days." She stared down at him, a dozen different emotions surging through her. "I'm just so happy that you both are back and still alive. Then I'm delighted that our debt from the Bar-B is finally paid. Now we can get down to running a real ranch here at the Circle-S.''

"And now you can start making your plans for getting married. I'll have one of the boys run you into town today so you can pick out a wedding dress and talk to the preacher. You'll want to have the ceremony here, I hope.''

"Yes, I should do that." Her smile brightened. "Yes, of course, I'll do it today, this morning!''

"Good, because I'm going to sleep for about a year.''

Morgan woke up at three that afternoon, went down to the kitchen and made himself a big sandwich. Heather had driven to town. Most of the men were still sleeping, and Willy Joe had ridden around and talked to the four guards, telling them they would get some relief before the day was over.

Morgan thought that now would be a perfect time for Bramwell to attack them, but then he remembered and shook his head. Bramwell would never be a threat again. Another day or two and they could pull in the guards. It was over.

They had made a better estimate of the herd after daylight. Willy Joe said he figured they had almost 2400 head of cattle, calves, bulls and steers. Not bad for two days work. Now to get them branded and healing up before they sold the steers.

Morgan had another sandwich, another cup of coffee and sat in the swing on the porch relaxing.

It was almost over. He still had to have a heart-to-heart talk with the sheriff. Or did he? Bramwell said that the wanted poster was still in force. The sheriff must have told him that. That could only mean that Tombstone had the same district attorney it did five years ago.

Morgan shrugged and settled back in the cushions for a short afternoon nap. He was still hungry, but he'd wait on that until supper. It was great to be unemployed again. Now he could just meander around, do what he wanted to.

He'd get Heather married off, maybe help a day or two on the branding, and then he'd stop by and see Elly.

A rifle shot boomed across the range, and Morgan came out of his swing running for the corral. He found a saddled horse, grabbed it and headed out. Willy Joe had also come running with a Spencer carbine, and he tossed the weapon to Morgan.

''The east sentry, straight east. I'll get a horse and come help.''

Morgan grabbed the carbine, felt to be sure the Colt was on his hip and charged past the ranch house to the east. What the hell? Some diehard man from the Bar-B?

The east sentry was on a small rise about a quarter of a mile from the ranch house. As he rode, Morgan heard another rifle shot and this time saw a puff of blue smoke.

Morgan sprang from his horse with the carbine in his hand and slid to the ground next to the lookout.

The men had dug a small hole to sit in and built

up a barricade with rocks and dirt.

The sentry looked up at Morgan and shook his head. "Don't see why somebody is shooting at us now. I sure as tarnation thought it was all over."

"It is, but not for this one. You think there's more than one out there?"

"Nope, just one. He came riding up and started shooting. Then he left his horse and dropped down. Guess he's in a little low place out there about two hundred yards."

"Is he any good with that rifle?"

"He put two rounds into our rocks there. Hadn't been for that I'd be dead by now."

"Stay here, and if he lifts up, put a slug in him. If you don't see him, throw out some rounds now and then to keep his head down. I'll be coming up on him from the side."

Morgan left the outpost and crawled on his hands and knees to a small gully where he could move out without the attacker seeing him.

He edged up to the top of the ravine and looked out. Morgan could see blue pants and a brown shirt of a man who lay behind a small mound about 100 yards away. Who the hell was he?

Morgan knew he should just sight in and kill the man, but his curiosity was aroused. Who would be so loyal to the owner that he could make what could be a suicidal attack after the owner was dead and his ranch probably gone?

Could be Hackett, Morgan decided. He was a good ranchman, but surely he would give up by now. Or did Hackett own the Bar-B now? Maybe he was planning on just assuming control and working it for as long as he could. Morgan had seen that done a time or two—ownership without benefit of law or deeds or transfers.

Morgan sighted in on the man's legs and fired. He could see the round slice through the gunman's upper thigh. The wound brought a scream of pain from the man who at once moved to the side until he was out of sight.

"Who are you?" Morgan roared.

"Guy who's gonna kill you, Morgan."

"Not shot up that way. Give it up and ride out."

"Kill you first."

"Who are you? Hackett?"

"Yeah, gonna kill you."

"Why?"

"You killed Bramwell. He was my ticket to getting my own ranch. Said he'd start me up in my own place."

"He was lying. Men like Bramwell lie a lot."

Hackett sent a rifle round toward Morgan, but it was ten yards off target.

"Give it up, Hackett. I'll bandage you up and send you into town to the doctor. You could always run the Bar-B until Bramwell's heirs show up. You know that nobody might ever come to claim the ranch. Why not just set on it for a while? You've still got enough stock to work a ranch."

"After you stole all of them?"

"We just took back what you and your crew rustled from us. You know that's fair. You could build up a nice herd there in a few years. Start with the thousand head you have. Better than trying to gun me down and run.''

''Hell, it was going damn well until you came.''

''Luck of the draw. Change seats in the poker game, Hackett. I've heard you're a good cattleman. Why not go ahead and prove it?''

''Hell, I got only six hands left.''

''That's plenty. Take them in on shares, and they'll work their tails off. Give it a try.''

''Damnit, I wanted to kill you.''

''What's that against having your own ranch, if even for only a few years? You'll be a rich man when the heirs get here, if they ever do. They'll pay you for your work.''

Hackett limped toward Morgan, hands in the air, and stopped 20 feet away.

''No tricks, no bluff, Morgan. I'm clean and I want you to bandage up my leg.''

A half hour later, Morgan had cut off Hackett's pant leg. Morgan was about to clean the wound when a buggy pulled into the ranch yard and Heather stepped down. She introduced herself and at once took over and tended the wound.

''That will hold for a while, but you best see the doctor in town in a day or two to check it.''

''Yes, ma'am.'' Hackett paused. ''You're about the prettiest little thing I ever did see.''

''Thank you, Mr. Hackett. You be nice and I'll invite you to my wedding next week.''

''Oh, congratulations. Thanks for taking care of my leg.''

''If all of you men weren't so offhanded about

shooting people, I wouldn't have so much nursing to do. I hope the gunplay is all over now.''

''Yes, ma'am, it's over. I intend to run the Bar-B on the straight and narrow. No more borrowing cattle. We'll make our spring and fall roundups together and separate the brands just the way we're supposed to.''

''Sounds good to me, Mr. Hackett. I hope we can be good neighbors.''

Hackett was ready to leave, but that was postponed until he sat down to supper with the three of them in the kitchen.

When the meal was over, he thanked Heather and went back to his horse. Hackett waved and rode due east toward the Bar-B.

Morgan put on his hat and settled his six-gun. ''Figure I should pay the sheriff a visit and get this little matter with him straightened out.''

''Now?''

''Can't think of a better time. Willy Joe can take care of things here. He'll get the branding done. Then in a couple of weeks be ready to ship some more steers and bulls. Might hold back on the bulls in case Hackett needs a few more for his Bar-B herd.''

Willy Joe nodded. ''Now get out of here, Morgan, but be sure you come back in plenty of time for the wedding on Saturday.''

''Saturday?''

''We had to move it up a day because the Reverend Allison had another wedding on Sunday afternoon,'' Heather said.

Morgan nodded and headed for the barn.

He rode at a steady pace toward town. Morgan

wasn't sure if he could or even should talk to the sheriff, but he had two hours to decide.

By the time he rode into town he had decided not to talk to the sheriff. It would only agitate the matter. Bramwell certainly could not make any more trouble about it. The sheriff probably had enough other business to keep him occupied.

Morgan rode up to the Plainsman Hotel and went up to the second floor. He knocked on room 211 and waited. Elly might be gone by now, down the tracks somewhere. She might have found a new friend. She . . .

Elly opened the door and grinned. "About damn time you came back to see me. You know how long it's been?" She grabbed him, pulled him into the room and kicked the door shut, then she kissed him with her whole body pressed tightly against his.

Morgan pulled away from her and laughed. "Now that's what I call a fine welcome."

"I'm going to San Francisco. I just decided. Why don't you come with me?"

"Can't until after Saturday. I have a wedding to go to. I'm giving away the bride."

"The girl at the ranch?"

"Yes."

"You ever fuck her?"

"No."

"You ever think about it?"

"Of course. She's young and pretty and almost as sexy as you are."

"Good, let's talk about me."

"You're beautiful, you're sexy, and you enjoy

laying on your back and spreading your fine legs.''

"Show me what you mean."

He did, fast and hard and a little rough. She loved it.

"You staying all night?"

"Yes."

"Good, I have some wine."

"When I drink I can't come as often."

"Don't care." She took a bottle of port wine from the dresser and tipped it up, drinking. Then she handed it to him to use.

"No cheese and crackers?"

She hit him on the shoulder.

They tasted the bottle again, then he spread her out on the bed. He ran his hands over her smooth belly and up to where her perfect breasts lay. Gently he massaged each one, bringing the nipples to full flower, deepening the pink of the twin areolas.

"Beautiful. Breasts are so beautiful, the most stunning part of a woman to look at." He bent and kissed them, and she pulled him down on top of her.

She pushed him up until she could focus on his face. "Sweet cock, I want to play a game. Can I play a game?"

"Sure, it's your bed and your room and your wine and your lovely little body. What game do you want to play?"

"Rancher. I want to play rancher."

"Not sure I know the rules."

"I do." She pushed him off her and got up on her hands and knees. "You see I'm this little heifer and you're a big range bull and you figure it's about my time."

He lay there on his back with his hands behind his head. "Yeah, you sure are a sexy little heifer, and it's definitely your time. What now?"

"Come on, don't be mean. Mount me from behind, like I saw these two dogs doing yesterday. That little male was just fucking up a storm, just humping and humping. Do me that way."

Morgan laughed, got on his knees and mounted her from behind. Elly groaned and then giggled.

"I feel more like that bitch dog than a heifer. Hump me, big dog."

They discovered four more positions they hadn't used yet as the night wore on, and when the bottle of wine was gone, they fell asleep in each other's arms.

Morgan awoke the next morning with a growling hangover. Wine did that to him. He shook his head and got up and dressed. He had no shaving gear, but it didn't matter. He didn't plan on going anywhere for two days.

It was Wednesday, and he had to be back at the ranch Friday. The wedding was Saturday. Good. While Elly slept, he looked out the window at Main Street. A few merchants were coming to work, and a milkman was making some deliveries. It gave him time to think. He should get back to Spade Bit up in Idaho and see if he still had a ranch.

He had more than the $5000 he had come with. Heather had insisted on paying him back the money he had spent on the ranch. She also gave him $500 extra as a "friendship gift" as she called it.

San Francisco with Elly? It would be fun for a while. Neither one of them wanted their association to be permanent. That made the decision easier, but he'd decide after the wedding on Saturday.

For the next two days he stayed off the street and spent most of his time in Elly's room. She began bringing up dinners to eat in her room, and the waiters thought that she really had a surprisingly big appetite. Of course Morgan was eating at least half of it.

Friday morning Elly lay on the bed naked as he got dressed.

"You're taking unfair advantage of a mere man," Morgan said. She twisted into a more provocative pose and crooked her finger at him.

"Just one more time. You're not supposed to be in a hurry this morning."

Morgan laughed. "You know that one more will lead to two and three more, and I won't get out of here until five o'clock. Nope. This time I'm gonna be mean and tough. Leaving in ten minutes."

She stuck her tongue out at him.

Ten minutes later at her door, Elly hugged him deliciously. She still hadn't dressed.

He caught her breasts, and his eyes widened. "I'll be damned. Look here. You aren't just a young boy after all. Look at these tits! You must be a woman."

She hit him on the shoulder, then kissed him again. "You be sure and come back, and we'll go to San Francisco on the train. We can get a compartment and fuck across six states."

"I'll decide when I get back. It's hard for me to plan too far in advance. You ever been in Idaho?"

She made a face at him, and he closed the door and walked to the livery. No sense in asking for any trouble with the sheriff now.

The wedding was beautiful. On his way back to the ranch, Morgan had picked up the buggy, a wedding cake, some flowers and a present for the bride and groom.

Morgan gave her away in the parlor, and half the hands were present, washed and combed and with clean shirts on.

The preacher had driven out in the morning. The afternoon ceremony was over quickly, and Morgan went up to kiss the bride. He pecked her on the cheek, and Willy Joe grinned. Morgan had never seen him in a suit before, let alone a black one with a string tie.

"Congratulations, beautiful bride. How does it feel to be Mrs. Willy Joe Dawson?"

"Oh, I haven't even tried to write my new name."

"Leave the Scoggins in and add Dawson. I think your daddy would have liked that," Morgan said.

The cook had made a banquet for the wedding dinner. They had a standing rib roast, whole roasted pheasants, six kinds of vegetables, three deserts and the three tier wedding cake.

Heather absolutely glowed.

Morgan caught her hands and held them. I'd say about four sons and two daughters would be right,'' he said. "That will give you at least two of them who will want to keep running the ranch.''

Heather blushed. "Lee, really.''

Willy Joe grabbed Heather and kissed her.

Morgan grinned. "That's a good start, Willy Joe, but that's not going to do the job. Let me tell you the facts of life. You see first there's this little mama bee . . .''

Heather pushed a piece of wedding cake into Morgan's mouth, and they all whooped with laughter.

When the dinner was over, Morgan got ready to leave with the preacher. He said his goodbyes to the couple in the living room.

"You come back at least once a year,'' Heather said, brushing tears away.

"I will. I want to see each new kid as he comes along.''

Willy Joe shook his hand. "We never could have done it without you, Morgan. "This place should be half yours, but you already said no to that. I mean it, you come back often.''

Heather threw her arms around him and hugged him so tightly he thought he'd have breast marks on his chest.

He waved at them in the dusk as he rode away behind the preacher's buggy. The preacher had been driving and nodded off after a half mile. Morgan took the buggy lines and picked up the pace.

He had to get back to town and find Elly. Tonight

they would decide just where to go and what to do. San Francisco? Chicago? Maybe even Idaho. He wasn't sure. Wherever it was he knew that he'd find something interesting to do until he got back to his ranch. Spade Bit kept calling him. Sooner or later he'd get back there. His roots and his ranch were still calling.

GUNSLICK

The bawdy Adult Western series that's
more fun than a Saturday night shootout!

#1: A MAN PURSUED by J.G. White. After two years in jail, Matt Sutton was thinking of three things: women, money, and a new life. He had the woman and the money, but some dangerous people stood between Sutton and a new life — people who shot first and asked questions later.

__2916-2 $2.95

#2: THE RAWHIDERS by J.G. White. On the road to California, Sutton's bedmate Diana was captured by a gang of horsethievin' cutthroats. And Sutton was willing to do anything to get his woman back — even die.

__2926-X $2.95

The Adult Western series with more
punch than a barroom brawl...

#32: THE MINER'S MOLL by Dirk Fletcher.
__2992-8 $2.95

#31: PORTLAND PUSSYCAT by Dirk Fletcher.
__2884-0 $2.95

#30: BOISE BELLE by Dirk Fletcher.
__2820-4 $2.95

#29: PLAINS PARAMOUR by Dirk Fletcher.
__2763-1 $2.95

#28: KANSAS CITY CHORINE by Dirk Fletcher.
__2714-3 $2.95 US / $3.95 CAN

SADDLER

**The hardest-riding, hardest loving cowboy
who ever blazed a trail or set a heart on fire.**

#1: A DIRTY WAY TO DIE by Gene Curry. When Saddler went to new Orleans for a good time with the ladies, he ended up accused of beating an old woman to death. He could have run, but if he didn't prove himself innocent his life would be worthless.

__2699-9 $2.95 US / $3.50 CAN

WILDCAT WOMAN by Gene Curry. Hired by a millionaire to find his spoiled daughter, Saddler knew the job was going to be tough. Soon the daughter's outlaw boyfriend was hot to put Saddler six feet under, and the wildcat heiress was even hotter to gun him down — between the sheets or anywhere else.

__2988-X $2.95 US / $3.50 CAN

BUCKSKIN

The hard-riding, hard-bitten
Adult Western series that's
hotter'n a blazing pistol and as tough as
the men and women who tamed the frontier.

#27: DOUBLE ACTION by Kit Dalton. Ambushed and left with amnesia, Lee Morgan swore he wouldn't rest until he had killed the cowards who had attacked him.
__2845-X $2.95

#28: APACHE RIFLES by Kit Dalton. Working as a scout for the U.S. Army, Lee Morgan tracked the deadly Chircahua Apache — and found a dangerous Indian maid who had eyes for him.
__2943-X $2.95

#29: RETURN FIRE by Kit Dalton. Searching for a missing prospector in Deadwood, South Dakota, Lee Morgan found the only help anyone would give him was a one-way ticket to boot hill.
__3009-8 $2.95 US/$3.50 CAN

LEISURE BOOKS
ATTN: Customer Service Dept.
276 5th Avenue, New York, NY 10001
Please add $1.25 for shipping and handling of the first book and $.30 for each book thereafter. All orders shipped within 6 weeks via postal service book rate.

Canadian orders must reflect Canadian price, when indicated, and must be paid in U.S. dollars through a U.S. banking facility.

Name _____

Address _____

City _____ State _____ Zip _____

I have enclosed $ _____ in payment for the books checked above.